The Spirit Catchers

ISBN: 978-0-9866620-6-5

1

All things considered, my death was pretty boring.

Let me ask you something: when do people start thinking they're going to live a long life? For me, it was around age ten. I wanted to be an oncologist. To this day I will never know what sort of divine influence planted that idea in my mind. All I know is that having cancer and treating cancer are as different as night and day.

I was nineteen when the first symptoms appeared. They started out small, as most things usually do: a bruise here, a nosebleed there. The fatigue was constant and immutable, mirroring my every move like a shadow until it became the darkness that swallowed me whole. Vial by vial my own compromised blood wrote the final chapter of my life, turning the page on everything I thought I'd have time to do. This is cancer: the thread that unravels the rug, interrupting the patterns of our lives and the tapestry of our expectations.

My attitude toward death had always been astoundingly cavalier. I never denied this possibility, even in the early days of my diagnosis when my body still responded to chemotherapy. I thought about death often and casually: between naps, during dinner, in the privacy of my bedroom on the rare occasion that I was home. Even then, I wanted to get it over with. I thought maybe it would be like hitting a reset button, and I'd wake up the next day feeling rejuvenated. But death doesn't work like that. Maybe if it did, we could finally break the stigma of being breakable.

My prognosis had been predictably bleak. I was told I had six months to live, but could buy myself two or three more if I consented to undergoing experimental treatment. I refused, saying there was no point in delaying the inevitable—not even if it meant that someone, somewhere, might benefit from my extended suffering.

I didn't get six months. Instead, I got four months, three weeks, five days, two hours, and seventeen minutes. My family didn't think this was enough time to say goodbye. I, on the other hand, thought it was too much.

A few days before my death, a woman named Joy appeared at my bedside. Joy had sat in the corner of my hospital room, next to my mother, who'd been dozing on a cot and woefully oblivious to the lean but impeccably dressed woman who'd come to claim my soul. I thought I was dreaming, but in actuality, I was just dying.

On the first day, Joy didn't speak. Instead, she studied me in the way one might study a Picasso or a Rembrandt, with care and polite curiosity. Having Joy around made me feel safe, and it wasn't long before I began to welcome the sight of her blue dress in a world worn grey with despair. Joy was what most people would call a guardian angel, but there are no angels at The Establishment. Collecting souls is both an art and a science, and requires far more than wings to achieve.

Enter the Spirit Catchers, a diverse cohort of supernatural entities tasked with escorting human souls to the hereafter.

Truthfully, the title is a misnomer: most spirits go willingly, so catching is seldom required. Being terminally ill had all but left me helpless, so when the time came for me to vacate the cancer-ridden shell of my once youthful body, I had no choice but to do whatever was asked of me. This was good news for Joy, but not for my family, who did everything they could to keep the hope—and me—alive.

On the second day, I asked Joy to tell me more about The Establishment: if it had towering iron gates and lush, manicured lawns, or ostentatious wooden doors with heavy brass knockers, or marble staircases that vanished innocently into the clouds. Joy said there was none of that. I was disappointed, but far from surprised, especially given the utilitarian nature of The Establishment's name.

On the third day, I was calling out to her in agony. Joy had materialized in her usual spot in the corner of the room the moment her name sprang from my lips. I begged to die. I pleaded with her until my whole body tingled with exhaustion. I cried until I couldn't breathe, until I was woozy from a lack of oxygen and the lasting effects of whatever painkillers I'd been given to ease my misery. I wanted out. When Joy didn't take me, it felt like betrayal. But she wasn't betraying anybody, only following protocol. If I'd been a little stronger, perhaps I'd have asked about this, too.

Joy didn't take me that day. She said I wasn't ready yet. I begged anyway. In the midst of my protest, she'd approached my bed and laid a hand on my chest. Light emanated from her fingertips as she illuminated me, erasing the layers that stood between my spirit and the world I no longer belonged to: first the itchy cream sheets, then the dull blue gown, and finally my translucent skin. By this point my body was producing bruises like a garden produced flowers and it was becoming harder to ignore the presence of ribs or the absence of fat that normally concealed them.

Joy bent her bright red lips close to my ear. She was cold and smelled like the inside of my grandmother's armoire, and it sent shivers of familiarity all the way down my aching spine.

"Ansel says not yet," she whispered, chilling me to the core. "Soon."

By the fourth day, I was ready to die. My life was over, and like discovering the blank page at the end of a book, I'd stared into the overhead lights and wondered who was responsible for ending my story here. I expected Joy to tell me more about this being named Ansel, but she never did.

My family came to say goodbye at 10:23AM on September 4th, 2005. It was a long goodbye. My parents cried. My brother, who never cried, sobbed until he hyperventilated. And I just lay there, waiting for Joy, who was waiting for Ansel to give her the go-ahead to collect my soul. No one noticed the fair-skinned woman knitting placidly in the corner, because I was the only one who could see her.

When it was finally time to make the transition, Joy returned her knitting needles to her bag, smoothed the wrinkles out of her dress, and walked the short distance over to my bed. I didn't look at her. I was too busy watching my family, who'd formed a prayer circle at the foot of my bed and were muttering tearful invocations under their breath.

"An odd habit, prayer is," Joy had remarked, folding her arms. "But I suppose it's par for the course: after all, this is your deathbed."

"Maybe they're hoping Ansel will change his mind."

"Ansel doesn't change his mind on much of anything. Can you imagine how complicated life would be if death was always second-guessing himself?" Joy then turned to me and smiled. "Ready?"

I nodded, the machine flatlined, and then everything I ever knew suddenly disappeared.

My name is Sarah Nicole Galloway, and my job is to help people die.

2

Joy's anecdotes did little to prepare me for life at The Establishment. Thankfully, my weeklong orientation made up for it.

The metamorphosis from human spirit to Spirit Catcher takes approximately two weeks, during which time recruits are outfitted with a new body, a uniform, and a specialized ring called a Keepsake. The Keepsake is our key to navigating The Establishment. In addition to alerting us to hazards in our environment, it also allows us to harvest and transport people's memories. It's the Swiss Army Knife of rings: lightweight, versatile, and an absolute necessity when working in the field.

Contrary to popular belief, The Establishment is neither a cornucopia of indulgence nor a cesspool of depravity. The Establishment is an enterprise, and like all successful businesses, its survival hinges on its ability to juggle supply and demand.

Before you start arguing that there's no demand for death, allow me to remind you that there is also staggeringly little demand for violence, epidemics, and natural disasters. Not all demands are desirable, yet, through generations of trial and error, society has consistently found ways to capitalize on human suffering.

As in life, death doesn't come with any promises. The Establishment is not in the business of making promises. To use one of my father's infamous sayings, reunions are as rare as wrinkles on a golf ball. This is because The Establishment is not a final destination, but another step along the path toward the next iteration of your life. There is no permanence in expiration, only another purpose needing to be served. And at The Establishment, your purpose is simple: collect human spirits, harness their energy, and then begin the cycle over again. You won't remember any of this, but you don't need to. It's not your purpose to remember. Your purpose is to live. And if you can change the world in the process, more power to you.

I didn't change the world; I didn't want to. With everlasting change comes monumental responsibility. Not everyone has enough force to warp humanity's protective shell. In fact, most of us function more like light, ricocheting off its various angles only to be fired back into oblivion—there once, gone forever. That's what I wanted: to skate across the surface of time and then veer off into the unknown, carried like a seed on the wind into a distant realm of infinite possibility.

Welcome to The Establishment. It's not paradise, but it's perfect for me. It's not much of anything, really, but it's everything I've ever needed, especially when the last leg of my life was rife with pain, suffering, and humiliation. And if you don't believe anyone would put death above earthlier desires like survival, ask yourself why misery corrals the anguished into suicide and drives the desperate into murder. Death is security. It's consolation. And in my case, it was a chance at a fresh start, one in which I didn't have to deny my own past or pretend to become a completely different person.

Growing up, I was a middle-dweller. I lived with two parents and an older brother in an average sized house in a midsized town. My mother, Desiree, was a part-time professional organizer and full-time karaoke aficionado. My father, Paul, was a dentist. At the time of my death, my brother Brody, who was twenty-one, was halfway through music school and gigging regularly with his band. We weren't a wealthy family, but we were rich in our own way, and that was good enough for me.

Before my diagnosis, I'd always considered myself genetically well endowed. I had hair that turned gold in the sun, eyes that matched the sea, and skin designed to be decorated. Whether it was my ability to adapt to virtually every social situation or my perfectly non-threatening demeanor I can't honestly say, but I don't remember ever being lonely. Friends came and went, but they were always there in some form or another. Being a middle-dweller meant I had friends on both sides of the tracks, and it taught me a lot about expectation—namely that you really can have too much of a good thing. The middle is a great place to be—for any animal, but especially for a nineteen-year-old female human being. Being in the middle makes you untouchable, and being untouchable keeps you safe.

But cancer's different. Cancer begins in the middle and works its way out. People are picky about a lot of things—including how they'd like to die—but I have yet to meet anyone who chooses cancer. It's not a dignified way to die. It doesn't even make for a good story. Plenty of Catchers entered through the cancer door, and they all sound exactly the same. That's because cancer comes with a script, and everyone knows the lines. If you're part of Team Cancer, no one asks you to elaborate. They've heard the story too many times, and they all know how it ends.

Soon, a fifteen-year-old girl named Sophia Jacobson will too, and all because of a cold that wouldn't go away.

The hospital is busy today. I'm on my way to see one of my regulars, and since I'm ahead of schedule I've decided to take the long way around. Ansel says there's no hurry, so I assume a leisurely pace as I make my way through the halls. This place has a soundtrack more familiar to me than any song: if you listen closely, you can almost hear the music in a pained moan or throaty wail of grief. The Living are too predictable some days. They expect too much, pray too hard, and love to point fingers when things go wrong. If the Living had their way, we'd all be out of a job.

I round the corner, where I discover a tall figure making his way toward me. I stop, briefly considering an alternate route, but it's too late: Gabe and I have already made eye contact. He raises a hand to wave as the distance between us shortens. I don't like Gabe, who loves to brag about his quotas and is always leaving everything to the last possible minute. The unfixable helmet hair and frosty green eyes are simply the icing on the cake that is his abominable personality.

"Let me guess," Gabe says when he's closer. "Ansel still hasn't given you your collection orders."

"Shouldn't you be scraping road kill off a highway somewhere?"

A smile dawns on his ashen lips and disappears a second later.

"Road kill," he echoes, nodding. "I like it. Very apropos."

I steer around him and keep walking.

"So I take it that's a no on those collection orders?" he says.

"Bye, Gabe."

"With quotas like yours you'll never get out of The Establishment. You know that, right?"

Despite myself, I turn around. I don't need him to explain quotas to me. If I was slow to die, it makes sense that I'd be slow to regenerate. Cancer is a slow business, but I'm not the one complaining here.

"And with quotas like yours," I counter, "you shouldn't be here."

"Sure I should. They're not all DOA."

"Well, maybe they should be."

Gabe smirks. "Maybe you should ask for a transfer," he says.

"Why? I'm finally good at something."

"And you still don't get to do it. Shame."

I keep walking. If I could kill him, I probably would—but then I'd be condemned to an eternity in The Establishment's basement, and that's a place I could do without seeing again.

Upon reaching the oncology department, I walk through the door and stand beneath the flickering fluorescent bulb. Feeble shafts of light pulse against the walls like a melody, causing the shadows of a few nearby linens carts to take up an erratic dance. Ansel is pretty adamant about not altering the environments in which we work. He says they should be raw and untouched, just like the souls we're responsible for collecting whenever he sends us out on a mission. Alteration is interference and interference is

10

unnatural, but I don't see the harm in making things a little more comfortable for the Living.

I press the tips of my fingers to the underside of the light. It hums like a hive of bees beneath my touch, protesting the infusion of energy, until the flickering stops. The shadows cease their tireless jive, and a second later I continue on my way.

3

Sophia Jacobson's room looks like an ad for a party store. Balloons cluster in the corners of the ceiling and there's a web of brightly coloured streamers dangling from the tiles over her bed. An army of teddy bears is assembled along the windowsill and someone has installed icicle lights above the window. The lights have been fastened to the wall using strips of scotch tape, except for one spot where the wire has managed to free itself and is now drooped crookedly across the glass. It's not Christmas yet—or even winter, for that matter—but as per the Cancer Script, Sophia's life has become all about lasts: last birthday party, last family vacation, last chance to see the city lit from within by holiday cheer before she succumbs to her illness and the lights go out for good.

She smiles as soon as I walk in, even though her eyes are still closed and I haven't made a sound. She and I have a bond now, one so strong it transcends the need for sensory input. Joy and I had this sort of bond, too, especially in the last hours of my life when I could detect her presence from across the hospital. We call this process fusion and it involves blending her spirit with mine. Fusion eliminates the need for fear or doubt, and since it requires more than one visit to complete, what you end up with is one terminally ill patient welcoming death, and their designated escort, with open arms.

"It's about time," Sophia says, grating out the words with what little strength remains in her voice. "Did you get lost?"

I traverse the room, adjusting this, straightening that, and setting the stage for her eventual transition. The Living don't like it when things are out of place, especially if it's the last place their loved one sees before passing on. You'd think they have better things to worry about besides a few limp balloons, but it's not my place to ask questions.

"It's pretty hard to get lost when you're everywhere at once," I explain, cupping my hand under a flaccid balloon. The rubber expands slowly, and a second later the balloon floats up to the ceiling to rejoin its brood.

Sophia studies the balloon. "Cool trick," she says, her gaze finding traction on my face. "Think that would work on me?"

"You mean extending your life?" I hook a thumb under the sagging lights and press the tape back into place. "Sorry, no. Ansel's orders are final."

She turns her attention back to the balloons. We've had this discussion a million times, but the Living are notorious for cultivating too much hope. You see, every once in a while, Ansel has a change of heart about collecting a person's soul. The Living call it a near-death experience. We call it spiritual restoration, and only the most seasoned employees can perform it.

After I've finished tidying Sophia's room, I take a seat on the edge of her bed and reach for her hand. My Keepsake begins to glow as her palm settles comfortably against my own. One by one, the last of her memories funnel into her multitude of veins before exiting her fingers and converging on the stone. While not a terribly complicated task, the extraction process requires a keen eye and a delicate touch—strong enough to maintain a consistent connection, but light enough to allow the recollections to flow uninhibited.

A smile lifts the corner of Sophia's mouth. "Do I get one of those?" she asks.

"Of course. Where else are you going to keep your memories?"

"I was under the impression I was leaving them behind."

"Memories are like a fingerprint," I tell her, "no two sets are the same. We use your memories to build a profile around your spirit, and then use that profile to determine how best to leverage your strengths. You'll learn all about this during orientation."

A few straggling memories zip through her fingers and spiral into the Keepsake like water down a drain. With the last of her recollections now safely contained within the stone's bottomless depth, I release her hand, causing Sophia to giggle.

"What?" I ask, smiling at her temporary joy.

"It tickles," she tells me as her eyes fall shut. A moment later, her expression becomes serious and she forces her eyelids open a crack. "Is it weird that I'm laughing on my death bed?"

"Not really. People do a lot of strange things at the end of their life."

Sophia's lids flutter back together. She has short, pale lashes that remind me of dandelion seeds right before they're cast adrift by the forces of nature. In fact, everything about Sophia's face appears to have this delicate, juvenile quality, like her entire being is one blast of wind away from being scattered in every direction.

"So I guess you know everything about me now," Sophia says. "The good, the bad, the ugly…"

The smile that curls around her lips tells me she already knows the answer to this question, but I have time to kill, so I reply.

"Oh, you bet," I tell her as one of the balloons bobs precariously above her bed. I extend a hand toward it and a second later it elbows its way back into the throng. "Not that I'm judging, of course."

"Liar."

Sophia sinks her head into the pillow. Her eyes are open now, revealing a pair of lovely hazel irises fringed with just the right amount of blue. Her gaze reminds me of the open ocean: devastating, unpredictable, and filled with just enough mystery to tempt people into a second glance. I bet she's drowned a few hopeful lads in that look. A quick glance at her memories would confirm this hunch, but I don't have the heart to check.

Sophia is fading, whether it's into sleep or something deeper I'm not exactly sure. I hinge forward and gently apply my fingers to her chest. As the layers dissolve, her heart appears, first as a pulsing presence, then as a cluster of chambers contracting in tireless rhythm. I wonder how many times in her fifteen years it skipped a beat, only to make up for it with a kiss or a well-executed surprise party.

I move on to her lungs, which bear an uncanny resemblance to the sagging balloons. The rest of her organs are blistered and swollen with tumors, but there's nothing I can do to help her. One by one, her systems will shut down, and when they do, her spirit—the essence of her being, the part that makes Sophia,

15

Sophia—will vacate its vessel. At this point, her suffering is purely physical: beneath the aches and pains, bruises and abrasions, pockets of blood and disfigured organs, her spirit is untarnished and ripe for the picking.

"How much longer?" she asks.

I remove my hand.

"Not long," I assure her. "Are you scared?"

"Not of dying," Sophia explains, looking elsewhere, "just of being alone. I don't know anyone on the other side, except you."

I smile. "It's a start, right?"

Unable to resist the seductive pull of sleep or her own impending demise, Sophia's eyes slip shut. When you're this close to the edge, every blink has the potential to plunge you into eternal slumber. I wait, watching the sheets shift with every shallow intake of air and wondering how Ansel could forget to give me my collection orders. Maybe Gabe was right: at this rate, I'll never get out of The Establishment. And really, I'm not even sure I want to.

"Sarah?" Sophia's voice wobbles like a newborn calf. "Stay with me?"

So that's exactly what I do: I sit, and I wait, until at last Sophia's lungs release their final, triumphant breath and my Keepsake explodes in a brilliant flash of green. My collection orders have finally arrived.

4

Society has a lot of names for The Establishment. Some people call it Heaven. Others call it the spirit realm. Most simply think of it as the other side. We don't call it the other side. We call it Headquarters, and it's our side. Other implies opposition, and there's nothing oppositional about death. Death has always been, and will always be, a part of life—not so much the end of one, but the beginning of another.

Shortly after Sophia's soul separated from her body, I led her across the hospital and into the sterilization chamber. The chamber is a large, cylindrical room unbound by the laws of physics: it has no seams, no buttons, and a door that only appears when we get where we're going. The floor and the walls are solid metal, but not a reflective sort of metal like the kind you might find in an elevator. That doesn't stop Sophia from searching for her reflection.

"Where is it?" she asks after several moments of circling the hermetic pod.

"Your reflection?" She nods, but her eyes have already lost interest in my reply. "You don't have one."

"Will I ever get it back?"

"There's a way," I reply as the outline of a door materializes inches from where Sophia is standing, "but it's not recommended."

I turn my head, nodding at the now-open portal, and a second later, Sophia reluctantly ventures out.

The door to the incubator stands to the left of a high-walled desk encircling a small, uncluttered workstation. On the front of the desk is a loop—some might call it a commercial—detailing The Establishment's purpose and values. Sophia stands perfectly still, transfixed by the images flashing across the screen. In the commercial, everyone is smiling. Ansel says smiles make people feel safe. I never got that feeling from a human smile, and judging by the look on Sophia's face, neither does she.

"Are you in this?" she wonders as I approach the desk and place my hand on the keypad.

"Nope," I say without turning around. "I was asked, but opted out."

Upon detecting my Keepsake, the keypad turns bright white: light-at-the-end-of-the-tunnel white, a universally recognizable hue that the Living typically associate with drifting off into the blue. "Crossing over," they call it, which sounds more like navigating a busy street than entering an entirely different dimension. Either way, now you know: that heavenly light you see when your spirit vacates your body is really just a fellow Catcher registering their latest assignment.

Sophia sidles over. Next to the keypad is a slightly larger screen displaying all of those pesky details I gathered during the final extraction process. Most of them, such as blood type, dietary intolerances, preferred sleeping position, and susceptibility to workaday ailments, are useless for our purposes. We filter those facts out first. Think of it as panning for gold, except the gold, in this case, is the more noteworthy aspects of a person's identity: their name, their date, time, and place of birth, and their memories; things that they alone would know, an intricate tapestry of intangible qualities spun from the yarns of trial and error. That's the meat and potatoes of a life. Everything else is just seasoning, and ultimately, it has no place in the catalogue.

Sophia stares at the screen next to the keypad, watching the summary of her brief life take shape before her eyes. Her image appears breathtakingly clear, from her asymmetrical hairline, to the faint dusting of freckles spanning the full width of her face. The remaining details trickle in shortly after, including her birthday, her zodiac sign, and her personal vices, which causes her to scoff—proof that, even without a body to inhabit, the ego is still as bruisable as a peach.

"I'm not fickle," she bristles. "I just like having options."

"And I'm not apathetic. I just get bored easily." When our eyes connect, I crack a smile and wait for her to reciprocate. It's what humans do, after all, and Ansel is a big fan of promoting familiarity.

Sophia turns around. Behind us, the chamber door opens and Gabe appears with his latest recruit: a young black man with kind eyes and a week's worth of growth fringing his jaw. His eyes fly over to Sophia, ricochet off of her face, and then return to the door through which he and Gabe just passed. He's positively stupefied, but Gabe doesn't seem to notice.

"Sarah," Gabe says, ignoring his flustered recruit. His eyes flicker to Sophia before returning to me a second later. "I see you got your collection orders."

I turn back to the counter, where Sophia is still watching Gabe's recruit. He's standing in the middle of the room with his head bent back and his jaw frozen at a forty-five-degree angle. If he'd discovered palm trees and ivory sand instead of a windowless room with no ceiling and a self-concealing door, I doubt his reaction would've been much different. Clearly, Gabe didn't give him the run-down on what to expect as a newly minted spirit, but it's not my place to school him on protocol.

Gabe begins to speak.

"Well, since Sarah's forgotten her manners, we'll just use mine. I'm Gabe. This is Kyle. And you must be…"

"Sophia," I say, beating her to the punch. "Her name's Sophia. Now we can all go back to what we were doing."

Gabe ambles over, leaving Kyle to ponder the nonexistent ceiling while Sophia toys with the uneven strings of her gown. Their collective curiosity has rendered them blind to our presence, so I resume cataloguing just as Gabe props an elbow on the desk beside me.

"I'm still trying to figure out how you made it back before I did," he says, "especially since you were late getting those orders."

"For one thing, I wasn't dilly-dallying around the hospital. Once the orders arrived, I got out of there as quickly as I could."

"I was not *dilly-dallying*," Gabe insists, planting the other elbow on the desk. "Unlike you, I actually want to get back to being a living, breathing organism." He furrows his brows and I grudgingly follow his gaze. "Capricorn," he says in a voice that belies his outward indifference. "Everleigh was a Capricorn."

"Fascinating."

"Don't forget to log her compatibilities," he tells me in that supercilious tone of his. "Also, if you're going to do this right, you should probably slow down."

I apply my hand more firmly to the keypad, causing the remaining details to flit across the screen. The sooner I can get Sophia into the system, the sooner I can be out from under Gabe's scrutiny.

"So you're not going to slow down?" he asks, eyeing me more closely.

"Nope."

"Not even if it means avoiding mistakes? You know how Ansel is about mistakes."

"Not a clue."

"Revel in your ignorance, Miss Galloway. Because I can tell you—from personal experience, I might add—that Ansel has no patience for mistakes."

"Your helmet hair would suggest otherwise."

This seems to do the trick and Gabe relents with a curt tip of his chin. However, my victory is short-lived, and a second later he launches into one of his signature, narcissistic tirades.

"I had a broken spirit," he reminds me with no shortage of passion or self-pity. "I was—and I'm quoting Ansel directly here—'unsalvageable'. So, in addition to being physically shredded on the interstate, I was also spiritually shattered beyond repair. And you know what happens to broken spirits."

"Get to the point already."

"My point," Gabe says haughtily, "is that the helmet hair was a small price to pay to make it here in one piece…which, frankly, is more than I can say for my body when it arrived at the morgue."

I don't flatter him with praise. Gabe is a bit of a legend around here, if for no reason other than because everyone's been forced to listen to the story of how Ansel had to temporarily leave The Establishment in order to gather the fragments of Gabe's soul. Ansel never leaves The Establishment, so naturally, Gabe believes himself to be above the rest of us, who were all escorted by more senior Catchers. Joke's on him, though, because when it comes to large-scale catastrophes, no one volunteers to help. That's what he gets for thinking he's the best: he gets to work alone.

Gabe is suddenly restless. "The girl's fifteen," he says impatiently, "how long can this take?"

"Oh, I'm sorry. I thought you wanted me to slow down."

He elevates his chin, fully prepared to sneer away my sarcasm, but a smile bubbles to the surface before he can stop it.

"You are quite something," he tells me, to which I give nothing in the way of a reaction. I don't like ambivalent

22

compliments. "Fine. In that case, I'm taking Kyle up to bay three."

"Then go. I'm not stopping you."

"Come on, comrade," he says, turning away from the counter. "The hypothetical clock's a-tickin'.'"

Gabe wanders toward the room's rear, where he raises a hand to the wall and waits for the door to reappear. It opens promptly, stealing both Kyle and Sophia's interest, and I wait until the portal seals itself behind Gabe before turning my focus to the catalogue's latest entry: Sophia Grace Jacobson.

"Well, that does it," I inform her. "You're in the system."

"For how long?"

"Until Ansel decides you're ready to assume a new form."

I remove my hand from the keypad. I turn to look at Sophia, but she's already poised in front of the incubator door and ready to tackle the next stage of her transition.

I move into position beside her. I halfway consider saying something to assuage her uncertainty, but I can tell from her unwavering gaze that she doesn't have any.

"So this is how it ends," Sophia says, sizing up the door.

"No," I reply. "It's not the end. You're just getting started."

"A new beginning," she says with a nod. "I can handle that."

I raise a hand to the door. It opens slowly, mirroring the uncertainty I had expected Sophia to feel, and she steps over the threshold without a second thought.

5

Ansel's office is the only room in The Establishment with windows. They run the full length of the wall behind his desk and offer an unimpeded view of the Verge, which is what we call the overlap between our world and the next.

The closest earthly thing I can think to compare it to is a two-way mirror: on one side—your side, the one shrouded in mystery and ignorance—all you see is your own humanly insignificance reflected back at you.

On the other side—our side—we see all of you: not as would-be catalogue entries with faces, names, and stories, but as a source of unlimited energy. Ansel built his empire on the infinite potential of the human spirit: without death, The Establishment would cease to exist. Without The Establishment, human beings would go extinct. It's a delicate balancing act: remove one force, and humanity is doomed to slide off its narrow plane of existence and straight into obscurity.

I let myself into the palatial room. Despite my hundreds of visits over the years, I never get used to the sight of Ansel's personal library, which fills two entire walls on both sides of his desk and consists of thousands of stiff, leather-bound books spanning every topic known to humankind. It's all here, every piece of every puzzle that society has ever endeavored to solve. With this much knowledge at my fingertips, the irony of the human condition is inescapable: the only thing the Living want to know is what awaits them on the other side, and by the time they finally get their answer, it's too late for them to do anything about it.

"I see you never lost your love for books," comes a voice from directly behind me.

I smile and trace the inscription on a crumbling green spine.

"It's hard to forget an old friend," I reply, turning around.

Ansel nods. His hairless head gleams like a lamppost at the edge of dusk. He's wearing a light grey suit and a slim black tie knotted perfectly beneath his throat. Ansel may not be the only member of The Establishment with a proclivity toward formal wear, but he's the only one who's permitted to wear a black tie, for obvious reasons.

Ansel appears to consider my response for a long time. Toward the end of his private musings, he closes the distance between us and produces a book from a shelf partway up the wall. A decade's worth of dust is cemented into the book's creases. I search Ansel's face for an explanation, but his expression is as blank as the pages.

"I haven't finished this one," he tells me, to which I offer no response. "Every time I try humanity embarks on another tragic escapade."

"But Ansel," I say, eyeing the empty pages, "there's nothing there."

"Is that what you think?"

I steel myself against the icy undercurrent of his inquiry. With all these books as witnesses, I'm reluctant to testify against my doubt.

He closes the book and sets it back on the shelf.

"Knowledge is a process of discovery," Ansel says, taking inventory of his collection. "History writes itself, but most people are existentially illiterate… In any case, I hadn't expected your assessment to be so shallow. I should think someone in your position understands that just because you can't see something, doesn't mean it isn't there."

Too embarrassed to speak, I turn back to the books. I miss reading: not so much the act of consuming what's written, which I can still do, but the ability to immerse myself in the solitary pursuit of meaning. I miss the musty fragrance of dog-eared classics and the weight of a thousand passing thoughts waiting to be unearthed in my hands. If I concentrate, I can call all of these sensations to the forefront of my mind, but memories are a mediocre substitute for reality.

Ansel ambles back to his desk and lowers himself into his chair. "I have an assignment for you," he announces.

I angle toward his workspace. I wait for him to look up, but he never does.

"An assignment," I echo, tasting the words as they tumble around in my mouth. Their bittersweet tang catches me off guard. "In what sense?"

"Mentorship," he replies, meeting my eye for the briefest of moments. "I was going to ask Jonathon, but I think you'd benefit from this exercise more."

"Who's the recruit?"

Ansel slides a stack of books aside in order to access a transparent screen. From here, he can see every entry in The Establishment's catalogue. I catch a fleeting glimpse of Sophia's profile as he scrolls through the endless entries.

"Funny you should ask," he says. "It's Gabe."

"Gabe," I say, measuring my tone, correcting my posture. "Gabe Conway?"

"Gabe Conway," Ansel confirms, pausing on a name I don't recognize. "As I said, my first instinct was to send Jonathon, but his skills aren't on par with the demands of this assignment."

"What's the assignment?"

"Train derailment," he replies. "I know that's not your beat, but Gabe won't be able to do this on his own, no matter how convinced he is of his own capabilities."

"And there's no one else you can send?"

"There's no one else I want to send, Sarah. I trust you. I don't trust Gabe."

"But Gabe attends derailments all the time. What makes this one so different?"

"The scale. It's a commuter train. Thirty-eight spirits will be escorted on site. The remaining seventeen will be collected at the hospital. Back up will be made available to you, but the important thing is that Gabe maintains a sense of order. That's where you come in."

Ansel reclines in his chair, trying to get comfortable, but his attempt at relaxation is lost on his face. Displeasure is chiseled into his stone-like features as he drums his fingers on the edge of the desk, keeping the tense silence at bay.

At last, he speaks.

"I know you prefer to work alone, and I assure you this arrangement is strictly temporary. But Gabe is hasty and doesn't know how to connect with the dying like you do. You need to be there, if only for the little ones."

I falter. "The little ones."

Ansel holds my gaze for the equivalent of a human heartbeat. "It has to be done."

I give a half-nod—accepting, but not agreeing with, everything Ansel has just said. He does what he has to do to keep humanity, and The Establishment, running smoothly, but that doesn't make it any easier for those of us who have to do the heavy lifting.

"I appreciate you doing this," Ansel continues. "I know you haven't given much thought to regenerating, but hopefully this will put you a little closer to your quotas."

"I was actually thinking of staying on for a while," I concede, which seems to surprise him. "I'm considering extending my training... specifically, into Quarantine."

Ansel levels his gaze at me. "You understand that we don't introduce recruits to the Ward until level three."

"I know, but I'd rather get the experience now, before I settle on a new form."

I pause, observing Ansel, who's staring down at his desk in mute contemplation. The Ward is a maximum-security zone at the heart of The Establishment where evil spirits are permitted to roam freely for brief periods of time. In order to gain entry to the Ward, Catchers must be qualified—meaning level three or higher—and they must be accompanied by Ansel himself. The Ward serves as training ground for employees graduating into Quarantine, and the only thing I know about the position is that no one volunteers for it.

"Help Gabe with his collections," Ansel instructs me, returning to his catalogue, "and then, maybe, we'll talk about the Ward."

His eyes travel downwards, in the opposite direction of his hand, which dismisses me with a flick. I retrace my steps, absently adjusting my shirtsleeves as the door slides open and I step out.

An empty hallway greets me on the other side, but it doesn't offer the tranquility I'm seeking. Lurid white light with no discernible source beams down on me at every angle. Behind me, the door to Ansel's office recedes into the wall before vanishing completely—there one minute, gone the next, just like the souls in his catalogue.

A shadowy figure floats into my periphery. I imagine the steady tempo of Gabe's footfalls driving away the silence with each approaching step, but his movement produces no sound whatsoever.

"Well, look at that." Gabe stops walking as his gaze traces the outline of my perpendicular form. "You beat me here, too. A little ironic, I'll admit, but I'm willing to give you the benefit of the doubt."

"Ansel wanted to speak to me," I say. "Does he want to speak to you, too?"

"I don't know. Does he?" Gabe gauges my energy field, which has become noticeably wider thanks to an uptick in confidence. "What did you talk about?" he asks, taking a small step back.

"Oddly enough, you." I face him and spread my arms. "Say hello to your new mentor."

Disbelief darts across his face. He blinks slowly, his dazzling green eyes drinking me in from a distance, until at last he shifts his weight and keeps walking.

"You couldn't mentor me if your regeneration depended on it," he says as he strides past "Not that I'm doubting your abilities, but you'd be hard-pressed to keep up with me. There's a reason you cover cancer and I cover freak accidents."

"So you're saying I'm too slow."

"I'm saying you're too slow to mentor me, or anyone on this beat, for that matter. Now if you'll excuse me, I have a quota to meet."

"Ansel thinks you're hasty," I call after him. "I'd tell you to ask him yourself, but I'm not sure he'd welcome the interruption."

"Well, lucky for him, I'm taking your word for it. I'm still not taking you with me, though."

"Too bad. I've already received the collection orders."

Gabe swivels back toward me. His field tingles with indignation and there's a deep crease between his brows where confusion is hunkered down like a bear in hibernation, but unfortunately, it's not enough to deter me from following through with Ansel's orders.

"So did I," he says with a shrug. "Shall I hold the door for you, oh holy one?"

"As if I need a man to open a portal for me."

"Good, because I wasn't planning to wait."

I smirk. "So much for manners."

"Blame it on my haste." Gabe takes up a spirited pace and adds, "If you want to keep up, you'd better start now."

I lengthen my stride accordingly. Within a few steps, we're shoulder to shoulder with each other, and even though Gabe refuses to look at me, his energy is considerably more subdued. He may have no reservations about taunting me, but he'd never disobey Ansel. He's been to the basement, too, and one trip is usually all it takes to keep the staff in line.

"So how do you want to do this?" Gabe asks as we step into the chamber. "Fifty-fifty? Seventy-thirty? Ninety-ten?"

"You take care of the adults. I'll look after the kids."

"Why? The kids love me."

"Because those are Ansel's orders. End of discussion."

I expect him to harass me, but he saves his energy. And it's just as well, because judging by the chaos that awaits us, we're going to need all the help we can get.

31

6

The look on Gabe's face is one of pure bewilderment. For someone who's seen his share of disasters, I hadn't expected him to be so appalled—and yet, as I begin making my way toward the wreckage, it takes him a moment to follow.

I turn around. Gabe is still standing in the chamber with his hands in his pockets and his eyes wide with surprise. Behind him, police have cordoned off the crumbling road and there's a wall of onlookers assembling behind the barricade. I motion for him to keep up, but Gabe is frozen in place and perfectly oblivious to my urgency.

"Gabe," I say when he still doesn't move, or even meet my eyes. "Come on. It's not like you haven't seen a train wreck before."

"Maybe you should do this without me—you know, since you're in charge and all."

I don't know what to say. This is Gabe's beat. Just because I'm here to teach him a thing or two about maintaining order doesn't mean I intend to do all the work. Ansel will know the difference. Somehow, he always does.

Exasperated, I walk back to the chamber. My brisk pace rattles him from his stupor, but does nothing to convince him to move.

"You can stop holding the door for me," I say. "I'm out."

Gabe's gaze finds my face. Amusement teases his lips, but where I'm expecting to see a smile, a grimace appears instead.

"You think this is about you?" he asks acerbically. "Typical."

"I don't care what it's about. This is your job. Ansel's orders were very clear."

Something akin to disgust makes an appearance in his eyes. Gabe frees his hands, readying himself for battle, and I step aside just as he charges out like a Thoroughbred in a starting gate.

"So you're Ansel's pet now, are you?" he says, exacting a distance between us in a few generous strides. "I wish I could say I'm surprised."

"If wanting to leave my mark on The Establishment makes me Ansel's pet, then so be it. At least I'm earning my regeneration." I quicken my steps. I'm keeping pace with him, but just barely. "And you referring to me as Ansel's pet is a little ironic, if you ask me."

"Is it?"

"You're Gabe Conway. The only reason everyone knows your name is because Ansel had to make a house call."

"And it's a good thing he did, otherwise I might've been haunting that overpass for all eternity."

"Doubtful. Ansel's against haunting."

We've finally reached the heap of mangled metal, where toppled train cars lie scattered in a twisted confusion across the tracks and surrounding countryside. A small fire has broken out in the engine and there's so much smoke that it's hard to tell where one car ends and the next one begins. A symphony of suffering reaches a desperate crescendo: between the garbled sobs, the resigned moans, and the unfettered pleas for help, I can just make out a softer, sweeter sound that ordinary ears would dismiss as the imagination's attempts at trickery. I close my eyes and concentrate my energy, filtering out the medley of competing noises until, against all odds, the wind relents and the whimper reaches me again.

"Gabe," I say, turning to him. "Did you hear that?"

He angles toward one of the cars, which is lying on its side at least fifty feet from the tracks. Broken glass litters the grass and there's a putrid stench wafting from one of the windows, as if someone forgot their dinner on the stove, but worse.

Gabe climbs onto the car and crouches next to the busted window. Long, slender fingers of smoke caress his gossamer complexion, but he doesn't seem to notice.

"Well?" I say. "You heard it too, right?"

He motions for me to join him. I scramble onto the train car just as he lowers himself onto his stomach and leans in for a better look.

Settling in beside him, I squint into the jagged opening. The dust is so thick it blots out everything except for the outlines of a few badly damaged seats. It is in this dense cloud of destruction that I detect the faintest glimmer of movement, confirming my suspicions once and for all.

I wave my hand over the window. Light streams from my fingertips, carving the plume of debris like headlights in a blizzard. I'm searching the shadows for a fresh clue when the light catches on something shiny and I tilt forward in time to see two bright blue eyes staring up at me through the smoke.

"There," I say, killing the light. I glance at Gabe. "Care to do the honours?"

He pushes himself back into a crouched position. "What happened to you handling the kids?"

"I found her, didn't I?"

Gabe nods and disappears through the window.

He lands effortlessly amidst the chaos that surrounds him. Still kneeling, Gabe raises a hand, casting just enough light to illuminate the face of a young girl with copper curls and plump, little cheeks now devoid of colour. She's wearing a collared blue dress, mismatched socks stuffed into a pair of shiny red shoes, and a string of dollar store pearls around her neck. When Gabe tries to approach her, she shrinks into the corner and wraps her arms around her knees.

"Gabe," I call down to him, "do the butterfly trick."

He acknowledges my suggestion with a lazy flash of his thumb. Hunching forward slightly, he scrapes the dust into a mound the size of an anthill before scooping it into his palms and rubbing it between his hands. It stutters and crackles like a bad connection, until at last he separates his hands and releases a colony of imaginary butterflies.

They flutter playfully around the train car, losing definition with each beat of their wings. The girl's face glows with glee. She crawls into Gabe's embrace and locks her arms behind his head, nuzzling his neck as he stands.

"Don't get too comfortable," he tells her, prompting her to wrap her spindly legs more tightly around his waist.

I back away from the opening as Gabe grapples over the seats and climbs out of the window. Annoyance is etched into his forehead, but still the girl holds fast, refusing to part with her rescuer.

"Come here little one," I say, hooking my hands under her arms. A pained whimper escapes her colourless lips as Gabe is liberated from her fierce affection.

"Is there anyone else down there?" I ask him.

Gabe saunters over to the edge of the car and hops down onto the tracks. When I try to pass him the girl, he pretends not to notice and begins walking away, leaving me to lower us both to the ground.

"Not that I could see," he says when we finally catch up to him. "My guess is she was late to the dying party and everyone took off without her. There were plenty of bodies."

"How many?"

"Hard to say… ten, maybe twelve. I don't know. I was a little preoccupied." His eyes flicker to the girl's face, but by the time she can summon the enthusiasm to smile, his gaze has already abandoned her.

Gabe leads us through the commotion. Black tendrils of smoke spiral out of shattered windows and pirouette above smoldering carcasses of tangled metal. Ansel could tell you

36

exactly what happened here, but the only thing I can say for certain is that fifty-five people are dead or dying and there's no way Gabe and I will be able to complete these collections ourselves.

"We need a system," I say as I adjust my grip on the girl's hand.

"More like a goddamned miracle. Whose idea was it to send two Catchers to do the work of ten?"

I stop and look around. A few disoriented spirits are wandering aimlessly up and down the tracks, while others are sitting on the ground looking alarmed and discombobulated. Sometimes death is kind and comes with a warning, and other times it cuts life short without the faintest twinge of compunction.

"Are you Sarah?" comes a voice from directly behind me.

I turn around, the girl still clinging to my hand as we scan the hubbub for the source of the voice. A leggy woman in black uniform emerges from behind one of the cars as she makes her way toward us. Her voice is as smooth as whiskey and she carries herself proudly, as if there's nothing else she's meant to do but collect souls like hockey cards from what is sure to be tomorrow's leading news story.

"I am," I reply when she's closer. "And you must be…?"

"Cheyenne, Mass Casualties. Ansel said you needed backup."

I nod and look around, but Gabe is nowhere to be seen.

"We do," I say. "We already have one soul, but the remaining thirty-seven are a little scattered."

Cheyenne shrugs. "It happens. As long as the separations are clean, it shouldn't be a problem."

Turning her focus over to the girl, Cheyenne hinges forward, plants her hands on her knees, and flashes her an electric grin. "Hi, sweetie. What's your name?"

The girl buries her face in my thigh. I smooth a hand over her hair, watching as the rusty strands wind around my fingers like vines. She hugs my leg a little more forcefully, refusing to meet Cheyenne's gaze, and I offer an apologetic shrug on her behalf.

"Any sign of the parents?" Cheyenne asks, extending to her full height once again.

"Not that I could see. If they survived, they're most likely conferring with police."

Cheyenne's thoughtful expression is blistered with confusion. She holds my gaze, weighing my words against the silence that follows, before finally shaking her head.

"No," she says slowly, panning her gaze over the frenzy of faces. "There's no way she could've died and they didn't. Look at how young she is. A child this small wouldn't be allowed to go anywhere without a parent or legal guardian."

"What are you suggesting?"

"I'm suggesting scouring the car for her parents. It's possible their souls are still in there somewhere."

"Gabe said he found only bodies."

"Double-check the bodies. Their souls may not have separated yet."

Cheyenne folds her arms as Gabe ambles over. When he catches the girl eyeing him inquisitively, he redirects his steps and comes to a stop on my other side.

Cheyenne smirks. "Well, if it isn't the infamous Gabe Conway, all dressed up and ready to disappoint."

"I never disappoint," Gabe says smugly. "Even when I crash and burn, it's a bloody spectacle."

Cheyenne shakes her head. Then she turns to address me, much to Gabe's displeasure.

"What were Ansel's orders, exactly?"

I brief her on the mission. On my right, Gabe's energy sizzles with rage, but I pointedly ignore him.

"In that case," Cheyenne says when I finish speaking, "you need a consolidation zone. Where did you enter?"

"A short ways down from the police barricade."

"Okay. So have your recruits assemble in the neighbouring field. As long as one of us is around to supervise, I don't foresee anyone wandering off."

I turn to Gabe. "I suppose we should get started, then."

"From the sounds of things, you already have."

I stoop to the girl's level. Where her spirit meets mine there's a faint blue glow extending from the web of her thumb to the heel of her palm. We call this crease the lifeline, and rather than serve as some arbitrary predictor of longevity, it functions more like a border between dimensions. Like all borders, one must be prepared to show ID prior to crossing. In the land of the Living, this is usually a passport. At The Establishment, it's their memories.

"We have to let go now," I say as her face scrunches like a paper napkin, "but as long as you stay close to Cheyenne, I promise nothing will happen to you."

The girl cranes her head to look at Cheyenne, and at last, her fingers detach from mine. She shuffles forward, left hand already outstretched, and Cheyenne proceeds to lead her away before I can think of anything to say.

Something akin to grief slithers through me. It strikes like a fist in the pit of my nonexistent stomach, so I scrabble around in my bag in hopes the feeling will pass.

"So where do you want to start?" Gabe asks, his voice slicing through the mounting cacophony. "Tracks or cars?"

I try my best to shake off the chill, but the discomfort persists, as does the feeling that something is missing. I consult my left hand; my Keepsake is still firmly affixed to my ring finger and the stone has turned a milky lavender colour—the default colour for documenting a child's passing.

I look at Gabe. If he notices my perplexity, he doesn't mention it.

"Cars," I say, needing to be alone. "I'll holler if I need you."

I begin to walk away, halfway expecting him to follow, but his eyes are the only things that move.

7

It turns out Cheyenne was right about the little girl's parents: death had claimed them last. When Gabe searched the car a second time, he found them huddled in the corner next to their daughter's body. They'd been so transfixed by her death that they were unable to process their own. Gabe says this is common with abrupt departures. He says the only thing that can prepare a spirit for separation is time, and even then there are no guarantees.

That's where we come in. Sometimes the spirits insist on reuniting with their bodies, even at the risk of suffering immeasurable pain, but unless Ansel authorizes a restoration the only way to go is into the chamber. The spirits who've experienced violent separations are often fearful and full of questions, but we don't answer any of them until they're safely sealed within the chamber walls.

It took two passes to gather all of the victims. Cheyenne and Gabe escorted the first batch, and with surprisingly little resistance. I headed straight to the hospital for the second group, whose members were considerably more headstrong. A few refused to cooperate, but quickly changed their tune when I detailed their punishment.

By the time I arrive at the incubator, Gabe and Cheyenne have processed nearly half of the first group, which is arranged in a line around the room's perimeter. A few of them shuffle sideways to allow me passage as I lead the second group onto the floor without even acknowledging Gabe's quizzical expression.

After instructing my recruits to join the queue, I set about performing my extractions. Most people are disappointed when they see their life laid out like this: not as the highlight reel they've been taught to imagine, but as an assortment of insignificant snapshots pulled from some invisible album buried deep within their psyche. Your life is not a movie, and the only time you see it flash before your eyes is when we're robbing you of your identity.

I approach my next recruit: a stocky businessman with a greasy comb-over and poorly knotted necktie. If I had to guess, I'd say he was running late for work and forced to catch the last train out of the station. This is how a lot of lives end: not with a final, tragic admission on a deathbed, but as a single step in the wrong direction. Sometimes I think this would've been a better way to go—suddenly, shockingly, and with my dignity still intact.

He smiles sheepishly and offers his left hand. He has the kinds of fingers made for manual labour, not clattering around a cubicle shuffling papers and rearranging photos of his family all day.

I turn his hand over and pour his memories into my Keepsake. One by one, they skitter and tumble like windblown leaves into the narrow passages of his capillaries. Most recruits like to marvel at the moments they've forgotten, but this one seems more interested in staring at me.

"So what did you do to end up here?" he asks. Even without lungs he sounds winded when he speaks, like he's asking for a raise and not how I died.

"Cancer," I reply without looking at him.

"Sounds like a better way to go. At least you had time to say goodbye."

I grip his hand more firmly, but there are only so many memories you can shoehorn into a single moment. Given the silver threads in his otherwise brown hair, I'd peg his age to be around forty-two. His pebbly voice is consistent with someone who recently quit smoking, and if the crow's feet are anything to go by, he was married with kids—probably more kids than he could realistically afford to feed.

Something feathers over me again. I'm tempted to call it grief, but it's not; there's no room for grief in a business that wheels and deals in death. In humans, grief usually manifests as a crushing, immovable force, like waking up with a lion on your chest and praying it doesn't swallow you whole.

But this sensation—whatever it is—doesn't feel like a lion at all. Maybe I'm imagining things, but that doesn't explain the icicles of dread that are now lodged in my otherwise unfeeling gut. Catchers aren't supposed to have feelings. Feelings are the hallmark of humanity, and they're the first things to be eliminated in the chamber.

"Sarah."

A brisk voice shatters my reverie as I glance down at the man's hand. Where there was previously light it is now completely dark.

His veins have cooled, along with my Keepsake, which is now a stormy red colour—not a bright, fire engine red, which indicates danger, but something far more sinister. Something I've only ever seen in orientations, but never in my day-to-day life as a fully licensed Spirit Catcher.

"Sarah," Cheyenne says, coming up behind me, "let go."

So I do.

Cheyenne frowns at me. Not wanting her to notice the ring's irregular hue, I cover my left hand and hope she won't choose this precise moment to probe me for an explanation.

Cheyenne holds my gaze. I massage the stone until it returns to its default colour.

"Maybe you should sit this one out," she says quietly, punctuating her command with a subtle nod. I mirror her gesture and then take my leave before I can embarrass myself further.

I approach the door on the right-hand side of the registration counter. Unlike the left door, which leads to the incubator, the right door doesn't lead anywhere in particular, only to another hallway and another series of unmarked doors. I keep walking, even without a specific destination in mind. I walk until I lose sight of the door through which I entered, then turn the first corner and keep traveling along my undefined trajectory until I abandon the desire to see if anyone followed me. Wherever I'm going, it had better take me away from whatever corrupted my Keepsake in the chamber.

I turn a few more corners and pass a few more doors. The Establishment is just a maze, really: a vast, maddeningly complex network of rooms and offices joined by hallways and tunnels connecting smaller wings to larger ones. If it weren't for my Keepsake, I'd be hopelessly lost in no time at all.

I slip through another door and race up a flight of stairs toward a platform. Once I reach the platform, I open the door and step out onto the terrace.

The terrace is the closest thing we have to a rooftop patio. It's the place where Catchers gather to socialize and forget about their latest missions. It's also the place where they come to sort out their thoughts when they're too afraid to approach Ansel, as I am now. He's not a belligerent leader, and to my knowledge he's never disowned a Catcher for going rogue, but that doesn't stop my imagination from assuming the worst. Catchers aren't supposed to have feelings, which indicate an error in the transition process. There is a solution, but as far as I know no one has survived it.

I approach the wall and peer over the edge. The indigo sky is peppered with stars; I watch a couple of them tumble into the abyss, white tails fizzling like fireworks as they vanish from sight.

The terrace door opens and Gabe appears. Concern makes a rare appearance on his face as he swaggers over to me. I'm not sure whether he expects me to speak, so instead, I turn back to the wall and hope he won't rub my mistake in my face.

"Good hiding place," he says mockingly. "Would've never guessed you'd come here."

45

I face him. He has both hands flat on the ledge and his hip is cocked at just the right angle to make me think he intends to stay, though for how long is anyone's guess.

"You puzzle me," I tell him.

He rounds his shoulders and casts his gaze out across the infinite expanse of stars. "Do I?"

"You care enough to come looking for me, but not enough to pass up an opportunity to make me feel incompetent. Would it kill you to show up and just be quiet?"

"Oh, believe me, I don't care," Gabe says. "I'm only here because Cheyenne asked me to check on you. And a little common sense would suggest you can't kill something that's already dead."

"Too bad," I mutter.

"So what happened back there? It's like you glitched or something."

I look at Gabe. If I tell him the truth, it'll just give him another excuse to be condescending. Not that he needs one, of course, but given half a choice, I'd prefer him to remain ignorant.

All the same, I need an ally, and a second opinion.

"It's nothing, really. I just thought I felt something."

"What kind of something?"

"I don't know… A draft."

"And this concerns you?"

"Deeply." I glance at him. "I have a theory, but it's terrible."

"I wouldn't doubt that."

I close my eyes, snatching a momentary respite from his infuriating smirk. I should've known better than to tell Gabe anything, but maybe not all is lost.

"Show me your guardian," I say as I face him again.

Gabe rears back and scowls.

"Why?" he asks cautiously.

I don't have an explanation, only a half-baked hypothesis demanding the crudest of experiments.

"Just do it, Gabe. Please."

He turns away from the ledge so that he's facing the middle of the terrace. I hadn't expected him to comply with my request so quickly, even if it did seem to take him by surprise.

Gabe makes a fist with his left hand and turns his arm over so that his wrist is facing up. He then uses the nail of his right thumb to draw a few beads of black energy from a superficial incision at the base of his palm. We call this practice bleeding out, and despite its resemblance to certain destructive impulses, the outcome, for us, is usually positive. Conjuring a grief guardian is about exposing ourselves to the environments in which we work. It's not glamorous, but it keeps us connected to our former selves long enough to do our jobs.

Gabe drags his fingers through the resulting puddle, then rubs the energy between his fingers until it sparks. The embers hiss and pop, and just when I think his hand is about to burst into flames, he lifts it above his head and sends a plume of rich, ebony smoke straight into the air. The smoke forms wings, and then a

47

rounded head, before finally developing talons, a hooked beak, and glossy obsidian eyes. Gabe waves his hand, sending the bird on its way, and it circles above the terrace with a few furious flaps of its wings.

"A falcon," I say as it swoops between us. "That explains a lot."

"Does it?"

"Well, I wouldn't have expected anything less from someone who met his maker while traveling at speeds of over two hundred miles per hour." I admire the falcon's acrobatics, then add, "It doesn't really explain the grief component, though."

"Sure it does," Gabe says, shifting his weight. "Have you ever tried to outrun grief? It's impossible."

"Well, that's one way to look at it." I shake my head. The discomfort I experienced in the chamber didn't feel like a falcon either, and even if it had, that still wouldn't explain why it affected me and not him.

"Let's see yours," Gabe says, snapping me from my trance.

"I'd rather not."

"Too bad. I'm curious."

Sighing, I expose my left wrist and bleed it out. I drag two fingers through the residue and distribute it quickly, coating the tips of all four fingers and my thumb until they glow with life. From there, the smoke begins. It gushes between my fingers and pools on the floor at my feet, where it tornadoes in on itself and eventually sprouts a long, flat head. An elongated body follows.

A forked tongue protrudes from the heap, and suddenly my relationship with grief begins to make a lot more sense.

Gabe nods. "A python," he says. "Largely solitary and capable of consuming its victims whole. Does that sound about right?"

"Unfortunately." The python slithers toward one of the walls and is gone in a blink. "That still doesn't explain anything, like why my Keepsake changed colour in the chamber."

"What colour did it turn?"

"Red. A smoky red, like a midsummer sky at sunset."

Something in Gabe's expression shifts. I'm not sure if it's disappointment or curiosity, but the way he's looking at me now, I'm starting to wish I'd never consulted with him in the first place.

When he opens his mouth again, his voice is a raspy whisper of surprise.

"Mine too," he says.

I stare at him. Could it be? Are Gabe and I actually agreeing on something, for once?

"You felt it too, right?" I say, trying to curb my excitement. "It was like a breeze—a warm breeze—like someone was breathing on you, but there was no one there, aside from the recruits. When we were in the field I kept feeling like something was missing, like I'd lost my Keepsake. I don't know, maybe I'm just going crazy, but maybe not..." I pause. Gabe is smiling, which is enough to make my proverbial blood boil. "Why are you smiling? You felt it too, right?"

He chuckles. Unlinking his arms, he removes his weight from the wall and takes a couple of steps toward me.

"Sarah, come on," he says, "I'm just fucking with you."

I slug him in the arm.

"You hit like a girl," he tells me as I and head toward the door.

"Go figure. I used to be one."

"Have you ever thought that maybe you're wrong about this?"

"You know, I hope I am. For your sake."

"Don't worry about me. I didn't need anyone before and I certainly don't need anyone now."

"You will if I'm right about this."

I turn back to him. He's standing tall, as he always does, but what he lacks in confidence he makes up for in venom. I brace for another onslaught, certain he'll spit a few extra words my way, but the impulse doesn't strike him.

"Well," he says, his voice as thin as his smile, "then I hope you are, too."

Content with this fragile truce, I nod and continue on my way. If we never agreed on anything else, then this would be good enough for me.

8

Today Ansel is taking me to the Ward. I'm nervous, which is the only proof I have that I'm making the right decision.

He's instructed me to wait for him in the barracks, which is what we call the series of windowless cells where Catchers escape for a little privacy. Each room is outfitted with a cot, a mirror, and four concrete walls that meet a glass ceiling about eight feet up. Most of the time the barracks sit empty, except for those rare occasions when Catchers are permitted to wear something other than the company uniform.

Because Quarantine requires additional precautions, I'll be wearing what all third-level Catchers wear: a specialized body suit designed to minimize the risk of possession. Like the wetsuits the Living wear to go scuba diving, it's form fitting but not restrictive. The outfit is made from holographic material and comes with reinforced boots intended to aid stability during turbulent transitions. After all, when it comes to ridding the world of evil, the holy men can only do so much. That's why Ansel keeps a cache of specially trained Catchers at the ready at all times, in case the Living find themselves faced with an evil spirit. We call these beings malevolents, and only those who've been to the Ward know how to control them.

I wind my hair into a bun and consult my Keepsake for the umpteenth time. It's been the same shade of yellow ever since I entered the barracks to find the uniform folded neatly on the bed. Yellow doesn't concern me one bit: all it means is that my energy has shifted from neutral to cautious. It does this all the time, especially in situations where the spirits promise to be confrontational.

I stand before the narrow mirror and watch the light frolic on the fabric of my uniform. It cascades over the slopes of my shoulders like children tobogganing down a wintery hill and appears to linger uneasily on the endless edges of my face. Even now, alone with my own reflection, I hardly recognize myself at all. I don't remember being this pale, or this muscular. Cancer taught me that curves come and go, so when I was sick I learned to embrace the inherent beauty of bone structure instead.

Satisfied with my appearance, I open the door. Ansel is already waiting for me on the other side. When our eyes connect, I lift my chin and square my shoulders, but my attempts at bravery aren't fooling anyone, least of all him.

"Scared?" he asks me.

I nod.

"You should be. The Ward isn't for the faint of heart."

"Then I suppose it's a good thing I don't have one."

A chuckle ripples Ansel's leathery cheeks. He nods slowly, and then assumes a relaxed pace as he leads the way down the hall.

"You always did have a sense of humour about things," he tells me as I fall into step beside him. "Especially dying. It's a gift really, being face to face with death and having the courage to laugh it off."

"I can't say as I had much to lose at that point."

"Oh, but you did. That was the most impressive part of it all: even when cancer had taken everything from you, it couldn't seem to get its claws into your positivity."

"Is that why you're taking me to the Ward?"

"Partly, yes."

We round a corner and keep walking. I check my Keepsake again. By now it's flashing orange, which is what happens when we go out of range. If it weren't for my excursion with Ansel, I'd be well advised to turn around.

"So these malevolents," I begin as Ansel concentrates on his footfalls. "Where did they come from?"

"These ones came from the basement, so they've already had exposure to the staff. Think of it as the difference between a wild animal and one born in captivity: both possess the instinct to kill, but only one is compelled to use it."

I match Ansel's confident strides. Storm clouds pack the space overhead and there's hardly enough light to illuminate the hall, much less Ansel's expression. In humans, fear shows itself in peculiar but unmistakable ways—in shallow breaths, sweaty palms, and watery innards. But just because I'm hollow doesn't mean I'm empty: fear is still a dear friend of mine, only now he makes his presence known in subtler ways. I bring my hands together in an effort to align my field, but there's so much interference that they end up repelling each other with a vivid blue bolt of electricity.

Ansel looks at me.

"We're close," he says. "Bleed out your fear. There won't be any room for it in the Ward."

I nod and do as he says. Trepidation trickles from the temporary gash on my wrist and studs my skin with bright cobalt beads. The droplets dodge each other like kids engaged in a game of tag before launching themselves over the edge and vanishing before they've even touched the floor.

Ansel comes to a stop at the end of the hall. A carpet of frost crackles beneath our feet, thickening as it moves toward the door. I examine the monstrous barrier, which is nearly double my height and features a specialized keypad for which Ansel alone knows the combination. The chill is spreading as we speak, and by the time he finishes entering the code, everything in our vicinity is encrusted in ice.

"I can't make any promises for your safety," he tells me, to which I only nod. "Sometimes things go wrong and the malevolents find a point of entry, but if I didn't think you could handle this, I wouldn't have brought you here in the first place."

I want to look at him, but I'm paralyzed by the frigid stoicism in his statement. No promises. The Establishment is not in the business of making promises. It is, however, in the business of keeping evil in check. If I didn't believe I could make the world a better place—even if it's just on a spiritual level—then I wouldn't have volunteered for this.

"Keep one eye on your Keepsake at all times," Ansel says. "It sees everything, even when you can't. The malevolent will be scouting for weak spots—doubts, insecurities, regrets… anything that could potentially destabilize your energy. Do not give in to it. If you do, there will be little I can do to help."

"And if it gets in?" I ask him. "Then what?"

"Then," he replies, "I'll have no choice but to destroy you both."

I watch the door. Fingers of frost weave a new blanket of ice thread by crystalline thread. I extend a hand toward the metal. Where my fingers meet its chilly glaze, the door expands like a lung, causing me to recoil in shock.

"You've awoken the beast," Ansel tells me in a calculated tone. "Now, you must tame it."

I'm not just afraid—I'm completely and utterly terrified. All the same, I have a job to do.

"Okay," I say. "Open the door."

Ansel obliges with a mute tip of his chin. The door grates open slowly, and a couple of steps later, I'm inside.

I walk to the middle of the room. Colossal concrete pillars are positioned at regular intervals around the arena, which is nearly double the size of the auditorium where Catchers assemble during orientation. A glass ceiling crowns the imposing cinderblock walls and offers an unobstructed glimpse into the holding tank where hundreds of malevolents are drifting like clouds across a blood-red sky. Bolts of energy infinitely more powerful than ours slither across the stormy canvas like lightning, forming a never-ending lightshow of catastrophic proportions.

The floor is solid ice. Through a hazy, circular window in the frozen foundation, all I see is a bottomless well of shadows. The darkness is deep, cold, and unforgiving, like a wrinkle in the earth's crust where only the hardiest organisms can survive. I've never seen the blackness in person, only in slideshow presentations delivered by fifth-level Catchers tasked with overseeing the transition process. Words and images simply don't do it justice.

A gauzy figure emerges from the abyss. As it nears the surface, its facial features become more apparent, and more repulsive. Dull yellow welts blister its grey face and its black eyes are streaked with ruptured blood vessels. Massive, overgrown claws click menacingly against the icy bottom, sending ripples of terror through my field. The being bares its pointed teeth, of which it has thousands, before pressing its mouth against the barrier and letting out a shriek so shrill that the malevolents circling overhead scatter instantly.

"What is it?" I ask, still eye to eye with the creature.

Ansel, who is still standing by the door, answers.

"Hate," he says simply. "The engine that drives the blackness, and the only thing capable of controlling the malevolent population."

"It feeds on them?"

"To the contrary: it spawns them."

Hate maintains its predatory fixation on me. I take a step back, and then another, but it doesn't budge, or even look away. It lingers, glaring at me until Ansel wanders over and banishes the being with an inconspicuous flick of his hand. The creature recedes, skirting the shadows with a few forceful pumps of its tail before trailing like an unfinished thought straight to the bottom of the pool.

"Now that you've seen Hate," Ansel says as he continues past me to the far side of the room, "it's time you learn how to control it."

"I thought we were here to tame malevolents," I say dubiously.

"We are. Every malevolent is an extension of hatred. But a king is only as strong as his army. Vanquish his soldiers and you nullify his power."

Ansel approaches the wall and taps it three times. From the uniform surface of its cement façade, the outline of a pedestal begins to take shape. It advances forward slowly, scraping across the floor until it is fully independent of the wall from which it emerged.

Ansel produces a wooden box from a glass case above the pedestal's hiding place. The box is made of dark, highly polished material—rosewood would be my guess—and is sealed with a delicate brass lock. Needless to say, when I found out that I'd be battling evil spirits, this wasn't exactly what I had in mind.

He places the container in the middle of the pedestal and turns to look at me.

"It's a vessel," he says, laying a hand on the lid. "Don't let its innocence fool you. Malevolents can attach themselves to anything."

He gestures casually to the box, causing it to jostle angrily upon its stone perch. It trembles violently, brass padlock rattling against the wooden face. I ground myself more firmly to the floor in anticipation of its content's liberation.

I glance down at my Keepsake. It's red—the same murky red it had been in the chamber only days earlier.

"Think of your happiest memory," Ansel instructs me as the vessel shudders beneath his touch. "Malevolents only prey on beings that are spiritually inferior to them, which is why they so often target humans. Humans cultivate hatred, hatred spawns malevolence, and malevolence perpetuates the cycle by feeding on the humans' fear. It's an endless cycle, but not an unbreakable one." Ansel observes me. "Do you have your memory?"

I do. It's an old one dating back to the summer of 1992, when my parents took Brody and me to the ocean for a family picnic. I love this memory: sea spray in our hair, sand between our toes, sunlight draped over our coppery shoulders like a blanket we'd never outgrow. All that sweet, temporary innocence offset by the salty permanence of the ocean, lapping and slapping playfully against our bronzed legs as we galloped back and forth along the shore.

I nod.

Ansel turns to the vessel. The lock snaps open and our eyes meet one last time. We exchange nods, and a moment later, he removes his hand from the lid.

The box bursts open, releasing a billowing plume of fiery black dust. It fountains out of the vessel with tremendous force, blotting out the ceiling in a matter of moments. A rancid, sulfuric stench fills the air as the malevolent spirals in on itself, forming a deadly vortex above my head. The sound it makes is deafening, like a million tortured screams echoing through an eternity of pain and suffering. It rumbles like thunder, disrupting my field in the process, and I cling to the memory of our family picnic with every shred of strength I can muster. Brody said he'd always be there for me, and I'd be a fool to deny it now.

"Good," Ansel says, "now build your orb. Quickly."

I close my eyes and center my energy. Electricity hums in the space between my hands. The distance between them widens, making room for the orb that will eventually form when all the pieces of this puzzle finally fall into place. I can see it all so clearly now, a million shimmering fragments banding together to form an indestructible shell around my field. Like grains of sand on a beach, they are nothing without each other, just as I was nothing without my family.

"Good," Ansel says again, more softly this time. "Now, call on the malevolent."

With the orb nestled securely in my right hand, I raise my other and summon the being from above. It descends rapidly, fully prepared to devour me without a whisper of hesitation. Just when it's about to penetrate my field, I turn my right hand over and slam the orb against the floor, shattering it instantly.

The shockwave is devastating. It radiates in every direction, sending the few remaining spirits scurrying for safety. The malevolent wails as it circles the ceiling like a startled sparrow. Unable to reach me through the protective dome encasing my field, the malevolent unleashes a squeal of defeat and promptly returns to its vessel. The lid slams shut, and seconds later, the Ward goes quiet.

I crumple to the floor and land on my knees. Between building the orb and withstanding its explosion, I've depleted all of my energy. I've been weak a thousand times, but never like this. Lethargy is shackled to my limbs and my thoughts are saturated with fog. The last time I was this helpless, I was bedridden and clinging to life by an IV line. I try and center my energy, but there's nothing left to work with.

Enormous, indistinct figures swim placidly around the pool, flashing their hideous faces at me in passing. Darkness rises up to greet me, and a minute later everything goes black.

9

I'm drowning. Not in the blackness—that would be too easy—but in the memory I trusted to keep me safe.

It's a cold, cruel irony: who would have imagined such a perfectly packaged gift could unravel with such explosive finality? And yet, here I am, somehow. No up. No down. Just water. The ocean is a spectacle of infinities and it feels as endless as it looks. I'm drowning. It shouldn't be possible, but it is, and I am. It claims me at my own pace: I opt to go slowly, holding my breath until desperation floods my body with water. There is no pain, just a persistent heaviness that carries me like an anchor all the way to the bottom of my suffering.

That's where I hear the voices. They sing to me in sweet, lilting lullabies that echo through the many miles that separate us. I don't recognize the voices, but the melody is unmistakable. My mother used to sing this song to me all the time. It's a comforting tune for a comfortable death, and I embrace it as if it will never end.

That's when I hear it: another voice, independent of the orchestra that surrounds me, sending ripples of familiarity straight through my waterlogged body. I've heard it before, but I couldn't tell you to whom it belongs. It's a loop, the same two words uttered over and over again, and I listen to it until the heaviness leaves my body.

Revive her.

Light floods the sapphire void. It's bright—brighter than the sun, brighter than anything I've ever seen in this life or the next. It dyes the water white, banishing the shadows and the chill, until at last I gasp for air and open my eyes.

Ansel stands over me. Across from him, a tall man dressed in white writes something on a metal clipboard. The man is a Healer, or one who repairs broken spirits. Like most of the staff, we've exchanged pleasantries in passing, but never stayed long enough to ask one another's name. He asks Ansel if he should give me another dose. Ansel says no, and a second later, the Healer departs.

"How do you feel?" Ansel asks me.

I try to move my arms, but I can't. All four of my limbs are secured in place by thick leather restraints, and the more I struggle, the tighter they become. There's one light located directly above my head, and it's blinding.

Ansel begins circling the table with his hands clasped behind his back and his eyes fixated on the floor. I fight the straps with every ounce of determination I can muster, but they hold fast.

"What happened?" I ask.

Ansel doesn't answer immediately. I consider asking him about the voices, but I'm too preoccupied with the immobile state of my limbs to care about much else.

"How do you feel?" he asks again.

"Besides confused? Fine."

"And your energy field?"

"Like new."

Satisfaction softens his features. I gauge him for an explanation, but it doesn't look like I'm getting one any time soon.

"Yes," he says to himself, "good. Very good."

"What happened?" I ask again, because now I'm getting impatient. "Did the malevolent return to its vessel?"

Ansel hesitates. "Not exactly."

Ansel concludes his trip around the table and sidles over to one of the restraints. I expect him to free me, but instead he studies the tendons in my wrist while I look on in frustration.

"As you know, when you discharged your orb, the malevolent became very agitated. Under normal circumstances, it would have returned immediately to its vessel, but this wasn't a clean quarantine. You chose a very powerful memory, but not an entirely pure one, and unfortunately, it gave the malevolent a point of entry."

I'm still writhing indignantly on the metal platform, only now Ansel has my full attention.

I reluctantly finish his thought. "I'm infected, aren't I?"

He unlinks his hands and loosens the restraint on my right arm. I flex my fingers, thankful for my newfound freedom as he continues to remove the leather shackles.

"Perhaps an analogy would help," Ansel says as the last restraint dangles off the edge of the table. "Suppose I were to give you a snow globe, one with a hairline fracture located directly at the top of its dome. The figurine—the very essence of the ornament—would be unharmed. However, its environment is now compromised. At this point, the snow globe's fate is undecided: either it remains defective but intact, or the damage spreads and the snow globe disintegrates. Only time and the right combination of external factors will determine its outcome." He offers his hand and helps me into a vertical position.

I stand next to the table. Someone has dressed me in a light, billowing gown and left nothing underneath to shield Ansel's eyes from the more noticeable areas on my body. I instinctively cross my arms, but it doesn't offer the privacy I'm seeking.

"That still doesn't answer my question," I say, trying to be discreet in my attempts at coverage. "Am I infected?"

"Not infected," Ansel says, "inoculated. The memory you chose was incomplete. I remember it perfectly, but you don't."

I nod distractedly. I look around for my uniform, or anything else I can wear that won't make me feel so exposed, but instead, all I see are a series of glass bottles filled with substances that mysteriously replenish themselves.

"You told me to choose my happiest memory," I remind him, "and I did."

"But the memory was incomplete. You don't remember how it ends, but I do."

"I remember it perfectly."

"If that were true, your orb would have been infallible and the malevolent would have returned to its vessel. It would have been a clean quarantine. But memory is a funny thing. Somehow, we never seem to remember things the way they actually happened."

Ansel takes a step toward me. His eyes wander over the angles of my body, but the length of his gaze would suggest he's not looking at me so much as through me.

"Brody loved to test his limits. The day of the picnic, he swam out too far and was caught in the undertow. Do you remember that?"

I remember a lot of things about this day, including the look on Brody's face right before he dashed into the frothing surf. He believed that if he swam far enough, he could eventually reach the horizon, but only made it half a mile before the current became too strong. Dad had raced in after him, his chiseled legs pedaling against the wet sand as my brother bobbed further out to sea.

I say, "Brody was fine. I don't see how such a minor oversight could have provided an entry point for the malevolent."

"Because a single second was all that stood between your brother and death. I should know. After all, I was the one who tried to claim him."

"But you didn't."

"Only because I changed my mind. Had I followed through with my original plan, that day would have ended very differently."

Ansel composes himself long enough to explain, "Even if you didn't understand death, you instinctively knew that something was wrong. You built that memory on the edge of disaster. Never in all my years of overseeing The Establishment has anyone ever chosen to repel a malevolent with such a volatile memory. Do you understand what I'm telling you? The malevolent may have found a way to attach itself to your energy, but as of right now, it has no means to destroy you. You are positively indestructible."

I still don't understand: if the malevolent managed to penetrate my energy field, why didn't Ansel destroy me, as he'd promised to?

"You said you'd destroy me if I became infected," I remind him.

"But you weren't," Ansel says in a voice that betrays his attempts at docility, "and that's where it becomes complicated. Had you been infected, the malevolent would have hollowed you out. But you weren't infected. You were inoculated. Your energy field remains intact and your memories are untarnished, only now you are immune to future possessions."

In case there's still any misunderstanding on my part, Ansel concludes his longwinded explanation by saying, "You had every piece of the puzzle, except for one, and that one missing piece was all it took for the malevolent to change the entire picture."

"So, what happens now?"

"Now," Ansel says, having finally tired of my interrogation, "you return to the field and complete your outstanding collections. Speak no word of this to anyone."

My uniform materializes on the table with a crisp snap of his fingers. By the time I turn back around, Ansel is gone and I'm alone. I have so many questions, like how long my immunity will last and what's expected of me now that I don't have to worry about being consumed by evil. It feels as though an enormous weight has been thrust upon my shoulders. I consult my Keepsake. I expect it to be black, or maybe even green, since I'm now behind on my collections, but instead, it's the dullest shade of grey I've ever laid eyes upon—and grey, as you can imagine, is never a good sign of anything.

I dress quickly. Ansel never returns, and neither does the Healer he'd been conferring with earlier. I wish I knew what they'd been referring to when they mentioned another dose. Around here, nothing good ever comes in doses. On earth, you can get a dose of courage, or a dose of cough syrup, but at The Establishment, it's all or nothing—unless, of course, you're delivering a neutralizer, then it's like taking insulin. This begs the question: if I truly am immune, as Ansel insists, then why is he favouring language that hints at treating an infection?

Having finished lacing my boots, I make my way over to the door and open it slowly. The stillness that awaits me is haunting. I look around for signs of life, but there are none—only a sparsely lit hallway that extends forever in both directions. Normally I'd have no trouble finding my way around, but today is not one of those days. For the first time since arriving at The Establishment, I have positively no idea where I am, how I got here, or how I'm supposed to find my way back to the main wing.

I glance down at my Keepsake. The ring sees everything, from unclaimed souls and rogue malevolents, to mediums trying to make contact with the spirit realm. But it also does something else: it enables transparency. Stone up, it makes us invisible to the Living. Stone down, it grants us unlimited visibility from any location within The Establishment.

I turn the ring over and suddenly I can see everything: secret passages, hidden rooms, and millions of unmarked doors in various states of closure. I see Catchers traveling between wings with enviable haste, Healers tending to the infirm a short distance to my right, and Programmers installing Keepsakes in the incubator below. The Establishment appears to operate like a hive, with countless workers overseeing innumerable functions with mechanical consistency. I'm dumbstruck by the complexity of this prosaic castle. I realize now that some people spend their whole lives this way, pacing the same narrow halls of thought until they become blind to the infrastructure that surrounds them.

I check in both directions. To my left stands a single, solitary elevator, which leads directly to the basement. To my right, I see everything else, including the infirmary, the Ward, and the barracks.

I scan the various levels with cursory interest, and then, having finally mapped my route, I begin walking.

10

As per Ansel's orders, I don't say a word of my ordeal to anyone. Even if I had any desire to create a stir amongst my coworkers, I doubt many of them would believe me. After all, the Ward doesn't discriminate: either you quarantine the malevolent and walk away unscathed, or Ansel does what he has to do to ensure the safety of his staff and the future of mankind. It's the perpetual struggle between good and evil, except sometimes good just isn't good enough.

I spend the next two weeks mentoring first-level Catchers. Most of them dote on Ansel to the point of exasperation, and several of them have gone out of their way to exceed their daily quotas, even if it means impinging on one another's beats.

My newest recruit is a fourteen-year-old girl named Chantal Evans. Chantal was found facedown in a pool of her own blood in the library of her high school where she'd sought refuge from a gunman. She'd had shotgun pellets embedded in her flesh and a once robust brain oozing like overcooked spaghetti from the chasm in her skull. Repairing the damage took longer than expected, and now, after nearly three weeks in incubation, she's finally ready to commence her in-field training.

"I still don't understand why we have to do this." Chantal crosses her arms and gives me a baleful look. You'd think I'd be used to the attitude by now, but it just gets worse every time she opens her mouth. "If Ansel wants souls so badly, maybe he should come down here and get them himself."

I debate educating her on Ansel's role at The Establishment, but ultimately decide to save my energy for more fruitful pursuits, like teaching her how to perform an extraction.

"Is that what you think—that the boss should do all the work?"

"Most of it. Besides, I thought the Grim Reaper flew solo."

In spite of my annoyance, I chuckle.

"The Grim Reaper isn't real," I remind her. "He's just a pop culture fabrication like all the rest."

I look around. Where the hallways of this hospital intersect there's a circular counter being manned by a couple of male nurses sipping coffee from Styrofoam cups. They're perfectly oblivious to us, as they should be.

"And to answer your first question, we have to do this because it's our job. No one can enter The Establishment without an escort." I nod toward one of the halls. "Besides, it's nice to have a purpose, you know? Your assignment is in room 210."

"And?"

I hold her gaze. She's wearing a dark blue uniform with black boots and a gold broach above her left breast. The pin serves two purposes: to inform other Catchers that her training is ongoing, and to maintain the lines of communication between mentor and mentee. Chantal's pin is synced to my Keepsake, as is the ring on her finger, so if anything goes wrong I can intervene before it becomes a crisis.

"And," I say slowly. "You have a job to do."

"Do we at least get breaks?" Chantal asks as I begin making my way down the hall, determined to get on with business.

"Breaks are for biological functions, something you don't have. You do, however, have a schedule to keep." I stop and turn back to her. Her petulance is wearing on me, but Ansel won't let me return to The Establishment until she can perform an extraction without any memory loss. "210. Now."

Chantal shuffles past me. Now, confusion, I can take. Many spirits suffer from extreme confusion in their first few days, hence the mandatory adjustment period where their only duty is to shadow a more senior Catcher and take copious mental notes. Confusion is the residue of effort, and effort is always better than resistance. I know she's young, new, and inclined to balk at authority, but I'm trying to keep her out of the basement. The least she could do is be grateful.

The patient in room 210 is an elderly gentleman with late-stage lung cancer. His name is Frank and he's eighty-nine years old. Frank hasn't seen his family since he was placed in palliative care nearly two months ago. I wish I could say I'm surprised, but when you're dealing with end-of-life care, the disappointments tend to outnumber the miracles. Frank says he's ready to die, not because of the physical suffering his cancer has caused him, but because the emotional neglect is taking its toll. He insists no one will miss him, but that remains to be seen.

Chantal glances back at me as she takes a cautious step into the room. I give her a reassuring nod, and soon after she disappears behind the yellow curtain.

"A Spirit Catcher," Frank says in a gravelly voice. "Don't you mean an angel?"

"No, sir."

He harrumphs. "Pity. Even the science of dying is leaving this old man behind," he grumbles. "Well, go on. Get it over with, then."

I round the corner and stand next to Chantal at the foot of the bed. Age is written on every inch of Frank's emaciated frame, from the constellation of dark spots patterning his arms, to the wispy white hair sprouting from his freckled scalp. His gaunt face reminds me of wet clay—lackluster and streaked with wrinkles—and his blackened gums are studded with yellow teeth. He used to be a professor, and even though his vision has lost its clarity, his intellect is still as sharp as the look he gives me when I approach the table next to his bed.

"Those are beautiful daffodils," I say of the flowers basking in the sliver of sunlight slicing through the blinds. "Did your daughter bring them for you?"

Frank shakes his head.

"Nurses," he says simply. "Thought they'd cheer me up."

I turn my attention over to my recruit.

"Rule number one of collecting spirits," I say when our eyes meet. "Have good bedside manners. People who feel respected will always be inclined to cooperate."

"Respect," Frank mumbles, sawing his chapped lips back and forth across his rotted teeth. "I wouldn't put it past the young bucks to know what that is."

72

"Well, lucky for you The Establishment upholds a certain standard of care for its recruits." I nod at Chantal, who takes a step forward. "Chantal is going to be doing your extraction today. You'll have to be patient with her until she gets a feel for things."

Chantal sidles up to the bed. I instruct her to maintain a firm grip on Frank's hand and then watch as their palms reluctantly unite. Eighty-nine years' worth of memories stampede into her newly minted Keepsake. I notice her grip slackening after forty-seven years, so I lay my hand over both of theirs in order to patch the holes in the transaction. You'd think a man Frank's age wouldn't care for a few missing memories, but that would be like crossing words out of a book and still expecting it to make sense.

The last of Frank's recollections stream into Chantal's ring, which is bright blue and practically smoking from the effort required to process this much data. This is normal, if somewhat frightening for newcomers, but Chantal doesn't look concerned at all. In fact, she doesn't look anything like she did ten minutes ago. Her eyes have lapsed into a blank stare and she's as rigid as a lamppost. I gently pry open her fingers, terminating the connection, but she's as inanimate as a mannequin and doesn't seem to hear me saying her name.

"Chantal?" I say for third time. I grab her shoulders and try to shake her from her catatonia. "Chantal, look at me."

Her eyes flicker over my face. She's stiff from head to toe, like she's suffering from some delayed rigor mortis, but I keep shaking her in hopes this is the result of a bug and not something more serious.

Chantal's eyes are the deepest shade of green I've ever seen: green bordering on brown, or the colour of a forest right after it rains and everything is dark. Her pupils are fully dilated and they spread like rumours into the surrounding foliage of her irises, blotting out the last of the colour until all that remains is a narrow band of blood encircling the inner edges of her eyes.

I check my Keepsake. Sure enough, it's smoky red.

I let go of her shoulders and take two steps back.

Frank's body is an orchestra of reactions, from the percussive tempo of his heart to the mighty rumble of his digestive tract. He thrashes in the sea of soiled sheets, his cries for help lost under the cacophony of nurses rushing to his aid.

I'm still staring at Chantal.

"Chantal," I say, ignoring the flurry of activity behind me. "Talk to me."

Chantal's eyes burn like coals in the pits of her eye sockets. She's finally looking in my direction—if not directly at me—but recognition doesn't follow. Blood leaks from the corners of her eyes, following an invisible path toward her pin. Where blood meets metal there is a faint hiss, like the sound a pop bottle makes when you break the seal. Her broach turns bone-white, making no noise as it hits the floor. Her body follows silently.

Then the whole hospital goes dark.

I approach the window and peek through the blinds. Outside, the sky is crystal clear and traffic is flowing without interruption. Anxious chatter fills the halls and there's a chorus of confusion at the nurse's station around the corner.

74

While the nurses help to calm Frank, I attend to Chantal. She's lying facedown on the floor with her arms crooked at her sides, just as they had been the day she died. I turn her over and shine a light on her face. She has no eyes, only two empty sockets with sooty edges and a lattice of blood trails crisscrossing her porcelain skin. Her Keepsake is the same shade of white her pin had been moments ago. There's nothing pure or innocent about a white Keepsake. White signifies absence: of colour, of life, and of the connection to The Establishment that makes all of this possible.

I lay a hand on Chantal's chest. Like all Catchers, her body cavity is devoid of organs, but where I'm expecting to see her essence—the spiritual engine that drives her soul—there's only a black hole.

Not wanting to waste any more time, I reach for her left hand and gently remove her ring. I place it in the middle of her torso, or roughly where her diaphragm would be, and turn the ring so that the stone points toward her chin. The Keepsake begins to emit a pale golden glow; a mist surrounds her, and seconds later Chantal is gone.

The hospital is pitch-black as I step into the hallway and watch the life flow around me like water. Nervous energy permeates the air, causing my Keepsake to oscillate between smoky red and dark amber. I should move, but I can't. There's too much commotion, and the mental image of Chantal's torched corpse isn't helping one bit.

The foot traffic is endless. Everywhere I turn, I see nurses darting between rooms, doctors trying to diagnose technological glitches, and patients shuffling anxiously in plastic chairs. Beneath the blushing glow of the Exit signs, the cell phones appear, lighting the halls in flashes like fireflies on a midsummer night. Panic hangs over the building like smoke. To the Living, it smells like fear. To me, it reeks abominably of sulfur and week-old garbage, which is exactly how the Ward had smelled after Ansel introduced the malevolent.

I begin making my way down the hall. I walk in a straight line, past the doors, past the people, past every shadow and halfhearted attempt to restore power. I walk against the current, diverting the bodies as I go, until at last I arrive in the ICU.

To my surprise, the department is deserted. There are no people here, but there are plenty of Catchers, including a handful that are trying in vain to rouse their downed trainees.

I approach one of the Catchers, a third-level employee named Hank who specializes in workplace accidents. Today Hank is mentoring a second-level Catcher named Callie, and when they see me coming, Callie's eyes go wide with surprise.

"Sarah!" she calls, waving her arm.

"What happened?" I ask, not entirely sure I'm prepared for an answer. "I just sent a recruit to disposal."

"You and half the staff." Hank nods at the surrounding bustle. We stand in silence for a moment, watching as the surviving Catchers process the remaining shells.

"Disposal count?" I ask.

"In here, eighteen. Until we can isolate the cause, I expect that number to rise." Nodding to himself, Hank adds, "If the symptoms are anything to go by, this was the result of a malevolent infestation. What I don't understand is the seemingly random pattern of infection, and the fact that it seems to have only affected us, not the Living. Normally the malevolents would feed on them first."

I survey the chaos. It doesn't make any sense: a typical malevolent infestation usually involves terrorizing the Living. Human beings make easy targets, and since they lack any sort of spiritual fortitude, they're largely helpless to defend themselves.

But this is no ordinary infestation. Even the most aggressive malevolents don't possess this many souls at once, and certainly not in such a sporadic fashion. Malevolents are choosy about their victims: they prefer the mentally unstable, the emotionally feeble, and the easily distraught. They prefer people and entities that will submit to fear and relinquish their souls with little resistance. There's a reason the hunters of the animal kingdom don't pursue the fastest animal in the herd, and malevolents are no different.

"Does Ansel know?" I ask Hank.

"How could he not? This isn't your everyday infestation."

Hank turns to Callie, who is chewing compulsively on her lower lip and anything else that wanders too close to her mouth. She gnaws on a hangnail with the alacrity of a hamster while Hank and I confer a short distance away. We're the lucky ones, but it doesn't feel that way when you're standing in the eye of the storm.

Hank's gaze returns to me.

"We need to quarantine. Ansel said you have some experience?"

I give a single, solemn nod. I wish I knew what Ansel told him, because I doubt it was the whole truth.

Turning back to Callie, Hank says, "I'm putting you on disposal assistance. Until we can determine the extent of this infestation, I'd suggest those left standing shelter in place. If anyone else succumbs, alert me."

Callie obliges and makes a beeline for the nearest recruit.

Hank faces me. He's older than most of the Catchers I work with, but still young, vigorous, and accustomed to giving orders. Hank used to be a foreman on a construction site, where he fell from a scissor lift and was pronounced dead at the scene. He left behind a wife, two kids, and enough debt to justify the premature ribbons of grey in his otherwise uniformly black hair. I've never worked with Hank, but something tells me I'm going to enjoy it, peculiar circumstances aside.

Hank lowers his voice. "Ansel tells me you were infected. Did they administer any neutralizers when you were in the infirmary?"

"I don't know," I reply, recalling the Healer's allusion to an additional dose. "I presume so, but Ansel claims I wasn't infected."

He scratches his brow in thought. If he asks, I'll tell him, but I'd rather no one know about my supposed ability to internalize evil. Besides, wasn't it Ansel who told me to keep my condition under my hat?

"Well, whatever the case, I'm glad to have you with us. Mass quarantines are challenging on the best of days."

"I presume you've executed one before?"

"Several. Thirty-three malevolents is my record. During my first large-scale quarantine I nearly succumbed, but only because I overlooked a key link in my recollection chain."

I nod. Unlike a standalone memory, a chain forms a more durable orb. Logic dictates that the longer you lived, the better your chances of survival, but not all lives are created equal.

Hank looks down at his hands. Soft blue light floods his calloused palms as they gravitate toward each other. Memories click effortlessly into place, generating sparks with each new addition, and before long he has a fully formed orb that pulses with life and the laughter of his two children.

I build my own orb. It's smaller, paler, and consists of significantly fewer memories—mostly of Brody and my parents, plus a sprinkling of faces belonging to friends I haven't seen since childhood. It's not a very impressive shield, but it does the trick.

"Okay," Hank says, making a fist around the orb until it whistles like a teakettle in his grasp. "So here's how this works: I'm going to walk the floor and try to get an estimate on the number of malevolents. On my signal, you'll discharge your orb slowly, one memory at a time. The key is to consolidate the malevolents in one area. From there, we'll begin the process of quarantine." He nods again, meeting my eyes. "Clear?"

"Crystal."

"Excellent." Extending a hand toward the doors, he smiles and says, "Ladies first."

With that, we abandon the safety of the ICU for the pitch-blackness of the adjoining hallway.

11

I'm standing alone in an empty stairwell, waiting for Hank's signal. He says the smaller the area, the better our chances of containment. He says this could take a while, given the sheer quantity of malevolents roaming the halls, so I lower myself to the floor and toy with my Keepsake while I wait.

The power outage is causing all kinds of trouble for the Living, who need electricity to go about their business. Computers are unresponsive and medical equipment comes and goes, setting off alarm bells at every turn. I've never seen so many people scrambling for a solution, and with so little success.

I look at my Keepsake. It's still a hazy red colour, only now it's frozen, meaning I can't access any of the memories stored inside. As in all emergency situations, all non-essential functions have been suspended until further notice.

I glance around the blackened stairwell. I don't need light to see, but I'm so used to the stark fluorescent glow that its absence is making me sick—not physically sick, but sick with worry. Because humans need light to function, malevolents use darkness to destabilize them. Fear leads to vulnerability, and vulnerability is at the heart of every successful possession. That still doesn't explain why we're being targeted, though.

Suddenly restless, I rise to my feet. Even if the building is teeming with malevolents, it shouldn't take Hank this long to drive them into a designated containment area. Unlike ghosts, who are notorious for lingering, malevolents are migratory entities. Malevolents are the ultimate shapeshifters, and they can reproduce with startling frequency. The key to executing a successful quarantine lies in inhibiting replication, otherwise controlling their numbers becomes a Herculean effort.

I climb the stairs and peer through the reinforced Plexiglass window on the door. There's no one on the other side, and nothing to see except for two empty, intersecting corridors. The Living have all left, leaving behind malfunctioning machinery and a haunting stillness that borders on apocalyptic.

I transcend the barrier and pause again to evaluate my surroundings. Empty, undressed beds with metal frames reflect needles of light into the unending sea of shadows. Rectangular pockets of light checker the floor on the left hand side of the hall, where four large windows overlook a parking lot crammed with displaced patients and befuddled practitioners. Microscopic particles of dust glint like jewels in the afternoon sun before parachuting to the floor to be churned up at a later time. I don't see anyone I know, but I know the malevolents are still in here; I can feel them, although pinpointing their location is another matter entirely.

An empty waiting room greets me at the next turn. Magazines with glossy covers catch the light at crooked angles and the chairs are grooved from years of use. I approach the vending machine in the corner and place my hand flat against its face. Light floods the enormous cooler, where dozens of plastic bottles shimmer in robes of condensation. I remove my hand, killing the only source of light, and then continue on my way to the first unoccupied counter.

Everything is black: the floors, the walls, even the computer screens on the cluttered desks. I lay a hand on one of the lamps, but the bulb stutters and dies beneath my touch. Whatever's going on here, it's infinitely more powerful than anything I can do to counteract the sudden absence of life.

I slip behind the counter and absently shuffle the papers abandoned across the desk. The Living may not understand the nuances of life and death, but you can't fault them for trying to keep the two apart, especially when dying comes at such a cost.

Something strikes me in the back and I lurch forward, landing on my stomach. A hand encircles my mouth, but I don't have the strength or the coordination to pry it off.

I glance over my shoulder in time to see a malevolent slithering across the ceiling. The stench it emits is putrid, like garbage left too long in the sun. It moves quickly, stirring up paper as it passes, and I wait until it slinks around a corner before trying again to free myself.

Gabe removes his hand. He crawls toward the mouth of the cubicle, checks in both directions, and then rises to his feet.

"Situational awareness," he tells me, brushing his hands together. "Use it or lose it, Miss Galloway."

I grapple my way to a vertical position and survey the disarray while I try to process this unusual turn of events.

"Have you seen Hank?" I ask as Gabe ventures into the hall.

"Who?"

"Hank," I say again, hoping my insistence will make up for not knowing his last name. "Big guy, mid-forties. He said he was

83

going to round up the malevolents so they could be quarantined."

His brows knotted, Gabe turns around. "There were others?"

"Dozens."

He shakes his head. The way he's looking at me, you'd think I've gone mad.

"Gabe, come on," I snarl, "the others, Hank and Callie and all the rest. They were taking shelter in ICU."

He shakes his head again—slowly, disbelievingly. I've never seen this look from him before, and it has me feeling hopelessly conflicted.

"Sarah," Gabe begins, all business, "there's no one here."

"I know. The Living left."

"No, I mean, there's *no one*. Look around. We're alone."

Still not convinced, I step out from behind the desk, remove my Keepsake, and slip it onto my right ring finger. If there's a Catcher nearby, my ring will find them.

Gabe shifts his weight. I expect him to patronize me, but he doesn't. I glance at the stone. When triggered by another member of The Establishment my Keepsake should turn silver, but instead, it continues to glow in that same burnt-out shade of copper. I thumb the stone, but the blushing hue persists, mocking my misguided hope for an ally in a place where the silence has suddenly become stifling.

"Like I said," Gabe says. "We're alone."

I return my Keepsake to my left hand and begin walking. I'm not ready to believe we've failed. We can't afford to fail with this many innocent souls depending on us to maintain order in the universe. They need us to protect them, and that's precisely what I intend to do.

We make our way across the hospital. Malevolents tend to congregate in areas where there is a reliable source of energy, but are not generally known to settle. Once they've depleted an area's resources, they waste no time wreaking havoc somewhere else—which is good news for us, since it means they are unlikely to return to ICU.

We walk through the doors and stop dead in our tracks. I don't know what I was expecting to see, but this certainly wasn't it. Bodies of Catchers lie scattered in every direction—limbs askew, blood caked into the creases of their uniforms, and shadows pooled in empty eye sockets. I try to take it all in, but there's too much to see.

"Jesus," Gabe mutters from somewhere behind me.

"We need to send them to disposal," I say, just for the sake of saying something. "They need to be properly disposed of."

Gabe crouches over a body. I didn't know the Catcher personally, but we've crossed paths enough times for me to recognize him.

Gabe places a hand on the Catcher's chest. Inside, his body is a forest of frayed nerve endings. Gabe applies his fingers more firmly to the fabric of his uniform, but the Catcher's essence maintains its charcoal consistency.

85

"Did you know him?" I ask as Gabe removes his hand.

He nods as he climbs to his feet.

"What was his name?" I persist.

"Charlie." Gabe gestures to the rest of the bodies. "So what do you think? Infestation or internal glitch?"

"It has to be an infestation. Ansel wouldn't do this."

"Malevolents don't attack Catchers out of the blue like this. It's not in their nature."

"I know." I look around, absently searching for a familiar face, but without their eyes they all look more or less the same. "The hospital is full of potential victims. Why come after us?"

Gabe ambles around a counter, where he discovers a Catcher with curly blonde hair and mutilated fingernails lying with one arm draped across her midsection.

"Population control," he says down to Callie's misshapen corpse. Turning to me, Gabe continues, "What if they're not killing for sustenance? What if they're killing for sport? Even the most powerful malevolents don't need this many souls to survive."

I nod. "Control us before we can control them."

"As long as they have a point of entry, they can multiply. The goal is to quarantine them before they can attach themselves to a new host." Gabe looks around and shakes his head. I've never seen him this subdued. "Either they've mutated or something's happened in the Ward. There's no way there would be this many floating around in a hospital, unless they're coming from someplace else."

"Ansel wouldn't do that. Not to us."

"Why? Because he's so loving and magnanimous?"

"Because he needs us to maintain The Establishment."

"Oh, girl," Gabe chuckles, "you have a lot to learn, don't you?"

Despite my fury, I hold fast, unwilling to tolerate Gabe's dismissive mannerisms or his guileless implication. Ansel is many things, but he isn't a monster.

"Why would he do something like this?" I ask as Gabe continues patrolling the floor, pausing to turn over the occasional body. "Ansel believes in controlling evil, not promoting it. Why else would the Ward be so heavily guarded?"

"Sarah, come on." Gabe doesn't turn around. "Malevolents are powerful—more powerful than you or I will ever be. Look at this bloody planet. We haven't had a major human die-off in decades. Ansel needs souls to run The Establishment, right? So who's to say he doesn't have a hand in this?"

He angles back to me, but I'm speechless. I refuse to believe any of this was Ansel's doing. He cares too much about keeping the peace to wage war on his own soldiers.

Gabe continues, "Unleash the malevolents and you have a few million new souls in a matter of days. Think of the potential."

"But why come after us?"

"Because the whole goddamned system's broken. The Living don't die, we don't regenerate. There's only so much energy and space to go around. A major, systematic die-off is the only way to make room on both ends. Hence, the malevolents."

"But if Ansel kills off his Catchers then who's going to control the malevolent population? It doesn't make any sense, Gabe."

"Don't you get it? Ansel doesn't want us to control the malevolents. He's sacrificing us to save The Establishment. It's the only way to guarantee the future of humanity—and himself."

He composes himself—or tries to—before his voice betrays his attempt at civil discussion.

"Ansel isn't a saint. He's his own boss, and when you work for yourself, you can do whatever you damn well please. If Ansel kills off a few hundred of us, it'll give his malevolents time to put a dent in the general population. He needs the souls. The Establishment needs the souls. You and I are just details, and insignificant ones at that."

I don't speak. I don't want him to think I'm validating his inane theories. Instead, I turn to the first burnt-out Catcher I see and begin preparing her for disposal.

"Why do you care what Ansel does?" Gabe asks as I tug off her ring and center it on the plateau between her breasts and her navel. "We're the lucky ones. Be grateful."

"Luck is temporary," I tell him as the Catcher's body fades.

"But we're still standing. If Ansel didn't care about us, we'd be emptier than peanut shells right now."

I pull another Catcher off the wall and lay him flat on his back, with his legs together and his arms straight at his sides. His ring shines like a moon on a midnight pond in the middle of his abdomen as he disappears before my very eyes.

I turn to Gabe.

"Have you always been this cynical?" I ask him.

"Only since before I died."

"Ansel saved you," I remind him, "he went out of his way to make sure you made it to The Establishment. Does that sound like someone who'd destroy his empire from the inside?"

"Just because he made an exception doesn't mean he cares. Like you said, he's against haunting."

I shake my head. I refuse to engage in petty disputes with ungrateful souls on any day, but especially today.

"Help me dispose of the bodies," I tell him.

Gabe scoffs and sticks his hands in his pockets. When we're within inches of each other, he tilts sideways slightly and crashes his shoulder into mine, causing just enough interference in my field to send microscopic bolts of electricity racing over my skin.

"Right away, your highness," he sneers, and then rounds a corner and disappears.

12

Gabe and I have no further interaction as we dispose of the bodies. I still don't believe Ansel is behind all of this. Accidents happen, even in death. A malevolent outbreak isn't inconceivable, even with the extreme security measures. Nothing is guaranteed in this world or the next. The Establishment is not in the business of guaranteeing things. We are, however, in the business of cleaning up after Ansel. So, that's exactly what we do.

In the corner of one of the rooms, Gabe is hunched over the body of a young female Catcher with jagged white hair and plump, ruby lips. Her name was Dana, and she was one of the most ruthless Catchers I've ever met. In Dana's world, claiming spirits was an art form: she romanced death, even danced with it like a masked lover at a masquerade ball. Though her specialty was suicide, she'd been known to tag along on other, more difficult missions requiring greater patience and more experience. She was the embodiment of everything a Spirit Catcher should be: cunning, perceptive, and above all, fast. She'd chased her share of spirits, and been lucky enough to catch them all.

Gabe straightens her limbs with uncharacteristic care while I stare down at Dana's long, slender frame and her equally long, red-tipped fingers. Had she survived, I have no doubt she would've enjoyed an illustrious career at The Establishment. Anyone can escort a soul into Ansel's domain, but few can do it with such elegance, grace, and stone-cold devilry.

"Did you know her?" I ask Gabe.

He angles her head so that her chin is pointing toward the ceiling. Then he takes both of her hands and gently layers them on top of her stomach so that her painted nails glisten like jewels on the canvas of her pitch-black uniform.

"What an odd question," he says as he removes her Keepsake and places it half an inch above her folded hands. "Of course I didn't know her."

I look around the room, taking stock of the drab yellow curtains, the wall-mounted hand sanitizer, and the recently vacated bed. Between the sudden cessation of power and the subsequent evacuation of the premises, housekeeping didn't even have time to remove the soiled linens.

"Your demeanor says otherwise," I persist, folding my arms.

"My demeanor is none of your concern, Miss Galloway. I'm just doing what needs to be done—and at your discretion, I may add." Gabe rises to his feet and waits until Dana's vessel vanishes completely before turning to face me.

I smirk. "Seems like you were trying to make it last."

"'It'?"

"Her disposal. Normally you function at blistering speed. What gives?"

His boyish grin reveals a line of slightly crooked teeth. Gabe crams his fists into his pockets, then passes through the door and into the hallway while I trail him by a few feet.

"We may have merged once or twice," he gloats nonchalantly.

91

A lag creeps into my step. "When did all of this happen?"

"A not-so-long time ago. She invited me to her parlour. What was I supposed to do?"

"You could've said no."

"And risk disappointing her?"

I shrug. "I'm sure she would've been disappointed either way."

He glances over his shoulder and sneers. I revel in silent satisfaction as he picks up the pace.

"And you? How did you know her?" he asks.

"Collections overlap. My recruit wanted to kill himself after his doctor said he was terminal."

"My story's cooler."

I roll my eyes and look away. We've disposed of all the bodies, but without the usual hustle and bustle of life clinging to its measly threads, the hospital feels emptier than ever.

"So, what happens now?" Gabe asks, turning to face me.

"I don't know," I reply. "I guess now we go back to The Establishment and give Ansel a report."

"That assumes he doesn't already know about this, and that would be impossible. Like I said, he probably ordered this fiasco."

"You're jumping to conclusions."

"Am I? Did we not just dispose of two-dozen Catcher shells? Did I not save you from certain possession when that malevolent was cruising the halls?"

"Well, yes, but that doesn't mean Ansel is responsible."

"So, who is?"

I cast my gaze over the uninhabited department. A swell of human voices echoes down the hall as I turn to see a couple of firefighters carrying flashlights.

I turn back to Gabe.

"Where did you enter?" I ask him.

"ER, like I always do."

"Then lead the way."

I follow Gabe across the hospital, past all of the empty rooms with their disheveled or missing beds. The main floor is crawling with emergency workers, several of whom have splintered off from the main group in order to investigate matters on the upper levels.

We arrive in the emergency department just as a fresh batch of uniformed workers floods the unremarkable entryway. It's still hopelessly dark in here, but I'm afraid to light up for fear of wasting energy. If what Gabe is saying is true, and The Establishment really has been compromised, then there's no telling how long our faculties will last.

I check my Keepsake. Its glow has dulled, which isn't altogether surprising considering that it's been working overtime scanning for malevolents. What worries me is what will happen if we can't get back to Headquarters. The Keepsake is like an umbilicus: it supplies us with the energy we need to function, including escorting souls, mentoring recruits, and, in rare cases such as this one, executing mass disposals. Without our rings, we can't communicate with Ansel or each other. Without our rings, we have no way of sustaining ourselves. Without our rings, we have no hope of survival.

Gabe approaches the wall between two vending machines. He places his hand flat against the paint, but to my confusion, nothing happens. The light spilling from his fingers penetrates the wall with ease, but there's nothing on the other side save for concrete blocks and the occasional steel reinforcement.

"What's wrong?" I ask.

"I don't know." Gabe removes his hand and reapplies it a second later. His fingers glide up and down the wall, but there's no door to speak of, only a smattering of white scars where the paint has endured years of abuse.

"Are you sure you came in this way?" I ask.

"Positive."

"So where's the portal?"

"I don't know. Maybe if I did, we'd have found it by now."

I study Gabe's movements. When his insistence fails to turn up any doors, he takes a generous step back and scans his immediate surroundings. The hospital is regaining its usual clamor, but the walls themselves remain inanimate. Ordinarily, there'd be portals every ten feet, but the only openings I see are the ones the Living have built for themselves.

"I don't understand," he says, flattening both hands against the wall. A weak glow fills the glimmer of space between his palms and the paint. His Keepsake begins to flicker, and a moment later the light goes out.

Against my better judgment, I grab his left wrist and slip my hand into his as if I'm performing an extraction. Gabe surrenders his search for the portal long enough to cast me a look of disgust.

"It's for your own good," I say, turning his arm over so that my Keepsake is facing upwards. His lifeblood—the vein-like conduit in his forearm that connects his ring to his essence—hums like a streetlight as I pour my energy into him. As quickly as it started, the stone stops fluttering and assumes a solid golden glow—the colour of charity, and of one Catcher extending the life of another.

"My own good, huh?" Gabe says, keeping his eyes steady on me. I try to take my hand back, but his grip is as fierce as his gaze. "You sure about that?"

I rip my hand free of his and nearly stagger backwards into one of the vending machines.

"Don't flatter yourself," I say as I fix my sleeves. "I need an ally. You're not much good to me if you're dead."

"I'm already dead, sweetheart."

"So there's no portal here," I say, canvassing the wall. "That much is clear. Where else would there be a portal?"

"Well, where did you enter?"

"Palliative."

"So we'll go to palliative. And if we get there and find that door MIA?"

"I don't know."

"Of course you don't."

Too incensed to speak, I set off at a brisk pace across the atrium. I conquer the stairs with ease before blurring down the hallway in the direction of my entry point. Unless the malevolents have polluted the entire system, there's no way they'd be able to seal every opening. The barrier between life and death is too porous.

In palliative, I approach the wall where Chantal and I entered what now feels like a lifetime ago. It's stationed between an artificial plant and a cart overflowing with sloppily sorted linens. I'm well aware of the futility of prayer, but I'll be damned if I don't murmur a few unintelligible pleas for help as I lay my hands upon the wall and promptly shut my eyes.

Behind me, Gabe scoffs.

"Are you sure you came in this way?" he asks, parroting my inquiry with palpable indolence.

"Shut up, Gabe."

"Face, it Sarah: the malevolents have this place on lock-down. In fact, it wouldn't surprise me one bit if Ansel has sealed the chamber from the inside. That sounds exactly like something your beloved boss would do."

"He's your boss, too."

"And that's all he is. I don't put people on pedestals."

"So don't," I grumble, hanging my head, my eyes still firmly sealed. "Just shut up and let me think."

"Thinking doesn't open portals. Only energy can do that."

I ignore him. If the portal is still active, then it should materialize in short order. If it doesn't, then I can count on two things happening before nightfall: Gabe and I will expire right here in palliative care, with no one to dispose of our vessels, and the rest of humanity will carry on in blissful ignorance, unfazed by the malevolents' violent transgressions or their own impending obscurity. This is exactly the kind of thing Ansel wanted to avoid: without life, there's no need for him or any of us. Without the ebb and tide of energy sloshing from one realm to another, we all fade into the void, where there is no life, no death, no light, and no hope.

I press my forehead against the wall. In my periphery, I can just make out the glow of my lifeline trying to forge a connection with the other side. Where there is a lifeline, there is life. Where there is life—or at least positive energy—there is hope. Hope may not open any portals, but neither does doubt, so in a stroke of desperation I opt for the lesser of the two evils.

Gabe lowers his mouth to my ear. A static crackle echoes in the space between us as our fields overlap. I try to turn around, but I'm trapped between his arms, with his body nearly touching mine.

"Give up," he says, "it's not like you were going to regenerate anyway."

Anger is knotted like a rope in my chest. Who the hell does he think he is, using my death against me like this?

97

His hands migrate to my hips, where I viciously tear them off.

"You'll be sorry when Ansel hears about this," I tell him. "In fact, I hear he's looking to fill a custodial position in the basement. I'll put in a good word for you."

Gabe scoffs and skates a finger down the side of my face. I go as stiff as a board, just as Chantal did right before she succumbed.

"I'd sooner go rogue," he says in a gravelly voice.

I'm suddenly boiling. "Seems you already have." I blink, causing a black tear to splatter on my hand.

Gabe rears back in surprise as I turn around.

"Something wrong, Mr. Conway?" I say with a smirk.

"Stay back," he warns as he moves away from me.

I wander over to where he's standing and lay both hands against the wall, trapping him in place. I steal a quick glance at a nearby painting and find two pitch-black eyes staring back at me from the depths of my makeshift mirror.

"Whatever you do," Gabe says, stiffening noticeably, "don't touch me."

"Do you not like being touched inappropriately?"

"Not one bit."

"I'll bet Dana touched you everywhere." I draw an invisible line from his throat to the zipper of his pants. "*Everywhere.*"

Gabe swallows. "She wasn't infected."

"Neither am I." My hand wanders back toward his neck, where it hovers over his Adam's apple. "What do you say, Mr. Conway? A kiss for the road?"

"Not if it opened every goddamned portal in this place."

I close my hand, causing him to gasp. Gabe tries to wriggle out of my clutches, but only manages a frantic shake of his head.

"I will find that portal," I growl, "with or without your assistance. Have I made myself clear?"

"Perfectly," he squeaks.

The outline of a door forms around him. I shove Gabe into the chamber as it glides open swiftly. He scrambles to his feet, but maintains a safe distance from me as my body begins to cool. I enter the cylindrical pod, and a moment later, the door disappears.

13

Gabe is the first one to exit the chamber. The way he's acting, you'd think I've disappeared. I bet he wishes I would. I bet he never imagined that I'd be the one pinning him against the wall, instead. For this reason alone, he shouldn't count on an apology. Every choice demands a consequence. Maybe next time he won't be so quick to try and take what isn't his.

Gabe is standing at the registration counter by the time I finally cross the floor. He has one hand on the keypad and the other in his pocket, where his fingers are curled as tightly as a sleeping bear in a winter cave.

I park myself beside him.

"Technical difficulties, Mr. Conway?"

He squares his shoulders and sets his jaw. He's as deeply rooted in his masculinity as an oak tree in a forest, but his false bravado isn't fooling anyone, least of all me.

"Hardly," Gabe says without looking at me. "I was giving you time to catch up."

"Well, I'm caught up."

The keypad comes to life with a jingle. When it detects Gabe's Keepsake, it directs him straight to the catalogue, but there are no entries listed. There isn't even the option to input a new recruit. I look at Gabe, but he's too mired in his confusion to notice me staring.

"That's odd," he says down to the screen. Craning his neck, he looks past me to the ancillary screen, but it, too, is blank. "Are we offline?"

"Shouldn't be." I shoo him away and he obliges with mute haste.

I apply my hand to the keypad. The system scans my ring, but instead of being transferred to the directory, I receive an error message instead.

"Catalogue not found," I say, turning to Gabe. "What does that mean?"

"Maybe your ring's not working," he hedges. "Maybe you fouled it when you decided to go rogue."

"*I* didn't go rogue. You did. And company policy clearly states that in the event of an employee going rogue, a coworker in his or her vicinity must act in a prompt and professional manner to ensure that the behaviour doesn't cause the Living undue distress."

"I'm aware of the policy," Gabe says, leveling his gaze, "but in my defense, we were in a dead zone. The only one suffering undue distress in that situation was me."

"Oh, really? And I didn't?"

Despite our solitude, Gabe checks his surroundings and lowers his voice.

"Section twelve, subsection three: Any employee found to be using unnecessary force against another being may face severe repercussions, including, but not limited to, custodial duties, demotion, and spiritual reassessment." He pauses. "Did you even read the contract?"

"Believe me, there was nothing unnecessary about my use of force in this situation." I fold my arms. "Section eighteen, subsection two: Unless explicitly agreed upon by both parties, no employee shall engage in lewd conduct with another. Any employee attempting to merge without consent may face severe repercussions, including, but not limited to, custodial duties, demotion, and spiritual reassessment." I smirk. "Did *you* read the contract?"

"You crossed a line, Galloway."

"Only to put you back in your place."

Not wanting to waste time debating semantics, I turn back to the screen. I don't understand: the catalogue is the backbone of The Establishment. Without it, we have no way of knowing who anyone is. If you're not in the catalogue, then you simply don't exist. You are undocumented, and undocumented beings are as good as gone.

"Maybe Ansel took the catalogue offline," I say, "you know, to protect it from the malevolents."

"Malevolents are catalogued too. Your argument is invalid."

"Well, then, Sherlock Holmes. Perhaps I should let you handle this mystery on your own." I turn away from the counter and make my way over to the incubator door.

"And where are you going?" he asks.

Outside the door, I tug my sleeves into place and assume the boldest stance I can manage. I can feel Gabe's eyes on me, but I refuse to give him anything to go on—not fear, or dread, or even plain, old-fashioned uncertainty. This may be our war, but it's my battle.

"To the Ward," I tell him. "If the malevolents are to blame, we may as well target the source."

"Target the source," he parrots, his voice sagging with exasperation. "If you're going to target the source, you're headed the wrong way. The bulk of the malevolents are in the basement."

"Then I'll go to the basement."

"You're out of your goddamned mind."

"At least I'm actually doing something. What are you doing?"

"Honestly," Gabe says, tilting his body so that it's resting against the counter, "nothing. Not my rodeo, not my bullshit. Like I said, Ansel probably set this whole thing up in an effort to trim the herd, and instead of celebrating, you're marching across enemy lines."

"So be it," I say with a shrug. "It's not like they can hurt me."

"Who?"

"The malevolents. They can't hurt me. You yes. But not me."

This seems to pique his interest, but I don't flatter his curiosity with an explanation. Besides, Ansel made me promise I wouldn't disclose my immunity to anyone.

"Send me a postcard when you get there," Gabe says, and then ambles away with whatever remains of his fragile pride.

○

There are two ways to get to the basement: the elevator, and the stairs. No one takes the stairs unless they plan to disembark at any one of the five hundred stops along the way. Since I don't have that kind of time, I opt for the blistering speed of the elevator instead.

Like the chamber, the elevator consists of a single, cylindrical room that can accommodate an unlimited number of riders, though the average is usually around twenty. Unlike traditional elevators, though, the one rocketing to and from the basement doesn't rely on cables and counterweights. Instead, it operates on its own independent energy source, but most new recruits are too concerned with their scrambled fields to pay much notice.

The basement is not for the faint of heart. It's dark, dank, and dripping with the evidence of society's most unspeakable crimes. The voices of the damned echo unendingly down every alley and sparsely lit corridor. When two malevolents collide, it produces a sound like a thunderclap. Some Catchers say it sounds more like an atomic bomb, but I suppose it depends on one's proximity to the tank, not to mention the malevolents' individual chemistry. After all, not all malevolents are created equal. Like everything else in this world, evil is a spectrum. Thus, compartmentalization is necessary to prevent more heinous malevolents from cannibalizing smaller, less dangerous ones.

The vilest beings are used to power the macro systems: incubation, authentication, and regeneration. Without them, we simply wouldn't have the power to stay in business day after day, generation after generation.

Beings that have committed violent crimes but on a smaller scale supply power to The Establishment's background systems, such as keeping rings fully-charged and cataloguing incoming souls. These slightly less sinister creatures are also the engines driving the more transparent functions, such as diffusing rivalries and ensuring every Catcher's needs are being met.

Then there are delinquents. These malevolents once took the form of vandals, thieves, and arsonists. We use them to light the halls and open doors. Of all the malevolents, these are the ones that stand the best chance of being successfully rehabilitated. Of course, once Ansel gives this small but largely innocuous cohort a loose rein, he also, inadvertently, gives them license to mutate.

The halls are empty. Given the sheer size of The Establishment, this alone is not particularly surprising. What it surprising, however, is the feeling that I'm being stalked. I don't turn around. I refuse to allow this sensation to govern my behaviour, especially at such a delicate juncture. Still, it lingers, like a vulture circling its next meal. I still don't turn around. Whatever it is that's shadowing me, it had better be prepared to work for its reward.

At the elevator, I adjust my bag and focus on distributing my energy. If I'm going to put a stop to this mayhem, I'll need to depend on all of my systems working together. I shine a light on myself. Inside, my essence smolders like coal in a fire, throwing heat and the faintest blue glow into the dimmest corners of my soul. I notice something else, too: my essence, which is the size of a fist and has a smooth outer shell like a snow globe, is laced with cracks, including one that zigzags diagonally across the core of my being.

The elevator door finally opens and I step inside. There's not much to see at this point, aside from the reflection of the hallway on the glass, so I brace myself for the descent and watch as the door slides shut behind me. It has nearly completed its closure when a hand shoots into the opening and the door glides open again.

I turn around. "What happened to celebrating?"

Gabe steps into the elevator. The look on his face borders on apologetic, but it's not enough to make me forget about what happened at the hospital.

"I took a rain check. Figured there wasn't much point if I couldn't drink."

Gabe hunches over the railing and stares through the glass at the concrete shaft in which our car is suspended. Below us, there's nothing to see but a bottomless pit of shadow that goes on for as long as time itself.

"You don't have to come," I tell him, hoping he'll take the hint and leave. "In fact, I'd rather you not. I don't want to be responsible for your possession."

"The way I see it," Gabe replies, continuing his assessment of the glass bullet encapsulating us, "the world's gone to shit and I have nothing to lose. If what you say is true and the malevolents give you a berth, then I don't see the harm in tagging along."

"Just because they'll leave me alone doesn't mean you're safe. The basement is not a safe place for anyone, but especially someone like you."

"If I didn't think you were going to insult me, I'd ask you to elaborate."

"Then it's best if you don't. After the stunt you pulled, you're not exactly deserving of flattery."

"The stunt? You mean helping you locate the door?"

I pierce him with a stare. Gabe just smiles and looks away.

"Keep this up and I may just leave you down there," I warn.

"And I'd just find my own way back, as I always do. Funny how you think you're the one doing me a favour here."

"Given our recent altercation, I'd say I am. Who knows? Be nice to me and I might think twice about feeding you to the malevolents."

Gabe slants me another stupid smirk. His eyes sparkle with mischief and indolence, and it makes me so angry that I debate strangling him again.

"Don't worry, Miss Galloway," Gabe assures me, "after the stunt *you* pulled, any man would think twice about getting in your way."

And then we plunge straight into the abyss.

14

The basement is the lowest point in The Establishment. Because of this, it's also the coldest. Frost is cemented onto every exposed pipe and pane of glass. The tanks themselves go on forever, forming an endless grid of aquariums where a staggering number of malevolents swim, thrash, and clash in a bath comprised of water and formaldehyde. The water is a necessary component for conductivity, and the formaldehyde is mainly to preserve whatever biological matter still lingers on their amorphous forms. After all, when it comes to malevolents, there's no such thing as a clean separation.

I gaze up at one of the tanks. The walls are at least thirty feet tall and consist of a composite material that is capable of withstanding all sorts of impacts, both internally and externally. Due to their territorial nature, malevolents often engage in highly physical confrontations involving high-speed collisions with the outer limits of their enclosures. To my knowledge, none of them have ever escaped, but that doesn't mean they haven't tried.

Affixed to each tank is a rickety metal ladder leading to an elevated platform. With the exception of a handful of Catchers who are responsible for looking after the malevolents, no one is permitted to climb the ladders or be anywhere near the platforms. Between the frost and the lack of reinforcement, they are dangerously unstable. One misstep, and you could easily become a malevolent's next meal.

I approach one of the tanks and squint at the figures churning the murky water. There isn't much light down here, save for a few sconces mounted along the room's perimeter, so I have to use my own energy to navigate the labyrinth.

"So what's the plan?" Gabe asks as I scour the glass for a clear spot to aim my light. "Or do you have one?"

At the next tank, I apply my hand to the ashen surface and watch as several malevolents drift through the hazy beam without even glancing my way.

"Simple," I tell him, even though I know the solution will be anything but, "find the tank with the breach and execute a quarantine."

"That assumes it's just one tank. Could be more."

I press my face against the window. A formidable-looking malevolent with cardinal eyes and a thick, ragged tail is paddling lazy circles at the bottom of the tank. When its eyes catch the light of my fingers, it snarls and lunges toward the glass, causing a few nearby malevolents to scatter.

I turn to Gabe.

"So we'll make it a mass quarantine," I say halfheartedly. "All we need is a memory chain and…"

Gabe holds my gaze. "And?"

"And then we save everyone else." I lower my hand, dimming the light in the process. Panning over the other tanks, I add, "The way I see it, if Ansel's behind all of this—if this is some sort of test—then we have nothing to lose by trying."

"Except any hope of regeneration."

"We won't even know the difference. Our memories will be wiped and it'll be like we were never even here at all. We have to do this for them."

"Define 'them.'"

"Everyone—everyone who has yet to transition. If they can't come to The Establishment, then their souls are doomed to haunt the earth forever." I keep walking. "Like I said, you don't have to help."

"You're right. I don't."

I hasten my pace, hoping to put a healthy distance between us, but Gabe matches my strides with infuriatingly little effort.

We maneuver the maze of tanks, the path becoming increasingly obscure as we enter the thick of the warren. This is where Ansel keeps his most ornery malevolents. Like caged canaries, the darkness has a calming effect on them. Here, they are more subdued and less likely to quarrel with each other. Here, at the heart of the basement where few have dared to wander, the number of beings in each tank is drastically reduced. If solitary confinement works on society's most reprehensible scum, why wouldn't it work on the diseased entities that helped execute the atrocities?

Water sloshes against my boots. I lower my hand, directing the light down at my feet where a puddle nearly an inch deep has settled in the various pocks and gullies peppered throughout the floor. The water appears to go on for miles, and it's still spreading.

"Hey, Gabe?" I turn around, but Gabe is nowhere in sight.

"Look up," comes a voice from directly above me. I crane my head back, and sure enough, Gabe is perched on the platform at the top of the nearest ladder.

"You want to see where the problem started? You gotta get higher." He gestures for me to follow, and amazingly, I do.

I scale the rungs. By the time I make it to the top, Gabe is standing in the middle of the platform with his hands dangling carelessly over the edge of the railing.

"We shouldn't be up here," I tell him. "It's dangerous."

"Danger is relative." Nodding down at the tank, he adds, "And really, after the day I've had, I'm not too worried about what some limbless fiend in a fish bowl might do. Perspective, you know?"

We stand shoulder to shoulder in silent understanding. I'm tempted to feel sorry for him, especially since he has no way of defending himself down here, but I know better than to let a temporary truce lull me into undeserved forgiveness.

"Any signs of a breach?" Gabe asks without looking at me.

"Aside from the water, nothing. Could be a false alarm."

"Or maybe you're right and poised to walk out of here a hero. Ansel will be so proud."

"What do you have against him, anyway?"

Gabe scissors his fingers and stares down at the surface of the pool. I don't know if I'm expecting a serious answer out of him, but seeing as we're alone and probably nearing the end of our employment, I don't see the harm in asking.

"Let's just say Ansel and I go back a bit," Gabe explains, relaxing his posture so that his right knee protrudes over the edge of the platform. At this point, I'm convinced he may be the only member of Ansel's staff who can stand on a flimsy metal contraption overlooking a sea of malevolents and not exhibit a single shred of caution or doubt. "Way, way back."

"How far back are we talking? Because apparently Ansel and I have a bit of a history, too."

Gabe glimpses my face. I want to tell him about my family's beach excursion and how close I'd come to losing my brother, but that would behoove me to expand on the hospital incident from earlier. The longer we spend trying to decipher the meaning of these irregularities, the more convinced I become that all of these events are somehow related, like an enormous, sprawling mosaic whose image can only be seen after all the tiles have fallen into place.

Gabe doesn't ask me to elaborate. Instead, he relaxes his other hip and frowns down at the tank just as the malevolent breaks the surface of the water.

"When I was five years old I lost my brother in a freak accident. We'd been messing around with dad's car when I accidentally put it in gear and drove over him. That was the first time I saw Ansel."

He pauses to look at me and I give a conservative tip of my chin to spur the story on.

"He'd been standing at the edge of the driveway, watching dad lapse into hysterics over Grant's corpse. I had no idea where he'd come from or how he'd gotten there. At first I thought he was just some creepy neighbour who was planning to rat me out for being an irresponsible dick, but when I asked my dad about the old man on the lawn, he just looked at me like I was crazy.

"After Grant's funeral, my parents thought I'd benefit from seeing a psychiatrist. Going off of my recent delusions the shrink diagnosed me with schizophrenia and suggested I be committed to a psych ward, for my own safety. My parents refused and said I'd stand a better chance in a normal environment with normal kids. After that, I didn't see Ansel for about three years."

"What happened when you were eight?"

"Honestly, I can't remember. I mean I could, if I really wanted to"—he holds up his Keepsake for emphasis—"but the details don't really matter. Point is, some kid I may or may not have been ragging on at the time collapsed during a game of dodge ball and died. Heart failure. Ansel made sure I saw him that time."

"I don't understand. Ansel never leaves The Establishment."

"He doesn't need to. His favourite little killing machine has finally come home to roost."

I try to make eye contact with him, but as usual, Gabe refuses to grant me this common courtesy. He knows I'll ask, because I need the full picture in order to see the problem clearly, but for once, I really wish he'd approach this conversation like a fellow human being and not a glorified apparition with a superiority complex.

113

"You know correlation doesn't imply cause, right?" I say, trying to stymie his remorse. "Just because you were present during those deaths doesn't mean you killed those kids. Sometimes shit just happens."

"Yeah, well, shit liked to follow me around. After that kid dropped dead people started thinking I was cursed. And do you know what happens to people who are cursed?"

"They get shunned?"

"I wish. More like they get the piss kicked out of them on the daily." Gabe continues, "So there I am, a gangly fifteen-year-old with no friends and a bad haircut, when this girl—we'll call her Sabrina—gets mowed down by some drunk driver in the high school parking lot. Can you imagine? Broad fucking daylight and this guy just rolls in and kills the girl. And who should happen to be bumming around looking guilty as hell but yours truly?"

"That doesn't mean you were responsible, Gabe. All it means is you were in the wrong place at the wrong time."

"And apparently so was everyone else, whenever I was around. When people saw me coming, they scattered. If you needed to clear a room fast, I was your guy.

"So now I'm twenty-one and legally able to drink myself to death. I'm drowning my sorrows at a bar in the south end of town when this homeless guy shuffles in and asks to use the can. 'Course the barkeep says no, so, he leaves. Next thing I know, some psycho comes barreling down the street, guns blazing, and shoots the hobo along with about eight other people who happened to be standing on the sidewalk. Guess who the police wanted to talk to?"

"Let me guess: Ansel showed up."

"Not right away. He did later, when I was passed out at my apartment. That was the first time he actually said anything in the sixteen years since our first encounter."

"What did he say?"

Gabe knots his shoulders as he hunches over the railing. His right foot is now suspended comfortably above the tank, where the malevolent is becoming so restless that foam has begun to form on the manufactured peaks. If I didn't know better, I'd think Gabe is contemplating spiritual suicide.

"He said 'Thank you.'"

"'Thank you'?"

"Given the context, I assumed he meant thanks for making my job a little easier. Like I said, I was the chosen one."

"Chosen for what, though?"

"To be Ansel's second in command. Why send a Catcher every time you need a soul, when you can send the Grim Reaper instead?"

I scoff. "The Grim Reaper." Gabe looks at me, his expression sober. "Wait, you're serious?"

"Did you think I was kidding?"

"But the Grim Reaper is a myth," I insist. "Everyone knows that."

Gabe smirks and shakes his head. "Oh, Sarah," he says as his gaze slides away from me, "get your head out of your ass."

115

"But Ansel—"

"—Is the head of the afterlife. He's not the Grim Reaper. I am."

"But why would he pick you?"

"Why not? I was a lone wolf with a chip on my shoulder and a bad reputation. And since I was a young, robust, mostly-healthy dude, I guess he figured I'd be as good a candidate as any. I was like a magnet for death: wherever I went, it followed. People kept dropping like flies, and I just kept running away. You ever tried to outrun death? You can't. So, instead of trying to hide, I embraced it.

"I scraped together enough money to buy a motorcycle and then went from town to town doing Ansel's bidding. No fixed address meant the law couldn't catch me, and even if it did, Ansel wouldn't have let them stop me. I was too valuable. Then, one day, I finally had enough. Clocked two hundred clicks on the I-18 and drove straight into the overpass."

Gabe presses his lips together, causing his chin to rumple in frustration. I watch the malevolent wedge its head into all four corners of the tank before returning to the spot where Gabe's foot is still dangling tantalizingly close to the water. If it were to snatch him, I doubt Gabe would put up much of a fight.

I wonder if this has been his plan all along: not to try and save the day, as I initially suspected, but to try and terminate his own suffering in the most morbid manner possible.

"But, as I now know, it never really ends. Sure, I was pretty useful when I was alive, but now that I'm dead? Well. Now I'm a fucking legend. Gabe Conway 2.0."

"I'm sorry."

"So am I. I would've preferred oblivion." He sneaks me another glance, but it ricochets off my face and lands on something in the distance. "Well. I guess we ought to be going, then."

Gabe turns to his right. Just as his foot hits the middle of the platform, the bridge gives way and plunges into the tank with a thunderous bang.

The malevolent unleashes an odious roar and careens through the cloudy water to investigate. The bridge is still attached to the ladder on the side closest to me, but it won't be for much longer. I'm clinging to railing with everything I'm worth. About ten feet below me, Gabe is wrapped around one of the spindles and trying desperately to grapple his way toward me. When our eyes lock, I do what any decent, morally upstanding person would do.

I offer my hand.

Gabe's fingers tangle with mine as I hoist him up. When we're side-by-side, Gabe places his hand on my back and pushes me toward the ladder. I pull myself over the edge, leaving just enough room for him to sling himself over the wall. The platform releases a final, triumphant groan and crashes into the pool, sending a wave of water over the outer limits of the tank.

The platform sinks to the bottom of the pool, where it lands in a haze of bubbles and unidentified debris. The malevolent continues to swim manic circles around its container, wailing and flashing its abundance of teeth until we lose sight of it behind a curtain of shadows and churning filth.

I've made it halfway down the ladder by the time Gabe finds his voice.

"So, you decided to save me after all, did you?" he says with a smirk.

I look at him. "Would you have preferred I leave you behind?"

"It wouldn't have been the worst way to die. Again." He descends the ladder quickly and skips the last two rungs. "I guess that makes us friends now."

"It makes you lucky," I tell him, "and in my debt."

"Name the favour, your highness."

I turn away, chin raised, and take up a leisurely pace as I steer down the nearest aisle.

"Well," I begin, with Gabe in tow, "you can start with an apology, for one. Bonus points if you make it sincere."

"An apology? For what?"

"Oh, I don't know. Maybe for trying to make me your next conquest?"

I face him. As predicted, he's adopted his usual, crooked stance, with both hands hidden in his pockets and his jaw canted in confusion. I relish this satisfying shift in our dynamic.

"My next conquest," he repeats. "Yeah, no. Nice try."

"So, you weren't trying to merge with me, then? I imagined the whole thing?"

"Look, if you're going to be anything, be flattered. I was just trying to make you feel appreciated."

I don't have the energy to be offended. Even disbelief is a stretch for me right now. Instead, disappointment is the most I can muster: not so much because of what he said, which isn't particularly surprising given his stunted character, but because for a minute, I'd almost allowed myself to believe he'd changed.

"You know what?" I say, to which he merely arches a brow. "Keep the favour. I don't need anything from you."

"Sure you do."

"Really, I don't. But keep telling yourself that, Gabe."

"You need me and I need you. That's a fact. And if you don't believe me, maybe you ought to take another look around. We're alone. You know why? Because your beloved boss is not the kind, compassionate, charitable being you think he is. Ansel is a monster, and the fact that we're completely alone should be all the proof you're ever going to need."

His gaze lands on something directly behind me. Apprehension supplants his previous abrasiveness, and a moment later I reluctantly follow his eyes.

A hulking figure emerges from behind one of the tanks. Two unblinking red eyes scan the aisle with cursory interest, and when they finally settle on us, the malevolent lets out a low, rumbling growl. Its rounded back is bristled with coarse, black hairs and its disproportionately long legs remind me of a circus performer on stilts. The creature's underbelly is covered in charred flesh, with patches of bright pink tissue poking through here and there. This malevolent isn't just hideous: it is an abomination. And it's coming for us.

"Is this the part where we quarantine?" Gabe asks.

I shake my head. I picture my orb, still buried at the bottom of my bag, but I'm afraid it won't be enough.

"No," I reply as the malevolent takes a step in our direction, "this is the part where we run."

The monster lunges, kicking up water as Gabe and I set off at a dead run down the nearest aisle.

We sprint past three tanks, hang a sharp left, and bolt as fast as possible in the direction of the elevator. Behind us, the malevolent gallops on all fours through the gridlock of enclosures, wherein the sudden commotion has caused the smaller malevolents to stampede in a confused frenzy around their containers.

A piercing wail echoes off the glass maze. We veer right. I can see Gabe in my periphery, his limbs pumping furiously against the gelid air. I seize his elbow and duck down another aisle, but the malevolent is undeterred.

It squeals like a frightened pig and lengthens its stride. The malevolent is now running parallel to us one aisle over. When it catches sight of us through a break in the tanks, it swerves sideways and collides with the corner of a pool, shattering it instantly.

Water explodes in every direction as four or five malevolents are liberated from their prison. As soon as their bodies make contact with the floor, they, too, sprout legs and stagger to their feet. The original malevolent is still in hot pursuit, and it bursts from between two tanks just as Gabe shoves me toward the elevator.

We've nearly made it inside when the beast extends its arm and hooks a claw into Gabe's leg. He yelps as he's dragged backwards, his arms pedaling for purchase on the dirt. I reach into my bag, determined to get us both out of here alive.

I diffuse the orb, blinding the malevolent long enough for it to release its hold on Gabe. He scrambles forward, stumbling into the elevator just as the creature shakes off its stupor. I slam my hand against the wall to seal the door, and seconds later we shoot like a bullet straight off the ground.

15

We hobble out of the elevator. The trip may have only taken seven seconds, but it was a long seven seconds: long enough for Gabe, who'd collapsed against the wall shortly after the door shut, to realize how close he'd come to oblivion, and for me to resign myself to the knowledge that in spite of our ongoing animosity toward one another, we are, for better or for worse, in this together.

Gabe limps into the hallway. He glances furtively in both directions, but I'm more worried about the grisly abrasion on his leg.

"I don't get it," he says, twisting to look over his shoulder at me. "Where is everyone?"

I shake my head. Our coworkers' whereabouts are the least of my concerns right now.

"I don't know. What I do know is you need medical attention, and soon."

"Sure," Gabe scoffs, "like that's going to happen. Spare me the last of my pride, will you?"

"You need a neutralizer and a new uniform."

"I'll be fine. Seriously. I just need to walk it off."

"So walk it off."

Too stubborn to relent, Gabe straightens his back and strides haltingly down the hall. He's barely made it three steps when my impatience gets the better of me.

"Without limping," I tell him.

Gabe falters. Slowly, he shifts his weight onto his right leg and stands for a moment to test its strength. Even though I can't see his face, I'm nearly certain he's wincing.

"As I said," he says, measuring his tone in an effort to disguise his pain, "I'll be fine."

"You're not fine, Gabe. You can barely put weight on your leg, much less run if the circumstances call for it. Let me take you to the infirmary and have them patch you up."

"Who?" Gabe spins back to me, but he's about as steady as a reed in a hurricane. "There's no one here, Sarah. Look around you. We're alone. If there was anyone left, they would've found us by now."

"Not necessarily. The Establishment is huge. Who's to say the others haven't hunkered down somewhere with Ansel and are waiting for everyone to regroup?"

I expect Gabe to belittle me, but to my confusion, a look of sadness comes over his face instead. I know I'm asking too much, standing here in a deserted hallway hoping that my one and only ally is wrong, but if the cost of my optimism is disappointment, then it's a price I'm willing to pay.

Gabe bends to examine his injured leg. He gently pries the two halves of the shredded fabric apart to reveal a wide gash oozing with sticky black energy and a few stray tufts of hair from

123

the malevolent's werewolf-like arms. Strips of tissue glisten gruesomely beneath the harsh glare of the overhead lights. A malevolent scratch may not be enough to transmit an infection, but it is enough to leave its victims permanently disfigured.

He looks up at me.

"If you think you can fix it, then be my guest," he says, extending to his full height once again. This time, the agony in his eyes is as clear as day and it puts the tiniest dent in my perpetual shell of indifference.

I angle in the opposite direction, toward the infirmary, and then wait for Gabe to fall into step beside me.

O

The infirmary is a ghost town. There are no Healers in sight, but if I want Gabe to live, then I have little choice but to administer the care he needs myself.

I open the door to one of the rooms and instruct him to take a seat on the raised metal table. With the exception of a few glass jars filled with unidentifiable liquids, the room could easily pass for a modern day earth hospital. The wall across from the table features an impressive display of drawers containing hundreds of sterilized instruments. Beneath the grid lies a wide metal counter, which sits above another row of drawers containing gowns and other fabrics. I search the room for a box of gloves and eventually locate them in a case next to the sink, which is surrounded on three sides by cupboards filled with basins, bandages, and other essentials.

The first cupboard I open contains precisely what I'm looking for: dozens of palm-sized bottles filled with a pale amber elixir designed to reverse the effects of a malevolent encounter. Even if Gabe hasn't been infected, it doesn't hurt to be safe.

"So you're the doctor now too, huh?" Gabe says, scooting backwards onto the table. "Is there anything your highness can't do?"

"Put up with your shenanigans, for one." I take down a vial of neutralizer and scavenge for a needle.

"Ah, but those shenanigans are part of my charm. Face it, Sarah: I'm a catch."

"Yeah, like catching a cold, that is: gross, tiring, and a perfectly good waste of my time."

Gabe chokes out a laugh.

"Oh, sweet Jesus," he says upon recovering his composure. "That was spectacular—the Cadillac of insults, really."

"Do you ever get tired of being insufferable?" I ask as I assemble the syringe and draw the neutralizer.

"I'm the Grim Reaper. I'm supposed to be insufferable."

"I thought you lost that title when you took your life."

"Yes and no. When I became a Catcher I forfeited my reaping privileges, but that doesn't mean Ansel can't reinstate my contract."

"So how does that work?" I wonder as I invert the needle and tap out the bubbles. "You sign some papers and all the sudden you're a real boy again?"

I turn around, needle in hand, and watch as a satisfied smirk flickers across Gabe's face.

"It's a little more complicated than that," he replies, tracing my curves with a quick pass of his eyes. His smile widens. "Of course, if you really want an answer…"

I approach the table. We're eye-to-eye with each other, but I can't bring myself to look away.

"Okay," I say, crossing my arms.

"Okay?"

"Tell me how it works."

Gabe's eyes abandon my face in order to peruse the needle languishing like a half-smoked cigarette between my fingers. He nods as he adjusts his seat and turns his focus back to my face.

"Step one: I tell Ansel I want to start reaping again. Step two: we weigh the pros and cons. Step three: we hammer out a new contract. Step four: we terminate my existing contract. Step five: he suspends my remaining collections. Step six: I regenerate. Step seven—and here's where it becomes complicated—I return to earth, except I don't start at square one like everyone else."

"Explain."

Gabe takes a deep pretend breath. I uncross my arms and wait for him to finish.

"If it were my first time on the reaping circuit, I'd have to learn the ropes, meaning I'd have to go through the rigmarole of being born, growing up, becoming America's Most Wanted. You know—the usual milestones. But here's the thing: once a reaper… always a reaper. Why start over when I can just pick up where I left off?"

I study him. "You're not saying what I think you're saying, are you?"

"Well, I'd need a vessel, wouldn't I?"

"But that's possession. Only malevolents can possess people."

"Exactly. And I'm the Grim Reaper, which technically makes me the biggest, baddest malevolent that ever lived."

I aim the needle at his knee and plunge it straight into his thigh. Gabe's grin disappears in an instant.

"Good Christ, woman," Gabe grumbles, too proud to meet my gaze, "what was that for?"

"For not telling me you're a malevolent," I say as I administer the dose and then withdraw the needle. "There are certain things you really shouldn't keep from people." I chuck the syringe into a nearby receptacle and turn back to him.

"To be fair, you never asked. And it's not like I could hurt you anyway."

I glance at him as I help myself to a couple of gloves.

"Would you?"

"Would I what?" he asks as he massages the injection site.

"Hurt me. I mean, it's in your nature, right?"

Gabe scoffs. "Presumptuous much? I don't have any reason to hurt you, Sarah."

I snap on the gloves and then scavenge for everything I need to suture Gabe's wound. It's a tricky task: before I can secure the broken skin, I need to flush out the clots and other contaminants. The muscle should eventually mend itself and the bone, though exposed, seems perfectly unharmed. I may have only lived nineteen years, but luckily for him, I spent two of them studying undergraduate medicine.

I cut away the fabric surrounding his wound and then cleanse it into a shallow metal basin. From there, I tie a standard surgical knot and begin the process of closing the gash. With each loop of thread, the two halves of Gabe's skin are gradually reunited. Rather than regale me with tales from his reaping days, Gabe waits quietly as I work on saving his leg, one careful pass of the needle at a time.

"Okay," I tell him as I secure the last of the gauze in place. "That should do the trick for now."

Gabe props himself on his elbows and peers down at his fully dressed leg while I tidy my workspace.

"Damn," he says, skating a finger over the patch of fabric. "I'm practically a new man."

I turn the gloves inside out and toss them into the disposal unit as Gabe eases off the table.

"You'll probably be favouring the leg for a while, so try to limit your acrobatics until it's strong enough to withstand the abuse," I say.

"Listen to you throwing around all these doctorly words. If I didn't know better, I'd think that was where you were headed."

"Well." Suddenly, I can't look at him. "Who knows?" I nod at his leg to take the focus off myself. "We should probably get you into a clean uniform."

"What, you don't like my just-mauled look? I think it's actually quite becoming of me." He turns a slow circle, arms spread as he poses in the light of the lamp.

I roll my eyes as Gabe strides into the hall. Then I take one last look at the mess I've left in the sink and gently close the door behind us.

16

The Establishment's wardrobe would put the average department store to shame. For starters, there's the sheer quantity of merchandise—enough to last until the end of time. You wouldn't think the dead require a change of clothes, but a lot of things can happen to necessitate a clean outfit, such as being attacked by a malevolent or graduating to the next level of work.

First-level Catchers are always outfitted in blue, with military-grade combat boots and a specialized broach to complement their Keepsake. Second-level Catchers wear black with silver trim, whereas third-level Catchers wear silver with black trim. Fourth-level Catchers are quite a sight to behold in their crimson habit, but since they're usually off hunting malevolents, few have actually met them in person.

As for fifth-level Catchers, they can wear whatever they wish. In Joy's case, this was a 1930s-style dress, white shoes, and dark red lipstick. Being a fifth-level employee means having the freedom to define one's style and choose one's assignments, and even though it carries the most responsibility, it also comes with the greatest reward: the power to leave an indelible mark on humanity.

Gabe follows me into the warehouse. I pause to absorb the mind-boggling assortment of clothes, but Gabe has already hobbled halfway down the nearest aisle and is now thumbing through the uniforms like pages in an enormous book.

"What size are you?" I ask, turning to the display opposite him.

Gabe lifts a uniform off the rack, scrutinizes it, and stuffs it back into the collection.

"Seventy-two," he replies. A capricious smirk slithers across his lips. "I bet you never thought you'd have to ask me that, huh?"

"I can't say as I pictured you making it this far in the first place. You know what they say about candles that burn twice as bright."

I locate a seventy-two inch uniform and pluck it off the metal rod. I hand it to him, and then turn to walk away.

"Where are you going?" he asks.

"Somewhere I don't have to look at you."

"Are you sure you don't want to stick around? You wouldn't want a stubborn zipper to undo all of your lovely work."

At the foot of the aisle, I stop to rein in my frustration. I wish I were as immune to his petty slights and underhanded insults as I am to the malevolents.

I angle back to him. Sure enough, Gabe is still standing exactly where I left him, only now he's naked from the waist up and trying to free his right arm from its sleeve.

"I studied medicine, not nursing. You can change yourself."

He gives me a theatrical pout as he continues to wrestle with the uncooperative sleeve. I keep walking, leaving Gabe to undress and redress his still tender leg without assistance.

I wander aimlessly through the warehouse. My fingers dance over the array of fabrics, appreciating the luxurious caress of satin, the edgy excitement of sequins, and the smooth, cool familiarity of supple black leather. I massage the prickly wool on an old sweater and marvel at the dazzling detail on an evening gown studded with crystals. I could've never afforded something like this when I was alive—maybe after I'd finished med school and repaid my mountain of debt, but certainly not before.

"Why don't you try it on?"

I turn to see Gabe, now fully dressed, standing lopsidedly at the end of the aisle.

"It's okay," I say, turning back to the clothes, "I'd rather not."

"Being shy now, are we?"

"If shy is the new professional, then yes, we are."

Gabe rights himself and takes a few cautious steps in my direction. When he finally reaches the dress, he fishes it out of the fold and unabashedly holds it up to my figure.

His eyes meet mine over the hanger. We both know his imagination can see straight through the dress and everything else, but his gaze is puzzlingly devoid of mockery or conceitedness.

"It fits you perfectly," Gabe tells me.

"I wouldn't count on that. Looks can be deceiving."

He gently lays the dress against my body, aligning the various scoops and angles despite my quiet fury.

Gabe tips his head, catching my eye in the process. "Trust me on this one, will you?"

"I don't see why I should. Trust is for people who care about each other."

"I'm not asking you to trust me with your regeneration. I'm just asking you to put on a dress."

"Believe me, Gabe, I don't suffer fools gladly. You and I both know the dress is merely a ruse for you see me without pants."

"So I have a vested interest. Sue me."

He holds up the dress again—this time against himself—and I begin to see the lavish garment in a new, albeit slightly unflattering, light. The crystals glitter like a summer lake and the bodice has a deep, sensual neckline I would've never allowed myself to be seen wearing in public. Still, it's a gorgeous dress— the kind of dress that can make me forget why we came down here in the first place.

"How about this," Gabe says, commanding my attention once again. "You try on the dress. If it makes you look like a beached whale, you can sock me in the mouth and we can forget any of this ever happened. But, if it makes you look the way I think it will, then I'll promise to put an end to my demeaning attitude."

I'd love to believe him, but I don't, and this dress is just a tad too short for me to extend an olive branch at such a crucial juncture.

Gabe hands me the dress, and for some reason—annoyance, capitulation, or some vague curiosity I don't have the heart to acknowledge outright—I accept it.

I drape the dress over my arm and carry it into the next aisle. Once there, I shuffle some of the clothes on the rack, ensuring there are no gaps through which Gabe may be tempted to peer, before setting the gown aside and beginning to undress.

Gabe is pacing the floor two aisles over when I finally muster the courage to emerge from behind my makeshift screen. I brace for what is sure to be his crudest evaluation yet, but to my surprise, he remains silent. I link my hands together—first in front of my body, and then behind it—and watch as he ambles over to investigate.

Gabe looks me over. "Well?" he says.

"Well, what?"

"What do you say?"

"What are you expecting to hear?"

He walks a slow circle around me. His eyes patter on every inch of exposed skin like a cold rain, and instinctively, I shudder.

"You can start by thanking me," he begins, "and I wouldn't be upset if you told me I was right, for once."

I debate challenging him, but the way he's looking at me—and the way it's making me feel—is so profound, and so thoroughly unexpected, that I let the impulse pass unheeded.

"You were right," I tell him, "but I'm not thanking you."

"Why not? Had it not been for me, you wouldn't even be wearing the dress at all." His gaze stumbles over me again. "Or looking so good in it."

"Don't push it. I'm barely tolerating you as it is."

Gabe is undeterred. He takes a step toward me with his arms at his sides and his chin shifted about half an inch to the left, but I don't budge. Instead, I keep my back straight and my shoulders square, ready to put him in his place if he so much as looks at me the wrong way. I search his expression for the usual suspects—vitriol, impudence, self-righteousness—but the only thing I find is a man whose eyes are still, amazingly, on my face.

"Do you dance?" he asks me.

"I'm not much for dancing," I admit.

"Pity. I could use a partner."

"It's not a requirement. If you'd like to dance, dance alone."

"You seem very bitter. May I ask why?"

I bite my tongue. I should've known better than to let anyone—but especially someone like Gabe—get this close to me. It's funny how the most innocent items can serve as artifacts for our juvenile sufferings. To him, this is just a pile of fabrics that does an impeccable job of highlighting my figure. To me, it's a reminder of the time I can't get back, when I was still young, vibrant, and as carefree as a cat.

"No," I tell him, "you may not."

He appears to surrender his halfhearted interrogation. Then, without blinking, without even looking away, he reaches for my left hand and places it delicately on his right shoulder.

"Shame. I could use a good story right now." He scoops my right hand into his left one.

"I'm not sure how good it is when it ends with me dying at nineteen." I glimpse our folded hands. I wait for the hand on my hip to commence its inevitable descent, but it remains firmly fixed in place.

Gabe concedes, "I'm bitter too. I never wanted to be Ansel's puppet."

"Why didn't you negotiate for your freedom, then?"

"You say it like I had a choice." Gabe pulls me closer and fixes the hand on his shoulder. We're turning slow circles in the middle of the aisle, but all I can see is a younger, wilder Gabe who traded his youth for an eternity of servitude.

"Ansel was grooming me to take over for him," Gabe explains. "He said I had potential, that I could follow in his footsteps if I paid the ultimate price. But it would've cost me everything I had." His pelvis grazes mine and I suck in my stomach in an effort to maintain our tenuous boundary. "Do you still think he's a saint?"

"I do. Your word isn't proof of anything."

"What would change your mind?"

"Real, indisputable evidence. Unless you can substantiate your claim that Ansel is a malevolent in disguise and we're just a bunch of mindless pawns on some invisible chessboard, I'm content to think you're lying—or, at the very least, exaggerating."

"You're a tough nut to crack, you know that?"

"Maybe I don't want to be cracked. Have you ever considered that?"

Gabe cants his head to the side; his face is unnervingly close to mine. Just when I think he's actually going to kiss me, I pull out of his embrace and nervously straighten the gown.

"You wanted a dance, you got one," I tell him, establishing a comfortable distance once again.

"You call that a dance? I don't."

"I'm not too concerned. You and I don't seem to agree on much of anything."

"And it's a bloody shame we don't. We'd make a stellar team."

"I'm going to go out on a limb here and assume your definition of *team* deviates slightly from mine."

"Does it? Because to me, it means two or more people working toward a common goal—the goal, in this case, being our desire to salvage The Establishment. Is that not your understanding of the term?"

I falter. "It is."

"So, we agree on this, at least."

"We do, but only to the extent that both parties function better in a state of civility. Don't turn this into some sort of ego trip."

He raises his hands. I know he won't quit this easily, but a ceasefire is always better than a sporadic, agonizing volley of never-ending verbal gunfire. Gabe and I agree on the essentials, and for now, that's all I need to forge ahead.

I begin to walk away. "We should go."

"One of these days, you'll see I'm right. And you'll thank me."

137

"Dream big, Gabe. What have you got to lose, right?"

"Actually, everything. Why else would I have told you all of this?" Impatience floods his voice. "I don't know what kind of fantasy world you're living in, but the reality is, Ansel only cares about himself. One day, you'll see this. Hopefully sooner than later."

I don't know what to say. On the one hand, I feel compelled to humor him. On the other hand, I know Ansel and I know he wouldn't do this. He spared me unnecessary suffering and outfitted me with a new and improved purpose. That's the work of a loving, compassionate leader, not a vengeful tyrant with an ulterior motive.

I return to my aisle, fully intent on getting out of this dress and away from my nostalgia, but by the time I get there, both my uniform and my bag are gone.

17

"What did you do with it?" I ask an alarmed Gabe as I storm around the corner.

He lifts a brow. "Do with what?"

"My uniform, Gabe. Where did you put it? I left it in the aisle and now it's gone."

He appears taken aback.

"Nothing," he says, bristling at my accusation. "How could I have even gotten a hold of it? I've been with you the whole time."

"Well, I didn't move it. And now it's gone."

"Maybe you misplaced it. Isn't that what women do?"

"Really? You think now is an appropriate time to introduce some antiquated gender stereotype? I'm asking you a serious question, Gabe. If you're going to engage, at least address me like the intellectual I am."

"How's the view from that high horse you're riding?"

"Give me back my stuff, Gabe."

"I don't have it! I haven't even taken one step down that aisle. Instead, I've been limping around like a first-rate cripple and encouraging you to lighten the hell up."

He tears his gaze from my face long enough to survey our surroundings, but we're the only ones here.

Gabe continues, "Maybe instead of defaulting to blame every time things don't go your way, you should stop and ask yourself why you always assume the worst in people. The world is not out to get you, and neither am I."

If I had lungs, I would force myself to take a deep, calming breath. Instead, I close my eyes and tuck my chin against my collarbone to consolidate my energy. It's not working; I'm too on edge, and having Gabe here is hardly helping.

Still, if he didn't misplace my belongings, then who did?

"You're sure you left your uniform in the aisle? You didn't set it down someplace else?"

I look up, but not at him. Something is wrong, and the only thing worse than being alone in a warehouse with Gabe, is realizing we aren't alone, after all.

He cants his head to the side, trying to catch my eye. "Sarah?"

"I left it on the rack," I say, avoiding his gaze. "I'm sure of it."

"How sure?"

"I'd stake my regeneration on it."

"In that case." He clears his throat and levels his gaze. I don't like where this is going. "What do you say?"

"I'm not apologizing, if that's what you're hoping to hear."

"Why not?"

"Because we have more important things to worry about, like inanimate objects supposedly growing legs and walking away."

"You know, you're lucky I'm still here. This whole situation is a big enough clusterfuck without you turning me into your personal punching bag, too."

"You flatter yourself. I need a partner, not a punching bag. But perpetual victimhood suits you, I must say."

Gabe scoffs and shoves past me, but I swing my shoulder back before it can absorb the force of his incoming assault.

"Perpetual victimhood," he mutters as he walks away, "victimhood my ass. I'm not the one moping around feeling sorry for myself."

"How am I moping around? I'm the only one doing anything of substance here. You're just along for the ride, comrade."

"I'm not your comrade. Don't flatter yourself."

"If you can't handle me, then leave."

"You know what? I think I will. I did better on my own anyway." At the end of the aisle, Gabe removes his hand from his pocket long enough to grant me a parting salute. "Best of luck, your highness. Looks like you're gonna need it."

"You're despicable."

"And you have a mighty long way to fall, so don't get too comfortable."

Gabe rounds the corner and vanishes without much fanfare. I'm convinced he's bluffing, so I cross my arms and wait for him to make his inevitable, shameful return.

He doesn't. I wait some more, but the only things that greet me at the end of the aisle are a long stretch of silence and an abundance of empty air. Sure, I wanted him to leave, but I didn't honestly believe he would.

I pad down the aisle and check in both directions. All I see is more of the same—more racks, more clothes, and more empty air. I consider calling out to him, but think better of it. If there's someone—or some*thing*—stalking us, then I'd prefer to keep a low profile.

I approach a rack dripping with black uniforms and scavenge for my size. Peeling off the dress, I kick it under the display and squeeze myself into the elastic material, all the while scanning for Gabe. I grab a pair of boots off a nearby shelf and draw the laces tight around my ankles, but Gabe is still nowhere to be seen.

I step out from behind the rack, fully expecting Gabe to do the same, but he doesn't. I switch my Keepsake to my other hand. I flex my fingers, and a moment later silver energy bleeds into the stone.

And then it goes bright red.

I look up. A short distance away, one of the racks begins to teeter, causing the clothes lining its rod to tremble. A soft clicking fills the air, and then the clothes two aisles down begin to sway as well.

The sound stops, but the clothes on the rack keep waving to and fro as if compelled by a gentle breeze. I watch them until they cease their swinging, but I can't move. I want to believe Gabe is behind all of this. I want to believe this is his way of getting revenge, but the ring tells me something else entirely.

"Sarah?"

I wheel around. Gabe is standing less than twenty feet away with his hands perfectly still at his sides.

His eyes skitter over my face. "Was that you making all that commotion?"

I shake my head. Behind me, the jingle of metal hangers tapers into silence. We stare at each other a second longer, appreciating one another's presence until I swallow my fear and lean around the corner.

I notice the back first, with its bony train of vertebrae and scarred, leathery flesh. The hair on its head is coarse, unkempt, and does little to conceal the constellation of scabs dotting its scalp.

The malevolent crouches over my mangled belongings. As far as malevolents go, it's not particularly big—Gabe's height, if that—but when it comes to demonic beings, size is irrelevant. Even the smallest malevolents can still do irreversible damage, if they're so inclined. And they are all inclined.

I turn back to Gabe, who nods at me, then the exit. I mirror his mute gesture and fall into step beside him.

We've nearly reached the hallway when I notice something that makes me queasy with apprehension: the door is open and the floor surrounding it is scarred with claw marks.

Gabe seizes my arm and leads me down the closest aisle. I can still hear the malevolent dissecting my bag a short distance away and I wonder how long it will take before it finally loses interest and goes in search of something else to destroy.

"I don't understand," I hiss, "how did it get in here?"

"Brute force and desperation, I would assume. I bet these things haven't eaten in weeks."

He steals a glance at the door, where a second malevolent has just appeared. It sniffs curiously at the claw marks etched into the titanium barrier and then pokes its head through the opening.

"Maybe there's another door," I hedge.

"There isn't. I already checked."

The original malevolent abandons its exploration of the bag in order to defend its territory. Gabe pulls me around the corner and clasps a hand over my mouth, but I couldn't speak if I tried.

The first malevolent gives a warning growl. It sounds like something out of a horror movie: a deep, guttural groan, like that of a dying animal in the final stages of suffering. The second malevolent shoulders through the gap and answers the first with a formidable rumble. We edge around the rack and into the neighbouring aisle, where the remains of my clothes have been reduced to a fine, fibrous dust and the contents of my bag are merely unidentifiable scraps.

Gabe slides to the floor and peers through a slit in the row of clothes just as the first malevolent unleashes a deafening screech. Like all animals, it's trying to appear more dangerous, but it has little hope of intimidating its rival, which is nearly double its size and armed with a plethora of pointed teeth. Regardless of who wins, we're still bound to lose, unless we can find a way out of here, and soon.

Gabe turns to me. "Any ideas?"

I shake my head. I have one, but I doubt it will work. "Nothing."

He turns back to the gap. The malevolents are still locked in a cryptic exchange of wails, whistles, chirps, and chatters, so for now, at least, we're safe.

Gabe lets the clothes fall back together. If he has any sense at all, he'll see that the best option for us right now is to simply wait: sooner or later, the malevolents' confrontation will escalate, a winner will emerge, and, having decided there's nothing worth possessing here, the victor will vacate the area, at which time we'll make our escape. It's not a foolproof plan by any means, but at least it'll get us out of here alive.

"We need to quarantine," he says in a hushed voice. "It's the only way."

"And send them where? They didn't spawn from a vessel. They're from the basement. Only Hunters can contain them when they're like this."

"Well, what's your plan?"

He's not going to like what I have to say. Even I'm not overly thrilled about our prospects. But a bad idea is still better than no idea at all, and I'm not generally known to sit and wait for something better to come along.

"We'll shelter in place. You know malevolents don't typically stay in one area for long." I check the status of the snarling creatures. "In the meantime, I need you to summon your guardian."

"Why?"

"Because we need to distract them somehow, in case they don't turn on each other."

"Seems inevitable that they will."

"Nothing is inevitable, Gabe. That's why I need you to summon your falcon."

Gabe does as I say. He's in the process of bleeding out when I notice that the warehouse has suddenly become hauntingly quiet.

I turn my head and find the first malevolent towering above the aisle. It appears to grin as our eyes connect, sparking a chill so deep that the racks in our vicinity become blanketed in a layer of thick, white frost.

My head snaps in the other direction, where the second malevolent is waiting. Darkness flows from its beastly presence, painting shadows along the floor. Ice coats the racks at the other end, and at last, the clothes stop swinging.

A fine mist clouds around my face. Whatever's happening here, it's wicked enough to deceive my body into thinking it still has lungs.

I look at Gabe and nod. He rubs his hands together until the falcon unfurls itself from the ashes. He opens his hand, releasing the plume of silky dust, and together, we watch as the bird zeroes in on the smaller malevolent and plunges its talons deep into its eyes.

Alarmed by the bird's attack, the malevolent staggers sideways, snagging a claw on one of the racks in its effort to fight back. The apparatus begins to wobble; the shifting weight of the clothes causes it to become unbalanced. In the confusion, the second malevolent scampers away, giving us a chance to make a run for it.

The racks begin to fall, crashing against each other in deafening succession as the malevolents continue to flail and screech. The falcon lifts and dives repeatedly, pummeling their tender skin with its dagger-like appendages while Gabe and I try desperately to outrun the enormous chain of dominoes.

We've managed to get ahead of the pandemonium when he grabs my hand and veers down an aisle. I look up. The next rack in sequence closes in on us, its hangers clinging precariously to its rods. We emerge from the shadow just as the rack clatters to the floor with an extraordinary clamor. Gabe's falcon is fading, but it's managed to keep the malevolents sufficiently distracted long enough for us to reach the door.

When the larger malevolent catches sight of us, it sets off in mad pursuit. Gabe shoves me into the hall and slams his hand against the mutilated door. Just when I think the malevolent is going to come crashing through the wall, there's a dazzling explosion of light. An atomic bomb would pale in comparison to this sudden, phenomenal eruption of energy. I instinctively raise my arm, shielding my eyes against the blinding glow.

I can't see anything—not Gabe, not the malevolents, not even the door through which we barely managed to escape. Any minute now, we're bound to wake up in the infirmary, with Ansel standing over us demanding an explanation. I wouldn't even know where to begin.

But I don't end up in the infirmary. Instead, I'm lying on my back in a ditch—hurt, confused, and very much alive.

18

I breathe in sharply, only for my body to sing with pain. This is a dream; I'm sure of it. I close my eyes and wait, certain that when I open them again, Ansel will appear and explain away this madness.

I open my eyes, but Ansel is curiously absent. Where I'm expecting to see a ceiling, there's only a wide arc of shimmering blue sky. Stiff stalks of grass jab the sides of my face and the dirt beneath my back is embedded with numerous, jagged stones. A passing breeze delivers a medley of aromas, from dirt to spilt gasoline. I try to insolate each individual sensation, but my pain trumps them all.

Footsteps patter up and down the asphalt, but no one is looking for me. In the midst of my rising panic, I listen to their distant drumbeat before curiosity and sheer desperation finally convince me to move.

I start with my fingers and toes. With each activated joint, the pain in my body multiplies tenfold. It licks up my legs and gnaws ravenously on the nerves cushioning my spine. My first thought is I've broken my back, but if that were true, then I wouldn't be able to feel my legs.

I drag my right hand toward my body and give my thigh a weak but determined squeeze. A single, salty tear dashes intrepidly across my temple as my leg answers the gesture with another sharp pang of discomfort.

Having confirmed my sense of feeling in both legs, I tackle the next seemingly insurmountable task: turning onto my stomach. If I can make it that far, then I'm hoping I can somehow make it to my feet.

I inhale deeply, trying to anesthetize my pain. An involuntary sob escapes me as I complete the transition onto my stomach and lie facedown in the ditch with my cheek ground into the dirt and my left arm dangling uselessly from its socket. I don't have the strength to relocate it myself. I fight for another breath. I resist the urge to cough as sharp, shooting pains explode in my side. I cough anyway, and the spasms very nearly cause me to go unconscious. Whatever's happened here, I get the distinct feeling I was not meant to survive it.

I manage to unpin my right arm from beneath the dead weight of my body. I then use my arm, in combination with both of my legs, to lift myself off the ground.

My first attempt at elevating myself is ultimately futile and I end up collapsing back into the grass. I breathe the earth in, trying to absorb an ounce of willpower from her mighty, unmistakable presence, and before long I'm ready to try again.

I make it to my hands and knees, where I bring my left foot forward and plant it under my body. From there, I straighten my knee and eventually my back. My right foot advances forward and comes to a stop alongside the left; reuniting them feels like a victory in a war that has only just begun. Who would've thought a body could feel so heavy, or hurt so much?

I shuffle toward the knoll and begin to scale it using my three functional limbs. I keep my left arm close to my body in an effort to minimize the existing damage, but all it's really doing is making me painfully aware of my battered ribs.

At the top of the hill, I grab hold of the guardrail and pull myself to my feet. Scraps of metal and other debris litter the road. Some of the shinier fragments bask in the glow of the sun, which beams down on me with a fierce, unrelenting intensity. Its warmth is like a lover's kiss: first the delicate reassurance in the spoon of my shoulder, then the passionate insistence in the crease of my ear. I think about that day at the beach, and wonder how I'd ever tolerated the sun's blinding presence.

I swing one leg over the guardrail, then the other. Every step is a struggle as I stagger into the middle of the road. Ribbons of shrapnel and shredded rubber crunch beneath my feet as I shuffle through the chaos. Less than fifty feet away, a silver sedan is lodged into the front of a red SUV. The sedan's hood is crumpled like a tin can and all that remains on its driver side front axle is a still-smoking rim. Several deflated air bags obscure the view of the cabin and there's a sea of shattered glass as far as the eye can see. I look for the driver amidst the metallic folds of the wreckage, but the car itself is hauntingly empty.

I shift my attention to the SUV, where I can just make out the outline of a human head propped against the steering wheel. Beside that, there is only a gaping hole spattered with blood and a landslide of glass extending from the windshield to the pavement below. My heart is beating a million miles a minute. How did I survive this?

I steer around the car, my right hand outstretched for stability and my feet scraping in an alternating rhythm across the asphalt, until I finally reach the SUV and lean in through the smashed window.

The driver is unconscious and slouched over the steering wheel. Against my better judgment, I reach through the window and tip him back, exposing his face and the puffy tissue around his nose where the skin is split and caked with blood. I look him over, hoping his untidy hair and chiseled jawline will clue me into his identity, but I've never seen this man before in my life.

"Ma'am," comes a voice from behind. I turn around, lock eyes with a paramedic, and see my own naked confusion mirrored in the depths of his sable eyes. "Let me help you."

My joints turn to pudding and I'm suddenly aware of the patch of crusty blood cemented in my hair. The paramedic looks me over, but even I can tell he's not quite sure whether to believe his eyes. They flicker between my head wound and the gaping windshield, processing the improbability of it all, and still I stand: knees weak, hair matted, and eyes damp with tears. Whether they're tears of joy or grief has yet to be decided.

"Ma'am," he says again.

I turn back to the SUV, where a second paramedic is now leaning through the window to place two gloved fingers against the driver's neck. I wait, anticipating the worst, when at last the paramedic withdraws his hand and looks straight through me to his colleague.

"We've got a pulse," he tells his partner, and I let out the breath I didn't even know I was holding.

152

The first paramedic assists me to the ambulance. There, he gives me a once-over, notices my dysfunctional shoulder, and tells me he's going to relocate it. I fight to stay conscious as he deftly pops it back into place.

The paramedics insist on taking me to the hospital, so I'm loaded onto a stretcher and into the ambulance. I'm told the driver will be transported in a separate vehicle. The paramedic secures my various straps and restraints, and before long we're on our way.

The ambulance zips down the highway, its siren whining periodically as we blaze through one intersection after another. I watch the world shrink into the distance, miles evaporating like water before my eyes. I hope the driver is okay. I need an ally, but beyond that, I need a whole lot of answers, and promptly.

At the hospital, I'm given a battery of tests, a gown, and a room of my own and told someone will seek me out as soon as they receive word on the driver's condition. Miraculously, the only fractures in my body are on my ribs. The doctors have started calling me Woman of Steel. They ask me if I'm even from this planet. I just smile and wait for them to leave.

And now I'm alone.

I nestle deeper into the bed and pull the sheets over my head. I picture the driver of the SUV and wonder if I know him. After all, I was his passenger. I scour my memories for a face that resembles the one I'd uncovered behind the wheel, but all I recall is a vivid flash of light and then total oblivion.

"A miracle," comes a voice from the corner of the room.

I push the covers off my face and lift my head. A bald man in a grey suit is standing next to the window with his hands clasped behind his back and his attention trained on something in the distance. He turns around and smiles, but still recognition eludes me, along with everything else.

The expressionless gentleman nods and approaches my bed.

"What did you just say?" I ask him.

His lips curl into a smile. Beneath the sheets, I feel for the call button and pull it closer to my body.

"I said it's a miracle. Odd wording, wouldn't you agree?"

"I'm sorry, do I know you?"

The man's conservative smile subsides into a smirk. He raises a hand and snaps his fingers, triggering an explosion of pain behind my eyes. I'm trying not to scream, and failing spectacularly.

And then I remember everything.

"I removed the other ones," Ansel explains. "I didn't want you to get distracted."

"Where's Gabe?" I pant, tears still rolling down my face.

"Down the hall. I'm afraid he got the worst of it."

"The worst of what?"

Ansel observes me wordlessly. The pain inside my skull has dulled somewhat, leaving me with a surprisingly organized compendium of memories dating back to my previous life. I remember everything now, including the incident in the wardrobe that presumably triggered this bizarre sequence of events.

"How do you feel?" he asks, ignoring my question altogether.

"Aside from a little sore… fine."

"Excellent." I look at him sideways, but Ansel doesn't notice.

I persist with my interrogation. "What happened? How did I end up here?"

He cants his head to the side. "You don't remember?"

"I remember seeing a flash of light, and then nothing." I compose myself and explain, "Gabe and I encountered two malevolents in the wardrobe. Rather than initiate quarantine, we thought it would be best to vacate the area and enlist the help of more senior staff. Needless to say, we were unable to locate anyone else."

"I'm aware of the situation in the wardrobe," he says in a level tone. "Thanks to you and Mr. Conway, I now have to rebuild."

My eyes snap to his face. "Rebuild?"

"Yes. Rebuild." He surveys the antiseptic room with vague disinterest, but the explanation I'm expecting doesn't follow.

"How did I survive the crash?" I ask when he still doesn't speak. "I saw the wreckage. It seems… hard to believe."

"The only thing you survived was a thorough mauling by two underfed malevolents, which is quite remarkable considering you and Mr. Conway were sorely ill-equipped to defend yourselves."

"But I'm alive," I persist. "I can feel again. I can *breathe*. Look—"

Lifting my arms, I examine the network of veins crisscrossing my skin while Ansel looks on in annoyance.

Finally, he speaks.

"You didn't survive anything because you were never alive to begin with. The only reason you're alive now is because I need time to finish what I started, and I can't do that unless I have the place to myself." He pauses, waiting for my reaction. A moment of silence passes between us as do a million questions I don't have the heart to ask. Thankfully, Ansel saves me the trouble of translating my own confusion.

"There's only one way for you and Mr. Conway to survive outside of The Establishment, and that's to inhabit a human vessel. Your injuries should mend themselves within a few days. In the meantime, I'd ask that you do your best to take care of the body you've been given."

I stare at him. "But the passenger—"

"Both the driver and his passenger died in the accident, Sarah. It was a very violent collision."

"But their spirits—"

"Have already been collected."

I sink into the pillow, trying to process this peculiar turn of events. Ansel glances at the open doorway just as the distant tread of footsteps grows louder. Then he turns back to me.

"You'll have to excuse Gabe's confusion. I wasn't able to purge his vessel in time."

"What do you mean?"

A nurse enters my room and Ansel disappears before I can get my answer.

The nurse cracks a practiced smile. I don't even blink.

"Would you like to see your husband?" she asks.

○

It's difficult to describe what I'm feeling. Hospitals used to be my second home. Now, they're just prisons for the ailing, with rooms for cells and the occasional white coat floating through my periphery like a guard making his rounds. Everything puts me on edge: the ringing phones, the downtrodden nurses, the looks I get from the other patients. The doctors have started calling me an enigma—a puzzle—but how can that be when I'm still in one piece?

The nurse steers my wheelchair to the left. We roll over the threshold and into Gabe's room, where I discover a large window concealed by vertical blinds, a table cluttered with plastic trays, and Gabe, lying at a forty-five-degree angle with his arm tethered to a jumble of machines. Without all the blood and broken glass, I can now see the full extent of his injuries: his nose and leg have both been fitted with a cast, and there's a cervical collar holding his head in place. It doesn't make any sense. If there's anyone who should be bedridden right now, it's me. I should be shattered, ripped apart—not capable of getting up and walking away.

Mary, the nurse, aligns my wheelchair with Gabe's bed. Before she goes, she hands me a transparent plastic bag containing Gabe's effects and suggests I bring him a change of clothes from home. I just smile and nod politely. I have no idea where home is.

I turn to Gabe. Bruises marble his skin and his hair is as crooked as ever, especially at the front where it sticks straight up like a rooster's comb. Two deaths later and still he looks like he just stumbled in off the streets. Unbelievable.

I turn my attention over to the bag. Maybe if I can figure out whom his vessel belongs to, it'll help me establish my own role in this nightmare.

I pull out the first item: a brown wallet with frayed white edges and more cards than room to store them. I uncover his driver's license first. Not surprisingly, "Gabe" is not actually Gabe at all. His name is William Russell Foster, and he was born on January 16th, 1983. He carries four credit cards, one debit card, and a smattering of fairly recent receipts, which have been stuffed into the pocket behind the slots. I take them out and smooth each one over my knee. His last three purchases took place at Frank's Convenience. Frank. Why do I know that name?

I shake my head and keep sleuthing. He bought milk, eggs, bread, coffee, and apples at a grocery store on Ellison Street. That same day, he purchased $47.81 in gas at a station on Warwick Boulevard. A small, savagely crumpled receipt reveals he made a third stop at the Conway & Matheson Pharmacy.

I lift my head and look at him. He's sleeping peacefully under the effects of a light sedative, so I carry on with my investigation and hope he doesn't awaken before I can determine my whereabouts.

I return the plethora of cards and receipts to the wallet and chuck it back into the bag. A black phone rimmed with scuffmarks catches my eye and I dig it out, only to spook at the sight of my smiling face on its rectangular screen. Except it isn't actually me at all, just the owner of my current vessel. So why do we look so similar?

He begins to stir. I sit ramrod still, but the only parts of him that move are his eyelids. They flutter softly for a moment, and then he returns to his medicated slumber.

I shift my attention back to the phone. The photo's subject is a young woman clad in an elegant grey turtleneck, midnight-blue jeans, and a pair of brown leather boots. The vibrant backdrop of autumn foliage mirrors the sanguine hue of her lips and brings out the natural rosiness in her cheeks. Her smile hints at knowing more than I do about what's really going on here. It's like looking into the past, present, and future, all at once.

I notice a second wallet buried at the bottom of the bag. It's marginally bigger than the first, with a creamy white exterior and numerous slots dividing its sand-coloured interior. I scavenge for a driver's license and find my face here too. I tell myself that this is not me in the tiny frame, with corkscrews of lush, golden hair spilling over my shoulders and those now-bare lips drawn into a fierce, unforgiving frown. I tell myself I don't actually look like this, even as I subconsciously trace the nick above my brow that is also mysteriously present in this miniature reflection.

Gabe inhales deeply and opens his eyes. When our gazes meet, I return the wallet to the bag and place the bag on the table.

"You owe me," he croaks.

"For what?"

He directs his eyes at the ceiling as they innocently slip shut.

"For saving you," he says in a throaty whisper, too burdened by his own exhaustion to manage much else. "Two seconds more and we'd be history."

I lean on the edge of the bed, but not even the shifting weight of the mattress is enough to make him stir. "What happened to us, Gabe?"

"Big flash," he says, which causes my heart to hammer against my ribs, "that's all I remember."

"But where'd the flash come from?" I shake his arm, but he's already fading. "Gabe. Where'd the flash come from?"

"Door..."

"The door? Did something happen to the door?" I wrap my fingers around his wrist, hoping the clammy quality of my skin will jolt him back to awareness, but instead he continues his rapid descent into sleep and the warm clinch of too much morphine. "Did something happen to the malevolent?"

A smile blooms on his lips. "Let me sleep, Tiff. We'll talk about it tomorrow."

I let go of his arm, but Gabe is already sound asleep. I try to explain away his incoherence by reminding myself that his brain is flooded with painkillers, but even in his drugged-up stupor, he sounds far too convinced of my name for this strange, new designation to be accidental.

I dive into the plastic bag on the table. I rummage for the white wallet, tear back the zipper, and fish for the license. Sure enough, next to the image of my face is my name: Tiffany Amanda Foster.

19

"Mrs. Foster?"

I roll over in bed just as a doctor appears wearing aquamarine scrubs. The young practitioner, who looks to be in his mid-thirties, scrabbles around in the pockets of his white coat before pulling over a chair and taking a seat beside me.

"How are you feeling?" he asks as he pulls out a pen and gives it a gentle twist.

"Better than I should be." When our eyes meet, I force a smile and wait for him to go back to his papers.

"So you've been in to see your husband," he says in a voice that makes me wonder whether this is an observation or a question. I nod anyway. "He's lucky to be alive, and so are you."

"He is," I agree.

The doctor jots an illegible note at the top of the page and flips to the next one. I wonder if Ansel is planning to come back and purge Gabe's vessel—which, judging by the context, I've taken to mean replacing William's memories with his own.

"Your MRI results came back," the doctor says without looking at me, "and I have to say, I'm a little surprised."

"I know. It's a mess."

His eyes find mine. "Actually, no. There's no sign of trauma whatsoever." He sets the clipboard aside and knits his hands together. "As I said, you're lucky to be alive. Aside from a couple of broken ribs and the laceration on your scalp, there's really not much to report."

I nod slowly and hope he doesn't ask me the kinds of questions only Tiffany would be able to answer. As far as I know, all of her memories are gone. All that remains of the woman I've replaced is her vessel, and it fits me like a glove.

"Do you have family you can call?" the doctor asks.

I picture Gabe's cell phone at the bottom of the plastic bag. "I'm sure I can get a hold of someone," I say evasively.

He nods and reaches for the clipboard. His pen scratches across the page again and I casually crane my neck to steal a glimpse at his notes.

"I'd like to keep you overnight, to see if your condition changes. In the meantime, if you need anything, you can call one of the nurses." He smiles politely, and then slips out of the room before I can think of anything to say.

When I'm sure he has no intention of returning, I rifle through the plastic bag again and pull out "my" wallet. Since it looks like I'm going to be here a while, I decide to pass the time playing detective. If I'm going to act like Tiffany Foster, I had better know my lines.

I open the wallet and dump its contents onto the bed table. From what I can gather, Tiffany also owned four credit cards and one debit card, leading me to wonder if she and Will had been arguing about money. It could explain the accident, especially if Will had been too busy making a point to notice the

163

oncoming sedan. I'll have to ask Gabe what he remembers as soon as he wakes up.

Unlike Will, Tiffany did not carry receipts. However, she did appear to have a slight obsession with loyalty cards. I arrange them alphabetically before tucking them back into the safety of their slots. All this plastic for a life that is as artificial as my sense of belonging.

When I'm done perusing the cards, I turn my attention back to the driver's license. I read her name until I can recite it without hesitation: Tiffany Amanda Foster. Tiffany Amanda Foster. Tiffany. Amanda. Foster. I wonder what her maiden name was.

I consult my finger, but there's nothing to see other than a pale, pink impression where a ring had been not long ago. My Keepsake would not have left a mark, but a wedding ring would. Maybe I was wrong—maybe the argument didn't begin in the car. Maybe that fire's been smoldering for months, and the accident was a fatal tipping point. And now Gabe and I are stuck in their bodies.

I skim the driver licenses. Will and Tiffany's home address is listed as 637 Jacobson Drive. I can't even begin to imagine where that is, but I'm reluctant to ask for fear that my inability to navigate the city will set off alarm bells. Then what? How many people would honestly believe that the only reason I'm alive is because an ageless man in a suit replaced someone else's spirit with mine? Even I don't believe it, and I was there.

I lean back against the pillow. My head is pounding like a drum and my ribs punish every breath that has the audacity to enter my lungs. I'm sore down to my fingernails, but lack the motivation to ask for morphine. And since I'm confined to a bed with nothing to do, I decide to pass the time counting the dots on the ceiling tiles. I hope Ansel comes back, but I'm not counting on it. After all, he's rebuilding—whatever that means.

I turn onto my side and gaze out the window. I close my eyes, eager to shut out the shafts of light streaming in through the blinds, and it plunges me into a deep, dreamless sleep.

○

The next morning, the doctor I spoke with yesterday hands me my discharge papers and urges me to return if my condition declines. I thank him and he leaves with obvious haste. Since I don't have a change of clothes, I pull on yesterday's outfit and do my best to tame my hair, which is flat on one side and flyaway on the other.

I decide to stop by Gabe's room on my way out. To my surprise, he's fully conscious and sipping coffee from a thick-handled plastic cup.

I pause in the doorway with the bag of items dangling from my fingertips. My gaze lingers on the triangle of exposed skin on his back, where the waistband of his boxers is visible. I glance around the room, searching for any indication that Ansel may have come and finished what he started, but all I see are a pair of crutches propped against the bedrails and a tray of picked-over food on the table beside him.

I give the door a few quick knocks. Gabe whips around. When he sees me standing in the doorway, his face explodes in a grin.

"There you are," he says in a jubilant tone. "The nurse said you'd be by."

"I'm not planning to stay."

I round the foot of the bed and lean against the window. When Gabe notices the cling gauze wrapped around my head, his smile slides into a frown and he motions for me to come closer.

"What happened?" he asks.

I shrug. "I got ejected."

Gabe tries to reel me in, but I plant my feet more firmly on the floor and refuse to budge.

"Good god," he says, thumbing my hand affectionately. "Did they keep you overnight?"

I nod and take back my arm. "The doctor says I broke a few ribs."

"Is that all?"

"Miraculously, yes." I flick my chin at the cast encasing his leg. "Looks like you got the worst of it," I add, parroting Ansel.

Gabe massages his temples. A storm of ruptured blood vessels encircles his eyes and he's breathing heavily through his mouth. It's so strange to hear him breathe. I'm used to detecting his presence in other ways—in electric shocks and unwelcome jolts, not laboured breaths and calloused thumbs.

"Yeah," he finally agrees with a sigh, "looks like I did."

"What happened to us, Gabe?"

His eyes snap upwards. "Who?"

"Don't play dumb with me," I grit. "I'm in a rotten mood as it is."

"Who's Gabe?"

I draw a sharp breath. I look him over—same hair, same eyes, same aggressively masculine jawline—but the expression on his face is as tender as a juvenile fern. He doesn't know who he is, but I do.

"You're Gabe," I remind him sternly. "Remember? You died in a motorcycle accident some time in 2008. We were in the wardrobe trying on clothes when those malevolents—"

"Tiffany."

I bite my lip. Gabe shakes his head.

"Maybe you should sit down," he says calmly.

"I'd rather stand."

"Tiff—"

"Don't call me that. That's not my name."

"I'm calling the nurse."

"No, you're not."

Gabe reaches for the call button, but I jerk it out of his hand.

His eyes lock onto me. His gown is sagging at the front, giving me an unimpeded view of his collarbone and the patch of dark, curly hair on his unmuscled chest. He makes a grab for the button, but I yank it out of reach.

"Tiffany," he hisses. "Sit down."

"Not until you call me by my real name."

"Nurse!"

I drop the device and the bag as a pair of ladies in pastel scrubs charge into the room. My eyes flicker nervously over to Gabe, who pushes back the table and pulls himself up by his crutches. I exchange flustered looks with the women in the doorway. Without thinking, I crash through the human shield and stumble into the hallway, where the air is cool and the only thing I can hear is the sound of my shoes slapping the linoleum as I race toward the exit.

I fly across the emergency department, through the automatic doors, and out into the sunshine. Every breath is a thorn in my throat and I'm dizzy with exhaustion, but I can't stop. Not now.

My desire for self-preservation takes me deep into the heart of the nearest parking lot, where I seek refuge amidst the rows of vehicles. I eventually reach the far corner of the lot, where, out in the open again, I have no choice but to soldier through the pain and hope I remain conscious long enough to lose my pursuers.

I've made it to a quaint little park about two city blocks from the hospital when a couple of police officers screech to a stop a short distance away. I change course and keep running, but my stamina is waning. I duck between a pair of trees and trudge through a sandbox, which consumes more energy than I'd anticipated.

I've managed to reach the far side of the park when one of the hospital security guards says something into his radio. His partner signals for me to stop, and I'm so weak from running that I sink to the ground before passing out completely.

20

On my first day in the big house, all I do is sleep.

The sleep comes easily, like a hug from an old friend. It takes me into its embrace and I surrender my troubles like a defenseless infant. Every now and then, a pudgy lady in a frumpy russet sweater shuffles in and replaces the tray of cold, untouched food with a steamy new offering. I've mastered the art of regulating my breathing, so whenever I hear her slippered feet swishing across the floor, I settle deeper into the bed and pretend to be sound asleep.

On the second day, I'm awoken by the sound of two people bickering downstairs. The male voice is unmistakably Gabe's, and I presume the female voice belongs to the woman who keeps dropping in to check on me. Some time later, the bedroom door opens. I resort to my dead-asleep pose and wait for her to deposit her latest offering on the nightstand.

I wait until I hear the door click closed before peeking out of my blanket cocoon. This time, it isn't a hot meal that greets me, but a framed photograph of Tiffany instead. She's wearing a contoured ivory gown and clutching a bouquet of white roses in her hands. I turn the photo on its face and bury myself in the bed once again, where sleep surrounds me like a current and swiftly sweeps me under.

On the third day, no one comes to visit. I don't budge. I don't belong here, and a hearty helping of pad Thai isn't going to change that. This is not my house. This is not my room. This is not my bed. And if anyone tries to insist that my name is Tiffany Amanda Foster, I'll have no choice but to prove how hopelessly wrong they really are.

It's shortly after 6PM. I have no idea what day it is and now I have a headache from sleeping too long. My stomach is eating itself and my ribs protest every hint of contact both inside and out. Deciding I've slept enough, I peel back the covers and amble into the bathroom to freshen up.

I flip on the light switch next to the door. The room comes to life and before I know it, I'm face to face with my reflection in the antique mirror above the marble vanity. I look like someone who's just crawled out of a grave, and given the circumstances, I'd say that's a fairly accurate description.

I turn on the tap and douse my face in cold water. Three days after leaving the hospital, I have yet to see or hear from Ansel. I have so many questions, like what happened after Gabe and I fled the warehouse or how long he thinks it'll take to rebuild The Establishment. I want to ask about the others and whether any of them survived, but I'm not sure I'm prepared for an answer right now.

When I've cleansed the sleep from my skin, I reach for a towel and bury my face in its heavenly folds. Then I slip back into the bedroom to hunt for a change of clothes.

I approach the armoire and open both of the doors, where I'm greeted by a tidy row of cashmere sweaters, silk blouses, and starched white shirts with the collars and sleeves properly buttoned. The two bottom drawers are lined with felt and contain countless pairs of crisp, folded khakis, socks, ties, belts, and lacy lingerie organized by pattern and colour.

Dismayed by my options, I shut the doors and turn back to the room, where the floor is faded from years of traffic. The decorative pillows have been pushed to the far side of the bed and there's a permanent groove in the sheets closest to the window. Everywhere I turn, I'm met with abundance: dozens of shapely bottles on the makeup table in the corner, columns of books on the nightstand, braided gold tassels on the thick, burgundy curtains bracketing the window. This is a room befitting of royalty, not a pair of debt-ridden suburbanites with marriage issues.

I venture back into the bathroom. Whoever owns this place put a lot of care into the presentation of the towels, which have been embroidered with a fanciful *F* – for Foster, I presume. A glass soap pump is nestled in a basket of potpourri, which sits between the matching sinks. A clawfoot tub sits in the corner, across from a bidet, which I've only ever seen in the most upscale hotels on TV.

I approach the bath and turn on the hot water. It surges out of the faucet with the urgency of a river, roiling against the pearly walls as I hold my hand under the stream. Its warm dependability melts my inhibition instantly, and before I can change my mind, I depress the drain stop and peel off all my clothes.

Naked, shivering, and fighting back tears, I stand next to the tub and try not to think about my family's trip to the beach. I shouldn't be here. The numbness I can live with, and death is all

172

about being numb. But this—being alive and trapped in someone else's body—is a little too much to take. My mind keeps returning to what Ansel said about rebuilding, and I begin to wonder if all of this is my fault. After all, I had no business being in the basement, and now humanity has to live with the consequences of my heroic intentions.

I lower myself into the bath. The water sloshes against my chin as I slip deeper into its embrace. I inhale deeply, remembering too late the temperamental state of my ribs. But there's no pain. If anything, my bones are rejoicing. I trace the blotchy, magenta bruise next to my breast, and at last, my ribs answer my gentle inquiry with a penetrating bark of pain.

Once the water has cooled, I drain the tub and wrap myself in a towel. My apprehension has returned along with the chill, so I pad into the bedroom and dress quickly. I opt for the simplest outfit I can manage—blue jeans and a sleek, white blouse—and then open the door and go downstairs.

From somewhere just beyond my view comes the garbled commotion of a TV. I take my time descending the stairs. Dozens of framed photographs line the wallpapered hallway on both sides of the stairs; I pause to appraise a couple of them in detail. On the surface, Will and Tiffany seemed happy, but I know better than anyone that looks can deceive an untrained eye. The signs of an unhappy marriage are all there, from the wandering eyes to the use of physical barriers, but their practiced smiles outshine them all.

I keep walking. Once I reach the base of the stairs, I stop and survey the multitude of rooms. There's a kitchen on my right, a narrow foyer straight ahead, and a grandiose sitting room with maroon walls and a steep, vaulted ceiling on my left. Another, slightly less pretentious den overlooks the backyard behind me, and there's a disproportionately small powder room in the corner. The house has more windows than actual walls, and they're all dressed to the nines in drapes of varying thickness and importance. The virginal hues in the kitchen stand in stark contrast to the bold, broody tones of the living room, which, in spite of its magnificent, steepled roof, is drenched in shadows and the artificial glow of the TV.

Gabe is stretched across the sofa with his broken leg resting on a pillow and his head propped against the armrest. He tears his eyes from the TV as I enter the room, but I'm too engrossed in my surroundings to initiate conversation. I note the assortment of bottles crammed into the liquor cabinet by the window and then casually turn my attention over to Gabe.

"Are we rich?" I ask him.

His interest hangs on the enormous flatscreen TV. "We were."

"Earned or inherited?"

"Both."

That's definitely not Gabe talking. I wonder if he's even in there at all.

My eyes flicker to the decanter of scotch on the bar. "Addiction?" I venture.

"Infertility."

I shake my head and make my way into the kitchen, where I open the refrigerator and pore over its contents without actually registering what I'm seeing.

Gabe lumbers in on his crutches. I think he's been drinking, but it's hard to tell when he's slouched over and favouring his leg.

"Are you hungry?" he asks.

"I don't know." I close the door. "It's been a while since I ate. I don't know what I like anymore."

"It's been three days, Tiff."

"Why do you keep calling me that?"

Gabe steers toward one of the cupboards. "How about some cereal?" he proffers.

"You've been drinking, haven't you?"

"I prefer the term 'self-medicating', but yes, I've been drinking."

"In your condition?"

"Because of my condition." He produces a slender box from one of the shelves and a grey ceramic bowl from another. Shaking some muesli into the bowl, he replaces the box and then rifles through the fridge for a carton of milk.

"Almond milk?" I say disgustedly.

"You're lactose intolerant."

"No, I'm not."

"Trust me, you are." He sinks a spoon into the mixture and passes me the bowl. "You think I wouldn't know my wife's dietary needs?"

I accept the bowl and bore into him with a vexed stare.

"We're not married, Gabe," I tell him for what I hope will be the last time.

"About that," he says, "why do you keep calling me Gabe?"

"Because that's your name."

His eyes flutter over the bandage enshrouding my skull. I know what he's thinking, but he's got it all wrong: there's nothing wrong with my brain. This life is not a permanent destination for me, merely an unexpected detour on the everlasting road to truth. I'm firmly of the opinion that Ansel put me here for a reason, and I endeavor to solve this riddle even at the expense of my alliance with Gabe.

"Listen, Tiff—"

"Sarah," I correct him. "If you're going to address me by name, at least use the right one."

"Sarah," he repeats slowly. I wait for an imaginary bell to go off in his head, but he doesn't appear to recognize me at all. "Please. Let me help you."

"Okay. Then you can start by telling me what you remember."

"That's a pretty vague request."

I narrow my eyes. "You're right," I concede, acquiescing with a brisk nod. I set down the bowl and fold my arms. "What happened before the accident?"

"Well," Gabe licks his lips and looks around the room, "we were at your mother's—"

"No. We weren't."

"Yes, we were."

"Gabe, be serious. What happened before the accident?"

"Maybe I should call the doctor."

"Maybe you should answer the question."

He tries to reach around me for the phone. As my hand makes contact with his chest, a spark of electricity jumps from my fingers. Gabe stumbles backward in shock and crashes against the island just as my hand loses its luminescence.

We look at each other. Gabe's face is whiter than the cast on his leg and he doesn't seem likely to move anytime, either.

I approach him slowly, thankful for his temporary paralysis as I lay a hand on his chest. His breathing becomes heavier as I channel my energy into him, illuminating the four chambers of his heart. The rest of his body lights up like a jar of fireflies, and before long recognition flickers in his eyes.

"Sarah," he whispers.

I remove my hand. "What do you remember?" I ask him again.

"Not much," he admits, righting his crutches, "but I do remember the flash. I remember other things, too."

177

"What kinds of things?"

Gabe pans over the room. "Well, this place, for one. You and me and…" He shakes his head. "What do you remember?"

"Ansel wiped all of Tiffany's memories. All I remember is The Establishment, plus whatever came before."

His face falls. "You don't remember us?"

"He didn't want me to get distracted."

I spot a sugar bowl next to the breadbox and concentrate my energy on it. The bowl divorces the breadbox and slides toward me as if drawn by an invisible string. I lay a hand on its lid and turn to Gabe as his face pales in disbelief.

I head for the living room, where I remove the screen on the impressive wood fireplace and gather a handful of ash from beneath the grate. Behind me, Gabe penetrates the silence with a disapproving intake of air.

"What are you doing?" he asks, leaning on his crutches. "You're making a mess."

I shoot him a sideways look. If he has any sense left in him at all, he'll do the wise thing and stay out of my way.

I roll the particles between my fingers. One by one, they come to life with a cheerful pop, filling the room with the redolence of burnt wood. The sputtering is soon replaced by an angry fizzle as the ashes are converted to energy. I open my hands, releasing a small flock of doves. Gabe follows their graceful movements until the birds disappear into a fine, white mist. He searches for the doves a moment longer, and then shifts his attention over to me.

"Who are you?" he asks with palpable confusion.

I freeze. "Sarah," I reply, "we already established this."

Gabe shakes his head. His memories are fading again, and so is any hope I may have had of finding a reliable ally.

"I don't know you," he says acerbically. "How did you get in my house?"

"For Christ's sake, Gabe, it's me, Sarah. Now, please, try and focus."

"I'm calling the cops," he says, staggering back into the kitchen. "You're not my wife. My wife doesn't know magic."

"It's not magic," I say, exasperation weighing on my voice. "It's manipulation. Did you retain nothing from orientation?"

"It's ringing," he calls from the neighbouring room.

I dash into the kitchen and snatch the phone out of his hands. I hang up the call, and then slide the device out of reach.

"Listen," I command, "I'm only going to tell you this once. Your name is Gabe Conway. You died in a motorcycle crash in 2008. After that, you ended up at The Establishment, where you met me. We'd been outrunning some malevolents when there was a bright flash and we woke up here. As of right now, The Establishment is gone and Ansel is rebuilding. The reason you're so confused is because he didn't have time to purge your vessel of William Foster's memories." I pause for a breath. "Anything?"

Gabe's expression is serious—seriously empty, that is.

"Would I have remembered if I'd died?" he asks.

I furrow my brows. "No. You wouldn't." I sigh. "All the same, we're not supposed to be here." I brush the last of the ash from my hands and perch them on my hips. Even if he doesn't understand what I'm saying, I still feel the need to explain myself.

"Regeneration can only be achieved by meeting a predefined collection quota, and you and I were nowhere near it. Well, you were, maybe, but I had at least a couple thousand more to go."

"A couple-thousand more what, exactly?"

I look him dead in the eyes. "Souls. We collected human souls."

"Oh, no," Gabe says, shaking his head emphatically, "that sounds like some Grim Reaper shit. Now I know you're making this up."

"How could I make this up? Did I not just convert ashes into doves? Did I not just electrocute you right here in the kitchen? Why would I make any of that up?" I nod at his bent leg. "For Christ's sake, Gabe, I stitched you up."

"I broke my leg," he says in a despairing tone, "if there was any stitching involved, I can guarantee you were not a part of it."

"Oh? Then care to explain the scar above your knee?"

Gabe's focus drops to his right knee. "There's nothing there," he says without really looking.

"Look again."

He grabs a handful of fabric and lifts the leg of his shorts. He cranes forward and squints, then touches his forefinger to the speck of raised flesh where I'd administered the neutralizer.

"That?" he says, straightening, his finger still aimed at the blemish, "I've always had that."

"Since when?"

"Since I was a kid. Remember? We were rollerblading around the cul-de-sac and I skidded into a big patch of gravel."

I arch my brows. "We?"

"Yes, we. You and I grew up together." Gabe shakes his head. "Who are you?"

"Who am I? Who are *you*?"

"Look, I wouldn't say this if I didn't care. But I think you need to see someone."

"I need to see someone about as much as you need another drink."

"You're talking like a crazy person, Tiff. I don't know who you think you are, but you're not the woman I married."

"Well, at least we can agree on that."

Gabe inches closer to me. He releases his grip on the right crutch and reaches for my wrist, but I swat him away with passionate contempt.

"What happened to you?" he asks.

"How much time do you have?" I ask sarcastically.

Gabe sighs. Nodding at the bar, he says, "Have a drink with me until I forget about all of this. Please."

"I'm not legal."

"You're thirty-one."

I don't know what to say. I've never had a drink in my life, and I'm not about to lose my alcohol virginity to something as pompous as scotch. Still, getting buzzed in a body I didn't choose, with a man I don't remember marrying, in a life that itches like a wool sweater, doesn't seem like a half-bad plan.

"I don't drink scotch," I say. "What else do you have?"

"Everything. I'm an aspiring alcoholic."

"Wine?"

"Red, white, or rosé?"

"Rosé. It sounds… dignified."

"Like you?"

"Just pour me a drink," I say, exasperated.

Gabe angles toward the cabinet, a smirk hedging his pale lips. "Right away, your highness."

21

If you'd asked me where I saw myself in my next life, getting drunk with Gabe wouldn't have been my first answer.

But times have changed, and since it doesn't look like Ansel will be unscrambling Gabe's memories anytime soon, I have no choice but to take matters into my own hands. Without a corresponding spirit, Will's memories should eventually disappear. To speed the process along, I'm making Gabe take a shot every time he calls me Tiffany or accuses me of lying. When he wakes up tomorrow, the only memories he should have are his own.

"You're full of shit. You know that, right?" Gabe says.

I nurse the wine. This isn't the best idea I've ever had, but it's undoubtedly the most entertaining. I recall Ansel's instructions to take care of my body, but it's just one night and I need an ally—even if that ally is a mess of a man with disheveled hair and an alcohol dependency that borders on clinical.

"Drink," I command him.

Gabe takes a shot before setting the glass back on the table.

"Is it working?" I ask, observing him.

"I'll tell you what *isn't* working: this marriage. And probably my liver, too." Gabe swirls his index finger around the rim before extending a hand toward the bottle of whiskey.

"I'll take that as a no." I take a sip of the wine.

"So help me understand," he says as he adds another splash of liquor to his glass and leans back against the cushions. "I drink myself half to death and then magically turn into someone else?"

"Ansel didn't have time to separate your memories from Will's, but without his spirit they won't last more than a couple of days."

"And how does alcohol fit into this?"

I shrug. "People drink to forget, right? What was that thing you said earlier... self-medicating?"

Gabe narrows his eyes suspiciously. "You're trying to make me forget about Will."

"Exactly."

"What if I forget Gabe, instead?"

"Impossible. Where there's a spirit, there are memories. Now, drink."

Gabe lifts the glass to his lips and swallows the whiskey in a single gulp, shaking his head as the bitter drink glides down his throat.

I frown. "Stop it. You're not a Magic 8 ball."

"Speaking of magic... why not break out a couple more party tricks for me? I'm getting bored."

"If you want to be entertained, get a dog."

This time, Gabe skips the glass and goes straight for the bottle. In agreeing to have a drink with him I had hoped it would wash away the remains of Will, but so far all I've achieved is a pounding headache that I'm nearly certain wasn't caused by the wine.

I modify my approach. "If I didn't know better, I'd think you were planning on visiting The Establishment yourself."

Gabe rests the bottle on his knee.

"Tell you what," he says. "If I die in my sleep, I'll send you a postcard."

"If you die in your sleep, we're both in trouble."

"We were in trouble long before this shitshow started. Do you want more wine?"

"I'm good." I look around the room to test my vision. "What would it take to make you believe me?"

"A visit from a scythe-toting skeleton would be pretty convincing." Gabe leans the bottle against his mouth only to frown in disappointment at the absence of alcohol that meets his lips.

"So is that what you think? That The Establishment is just a revolving door of clichés?"

"I never said that."

"Not explicitly."

"So what does that make you, then? An angel?"

"A Spirit Catcher. Angels are a myth."

Gabe drags a hand across his mouth, erasing the evidence of his binge just in time for a smile to bubble to the surface.

"What?" I ask.

"Nothing. I just can't believe we're having this conversation."

"Well, that makes two of us."

Gabe smirks and places his hand on my thigh, causing my body to stiffen. His fingers fan over my knee in slow, circular sweeps.

"What are you doing?" I ask.

"Seeing what you remember." Gabe's hand drifts toward my hip.

I shove him back against the sofa and set my glass down on the table.

"Okay, new plan," I say, sweeping some hair out of my face as Gabe ogles me expectantly. "I'm going to go to bed, and when I wake up tomorrow, you're going to be back to your insufferable, narcissistic self."

"Good idea," Gabe says, "let's settle this in the bedroom, just like old times."

"I never thought I'd say this, but I'm really glad you broke your leg."

He stares down at his hands. Amidst the confusion of partially consumed alcohol, I feel the slightest twinge of pity toward my emotionally encumbered companion. Even without any of Tiffany's memories, it isn't hard to see where it all went wrong. Perhaps Will turned to drinking as a way to cope with their lack of children, and maybe Tiffany found the same temporary satisfaction in shopping, hence the loyalty cards. A picture may be worth a thousand words, but it takes more than that to tell the whole story.

"I need to tell you something," Gabe looks up at me. "I had an affair."

I reach for my wine. I'm not sure how to process this admission, which was clearly intended for another woman's ears, and I'm nowhere near drunk enough to forget it happened.

And that's when it hits me: maybe I'm going about this the wrong way. Maybe the best way to purge Will's vessel isn't to bury his memories, but to give them a new home in the walls of this house. So, I slip into character and hope for the best.

"How could you?" I snap. "After everything we've been through!"

"Tiff, I'm sorry. I was drunk."

"Really? That's your excuse?" I don't have much to work with here, but I'm prepared to improvise if need be. "Maybe it's a good thing we never had children. No one wants a drunkard for a father."

"Do you really want to go there?" Gabe growls.

"Oh, you bet I do. Look at you. When was the last time you shaved?"

"A week ago, when you told me you wanted a divorce." He seizes a handful of hair and shuts his eyes. The pain on his face is as sharp as the accusation in his voice.

"You and I both saw this coming," I persist as Gabe doubles over. "Between the debt and the infertility, we didn't stand a chance."

He slams the heels of his palms against his temples. Where I'm expecting words, there is only an ungodly roar of pain. Saliva drips from his lower lip onto his lap, but he doesn't seem to notice.

"I wanted to make you happy," Gabe says through the tears, though whether they're in response to his memories or the pain is unclear. "I gave you everything, but it was never enough, was it, Tiff?"

Gabe's face is the colour of Bordeaux as he cries out for mercy. His fingers make a fist, trapping the hair between his joints as he rocks back and forth against the cushions.

"That's it," I whisper, "come on, Gabe."

"Nothing was ever enough," he continues, "not this house, not our marriage, not me. When did I stop being enough for you?"

He hunches over his knees and sucks in a massive breath. Just when I think his head is going to explode, the redness drains from his face and he calmly removes his hands.

"We should've quarantined those malevolents," Gabe says.

Relief floods my veins. I let out a long sigh. "You're right. We should have."

"Why didn't we?"

"I don't know."

Reaching for his crutches, Gabe positions them under his arms and spends a moment surveying his environment. Then he turns to me.

"I have a headache," he announces. "I think I'll go lie down."

Gabe makes his way into the neighbouring room, his crutches thumping rhythmically along the hardwood as he departs. The crackle of burning wood drowns out his murmured grievances as he works to settle in, and minutes later the fire is the only thing I can hear.

22

The photo albums have been sorted into four piles: wedding photos, family photos, vacation photos, and other photos, which includes snapshots from birthdays, baby showers, bridal showers, baptisms, and the occasional bathroom renovation. I've gone through each album at least a dozen times, trying to make sense of a life that doesn't belong to me at all. I see my face in every frame, but these are not my pictures. This is not my story. And the man sleeping on the other side of the wall is not my husband.

I reach for one of the albums, where I discover a picture of Tiffany in the upper left-hand corner of the first page. She's standing on the lawn wearing an aubergine sweater and knee-high Wellingtons, and the look on her face is so bright it can make you forget that the rest of the frame is dreary and grey. Two overgrown bushes flank the cement steps leading up to the house and the shutters are in need of a new coat of paint. Like Will and Tiffany's marriage, the house is shrouded in neglect, frozen in a moment of tranquility behind an inextinguishable smile.

I turn the page. Whoever snapped the photo of Tiffany also captured a couple of shots of the view from the veranda. The For Sale sign pounded into the lawn has been slashed with an even more audacious SOLD sign and there's a black Camaro parked in the driveway. I skim the caption at the bottom of the page: *Move In Day! Pictures courtesy of Will Foster*

I close the album and set it aside. I think about what Ansel said at the hospital, and it's the first time since settling into my vessel that I've felt the weight of Will and Tiffany's absence on my shoulders. I think about the woman who visited me after the accident and wonder if she could tell anything was different—if she could tell I wasn't Tiffany. Gabe may have been able to fool her into believing he was still her son, but time has a way of favouring the truth. And the truth—at least as far as I can tell— is this: nothing is ever as it seems, not even the laws of life and death.

I stare at the hearth as I debate getting up for another log. The pain in my ribs has returned and my stomach is rumbling, even though food is the furthest thing from my mind. Assuming Ansel expects me to use my powers for good, why would he grant me such a cumbersome—and, frankly, inadequate—form?

I hold my hand over the album and feel a faint tug on my fingers as the book absorbs my energy. I slowly rotate my hand ninety degrees to the right, as though I were physically intending to lift the page. Sure enough, the cover arcs through the air and clatters against the hardwood. It's a neat trick, but not a terribly useful one. Even I can't whip up any enthusiasm for my abilities. With no way of getting back to The Establishment, my powers are pointless, especially in a vessel that demands continuous maintenance.

Getting to my feet, I make my way into the kitchen and over to the refrigerator, where I open the door on a daunting array of cartons, bottles, and other containers. When nothing in the fridge piques my interest, I shift my focus over to the pantry, only to discover a dizzying plethora of cans and boxes containing organic soups and gluten-free cereals. I know I should eat; I have to eat, if only to stymie the headache unfolding behind my eyes, but like Tiffany's memories, my appetite eludes me.

I shut the door and turn toward the counter. My eyes traipse over the usual kitchen trappings, from the ceramic cookie jar to the spice carousel in the corner, before eventually glossing over the smaller appliances and settling on the knife block. There's only one way to get back to The Establishment, and it certainly won't be through a portal.

I withdraw one of the smaller knives and inspect the implement in the meager glow of the cabinet lights. The edge is as clean as a whistle, leading me to think it was recently sharpened. I thumb the tip; it pricks my skin like a burr and I give a satisfied half-nod, knowing exactly what I have to do.

"Sarah?"

Gabe's figure manifests from the shadows. He has only one crutch and his eyes are cloudy with sleep, but the alarm on his face is as clear as day.

"What are you doing?" he asks, his voice pebbly with concern and the lasting effects of the whiskey.

I let the knife languish at my side. Across from me, Gabe swings his solitary crutch forward and comes to rest against the counter, his hair flopping awkwardly over his right brow.

"What are you doing with that knife?" he asks.

"You wouldn't understand."

He continues to make his way toward me, step by halting step. His eyes don't leave my face for even a second.

"I would if you explained it to me." Gabe braces his arm against the counter, sizing me up. "Could you explain it to me?"

"I'd rather show you."

Raising my left arm, I use the first two fingers of my right hand to isolate the faint blue vein bulging beneath the surface of my skin. I'm nervous: I've bled out a thousand times before, but never in a vessel that could feel pain.

"Sarah"—Gabe's voice is nasally with fear—"give me the knife."

"Ansel will know what to do," I tell him, applying the blade to my wrist. "I'll confer with him and come back for you."

"Don't do this, Sarah."

"You were right, Gabe. It was a test of our loyalty." I nod and squeeze the handle, bracing myself for the blade's inevitable bite. "Sooner or later, we have to go back. I just need to know what we're dealing with here."

I twist the knife until it finds traction on my skin. I'm just about to draw blood when Gabe grabs my wrist and jerks the blade away from my arm, foiling my half-baked plan.

"Don't do this," he snarls, bearing down on me with his hot, whiskey-laden breath. "I'll get you whatever help you need, but only if you promise to cooperate."

"I've cooperated with you for long enough," I shoot back, "now you can do the same."

Gabe sinks his nails into my skin, determined to apprehend me in spite of his unreliable grip. In a desperate gamble for control, he loosens his grasp on my wrist and clamps down on my elbow instead. I yank my arm sideways, causing him to stagger. His chest collides with the side of my arm, and before I can process the next step in this fatal chain reaction, my grip slips and the knife enters my body. Warmth soaks through my shirt. When I finally muster the nerve to look down, all I can see is the butt of the knife jutting from the middle of my stomach.

Gabe catches himself, but it's too late; the damage has already been done. When he sees the ruby stain on my plain white blouse, his face blanches instantly.

"Sarah—"

"It's okay." I wrap both hands around the handle. I'm bleeding profusely. "I just need a few minutes."

Gabe jettisons his only crutch and stumbles forward to catch me as I fall, gripping the edge of the counter for stability. I come to rest on the floor beneath the sink, a trail of blood streaking the cabinets behind me. I'm fading fast, so I use the last of my breath to convey my dying instructions.

"Wait until my heart stops," I say, "then call for help. But not before."

"Sarah—"

"It's the only way. Either someone will come and get me, or I'll end up back here." I look at him. "Ansel will know what to do."

Gabe pulls me into his trembling arms. He has one hand cupped around the knife and the other flat against my back, where the blood is gluing my shirt to my skin and my spine is prickling in pain. His lips nuzzle my hair, tentatively at first, then more forcefully as the weight of my actions settle over us. We're both quiet. Any minute now, the walls will blend with the floor and the shadows will swallow the light, and when that happens, the pain will abscond like a thief in the night. I've walked this road before, and it always leads to the same place.

Gabe draws a breath to speak. "Now?" he asks in a whimper.

I count my heartbeats—sixty-seven and falling. It's a long, slow descent, like a leaf blown loose from a tree, and I watch the shriveled offerings of my ephemeral life float indecisively above the rock-bottom finality of the cold, dark earth.

"Not yet," I whisper. "Soon."

Fifty-two...

"They'll come and take me away," Gabe says, his voice a washboard of panic. "They'll know I did it."

"No, they won't."

"I killed you."

"I know."

Forty-four...

Gabe adjusts his hand. The infinitesimal movement of the blade causes the wound to bleed anew. It gushes in warm, thick rivulets down my abdomen and into my pants, which are now black and stiff with blood.

Thirty-eight...

"I'll come back," I say as the ceiling fades in patches, revealing a swath of sky speckled with stars and forlorn planets, "I promise."

Thirty... The ceiling is gone, and so is the light in Gabe's eyes. He burrows his face in my neck and proceeds to sob uncontrollably.

Twenty-two...

I let go of the knife.

"Now?" Gabe asks, damp-faced and breathless.

Fourteen... The cabinets are a distant memory.

Nine...

I look at him. His loyalty is as fierce as it is surprising.

Five...

"Now," I tell him. And then he, too, disappears.

23

I open my eyes. I'm lying on my back in the middle of a polished white floor. There are no walls, no doors, no ceiling. No incubator, no registration counter, no chamber. No Catchers. No Healers. No Ansel.

I lift my head to look at my stomach. The knife and the bloodstain are both gone. There's not a single fiber out of place on my ivory blouse. If I didn't know better, I'd think I dreamt the whole ordeal. But I didn't: my pulse is still and I'm cold as ice. Wherever I am, it's not where I should be.

I get to my feet slowly. There's no pain, no discomfort, no relief. There's simply nothing, and it is profoundly humbling.

I turn a quick circle, taking it all in and wondering how the absence of anything can be so overwhelming. The silence is infinite and crushing like the ocean, but with so much air that you can't help but breathe in the emptiness. I imagine it smells like sea salt, but it doesn't. It doesn't smell like anything, but the void is so vast that it practically demands interpretation.

"Did you really think this was the best way to contact me?"

I turn around. Some twenty feet away, Ansel is standing as proud as a statue and has his hands clasped authoritatively behind his back. He's wearing his usual grey ensemble and his hairless head is as smooth as marble. The way he's looking at me, you would almost think nothing is different.

"What happened to The Establishment?" I ask him.

Ansel nods at the nothingness that surrounds us.

"It's still here," he replies, prompting my confusion. "Let's just say a little housekeeping was in order." He ambles over to where I'm standing, but my legs are stone beneath my body.

"Gabe claims you unleashed the malevolents to execute a mass die-off," I deadpan.

Ansel scrunches his brows, causing the rest of his withered face to pucker in thought.

"And you believed him?" he counters, circling around behind me.

"I don't know what to believe anymore."

"Why the sudden change of heart?"

I gesture to the stark white panorama just as Ansel edges into my periphery.

"There's nothing here," I say, "and seeing is believing. Isn't that what everyone says?"

"People say a lot of things. Just because you can put a thought into words doesn't make it true."

"But The Establishment," I persist, growing distraught, "it was here. I remember it perfectly."

"And yet," Ansel counters, sympathy rounding out his voice, "you remember very little, if anything, about your life before your death. If we were to apply your logic to this predicament, then one could argue you never existed, either."

"But I did."

"Did you?"

I hold his gaze. Ansel shrugs and continues pacing, visibly unshaken by my need to understand the impossible.

"Did The Establishment exist to be seen, or did your unfulfilled need for purpose and belonging will it into existence?" Ansel continues, "Realistically speaking, what purpose does the imagination serve if not to create, to render the nonexistent real? Without the imagination, all we know is what we have... what we see."

"I know what I saw," I maintain. "The Establishment was real. It's always been real to me."

"Just as the characters in a book appear real to its author, so, too, does The Establishment appear real to you. But what is reality? Is reality predicated on perception, or faith?"

"Perception," I say with frosty conviction, "the senses don't lie."

"Of course they do. Have you never experienced a hallucination before?"

I look away. The architectural complexities of The Establishment alone are enough to convince me that this world is as real as life itself. Every wall, every door, and every room... it was all here within my reach. And the other Catchers—where did they come from, if not reality itself? If what Ansel is saying is true and I've manufactured my own version of life after death, then it stands to reason that I engineered my coworkers, too.

"Impossible," I say, meeting his eyes once more. "There are too many details."

"Your statement implies the imagination has limits. If this were true, then modern society would cease to exist. I suppose you could say our collective imagination has brought us to this precise moment in time, and possibly even beyond." Ansel observes me coolly. "Suppose the devil is truly in the details. Would this not explain our inherent tendency to anticipate the worst? Our survival as a species hinges on our fundamental ability to recognize and process details, so your argument is weak."

"The devil doesn't exist," I assert, "and neither does God."

Ansel smirks. "So, who am I?"

"You're Ansel."

"And how do you know this?"

"Because you told me."

"And you believed it?"

"I had no reason not to."

Ansel raises a finger. All at once the nothingness begins to whirl around us, forming a dense, protective shell of dust, debris, and other cosmic particles. A gentle, whistling wind morphs into a howling gale, and before long the floor and the ceiling are stirred into a single, existential storm. The nothingness has suddenly become everything at once—light and shadow, beauty and chaos, life and death—and as it orbits apoplectically around us, I begin to wonder if everything else I know is a lie, too.

"Welcome to the in-between," Ansel tells me, right before he delivers a jolt of electricity through my heart and I awaken to the sights and sounds of a hospital emergency room.

Faces half-hidden behind masks converge on me. They converse in murmured tones as a hailstorm of metal implements flies between them. An opaque bag of blood hangs from a hook on a metal pole next to my head. I look around for Gabe, but the only people I see are the doctors and nurses and they're all preoccupied with the knife still embedded in my stomach.

One of the doctors swoops into my field of view. The only thing on his face that isn't covered is a narrow strip of skin around his gunmetal eyes, and they crinkle kindly as they make contact with my own.

"We almost lost you," he says as someone hands him a fresh wad of gauze. There's a rumple of discussion about my wound, and before long he loses interest in making small talk with me.

The knife is removed from my stomach and the doctor sutures me shut. I watch the mechanical precision of his gloved hands as the thread is tugged through my skin and eventually knotted half an inch above my navel. I make a mental note to examine myself as soon as I'm alone, and before I know it, the wound is dressed and I'm wheeled into a separate room. The nurse instructs me to lie still and relax, so I position myself on the large white pillow in such a way that my head, neck, and shoulders are all sufficiently supported, and wait.

I close my eyes. If I can center my field, then perhaps I can trick myself into believing I have enough energy left to get to the bottom of whatever keeps bouncing me back into this strange, parallel reality.

The energy encompassing my body gravitates toward my limbs and enters my skin through my pores. One by one, the individual atoms commence their pilgrimage to the core of my being. The incoming energy has a cooling effect on my blood; I flex my fingers to relieve a bit of the discomfort. Normally I wouldn't feel anything, aside from a mild shock when the two halves of my field become one. I flatten my tongue against my palate, trying to quell my nausea as the last of the energy is consolidated in my heart. It palpitates furiously for a couple of beats, and then all of my systems find their equilibrium.

I look around. I'm expecting Gabe to show up at any minute, but the two faces that appear at my door look as though they won't let me leave anytime soon.

"Mrs. Foster?" says the one on the right, whose chin is loose, flabby, and rough with midweek stubble.

I nod. His partner takes a step into the room.

"We're sorry to bother you. We just had a few questions." The second man is wearing a black windbreaker over his white shirt and jeans that are still stiff with youth. "I'm Officer Hammond. This is my partner, Officer McKinnon. We were hoping you could tell us a little more about the incident with your husband."

"You mean Gabe?" I reply, already tiring of their presence.

Officer Hammond consults his notes.

"I'm sorry, there must've been some sort of miscommunication. Is your husband's name not William?"

Not wanting to draw attention to my unusual behaviour, I nod and say, "It is. I must've been thinking of someone else." It's a terrible answer, to be sure, but it beats the truth any day.

Officer Hammond appears unconcerned by my faux pas.

"Could you tell us a little more about the events leading up to your attack?" he continues, his pen already skating along the notepad in his hand.

I blink, momentarily blindsided by what I imagine is a pretty standard inquiry. If I tell him the truth, he'll think I'm lying. But if I lie, there's no telling what will happen to Gabe and how it will inevitably affect me. He's my ally, my only source of hope in a place where it stubbornly refuses to grow. At this point, I really can't afford to lose him.

"I don't remember," I fib, resorting to a line I've heard so many times, "it all happened so quickly."

Officer Hammond nods and scribbles something on his pad.

"What's your relationship with your husband like normally?"

I stall. "I don't understand the question."

Officer Hammond flashes his partner a brief, unreadable look.

"Would you say your husband has a drinking problem?" he persists.

I picture the liquor cabinet in the living room, the empty bottles of whiskey on the coffee table, and Gabe's intoxicated slumber. His exact words had been "an aspiring alcoholic", but I don't mention this to Officer Hammond.

"Not really. He just has expensive tastes."

"And how does he usually behave, after he's had a couple of drinks?"

"My husband didn't stab me, if that's what you're getting at. He'd already gone to bed by the time I'd found myself in the kitchen."

"And what were you doing in the kitchen?"

"Getting something to eat."

He nods and jots a few more notes.

"Mrs. Foster—"

"Tiffany," I say, cutting him off. If he's going to use a name that isn't mine, I'd rather it be the one that carries the least responsibility.

"Tiffany. Could you tell us roughly when your husband entered the kitchen?"

"I don't know," I say, annoyance simmering in my voice.

"And what was he doing there?"

"I don't know."

"Were you two arguing?"

"No."

"At what point did the knife enter the altercation?"

"There was no altercation."

"Are you sure?"

"Positive."

Officer Hammond adds the finishing touches to his report. He exchanges another cryptic look with his partner and then turns back to me, a mask of stoicism upon his elongated face.

"Thank you for your time, Mrs. Foster," he says, nodding. The pair begins to take their leave.

"Where is he?" I ask.

Officer Hammond faces me again. "Your husband?"

I nod.

"Not to worry, Mrs. Foster," he says reassuringly, "we have him in custody. He can't hurt you anymore."

"But he didn't attack me. It was an accident."

"It's okay, Mrs. Foster," Officer Hammond says, more firmly this time as if attempting to silence a petulant child, "you don't have to make excuses anymore. You're safe now."

I watch them depart. Minutes later, the doctor who stitched me up appears to present me with my discharge papers. We continue our stilted dialogue between questions about my living arrangements and a prescription for antibiotics, but I can sense his unease as clearly as I can feel my own. Our conversation meets its premature conclusion, and before long I'm left alone to arrange a ride home.

But first, I need to confirm a couple of suspicions of my own.

I divide the layers of fabric and peel back the tape framing the square of gauze in the middle of my abdomen. The cotton separates from my skin, but where I'm expecting to see a neat ladder of thread, there's only a clean, smooth patch of skin.

I remove the rest of the dressing. The skin underneath is unbroken—no nicks, no scratches, no indication whatsoever that my body had ever experienced the cold rush of metal or the warm surge of blood that followed.

I turn my attention over to my ribs. I apply my fingers to the space between the bones, but all I feel is more skin. It, too, is mysteriously unblemished.

I swing my legs over the edge of the bed and stumble over to the mirror on the wall. My head has healed, too, and without even the faintest suggestion of a scar. I part the hairs around the injury site, but there's nothing to see except for the alabaster dome of my scalp.

Panicked, I turn back to the bed. If I can prove Gabe didn't hurt me, I might stand a chance at saving him. All I have to do is figure out where he's being held.

I approach the bed, where I discover a change of clothes and a brand new Keepsake. I pick up the note folded neatly on top.

Find Gabe. Then find me.

24

I leave the hospital quickly. In my condition, I shouldn't be able to walk, much less with such noticeable strength and vigor. I stride down the long corridor with Ansel's note folded in my pocket and a stony expression on my face. I'm as unhindered as a bird, possessing nothing but my powers and a mint-condition Keepsake containing everything I need to know, including where to find Gabe.

The automatic doors whoosh open. Outside, I stand for a moment on the sidewalk, scoping out the scenery and relishing the tranquility of a crisp autumn night. According to my Keepsake, the police station is located at the corner of Dawson Street and Cleary Boulevard, roughly six and a half city blocks away. Minding the urgency in Ansel's note, I visualize my route and then set off at a brisk pace toward Gabe.

○

I arrive at the station roughly twenty minutes later. I haven't even broken a sweat, and the only evidence of any physical exertion is the slightest rosy tint to my cheeks.

I approach the doors and pull one of them open. Inside, the air is cool and reeks of stale coffee and undeserved importance. I glance around at the smoky grey walls and reflective linoleum floor before taking a breath and making my way over to the counter.

The lady behind the glass sizes me up. "Can I help you?" she asks when I get closer.

I don't know what to do with my hands, so I lay them flat on the counter. When the female officer notices my ring, I remove my left hand and bury it in my back pocket.

"I'm looking for my husband," I tell her.

"Name?"

"William Foster."

She turns to the computer and types quickly, filling the stuffy silence of the lobby with the determined clack of keystrokes.

Finally, she turns back to me.

"It says here that your husband was brought in about an hour ago and that he's currently being held for questioning," she says, looking me over again.

"Can I see him?"

"I'm sorry, but no. He'll need to remain in custody for at least twenty-four hours."

I nod. I don't have twenty-four hours.

Not wanting to cause a scene, I thank her and leave the way I came in. I pause to search for a familiar constellation, but between the ambient light of the city and the meager glow of impending daybreak, there's only a distant dusting of galaxies. I locate the eastern skyline through a break in the trees and see a ribbon of sunlight unfurling along the horizon. Twenty-four hours can feel like a heartbeat or an eternity, depending on which side of the lifeline you're on, and tonight, I'm on the wrong one.

Something rustles the leaves of a nearby bush. I look around, halfway hoping to see another human being, but the parking lot is empty and I'm perfectly alone.

I approach the agitated bush. Fear ripples through my field as I step onto the grass and concentrate my energy on the disturbance. Through the tangled clumps of foliage comes the outline of a small, tightly bundled creature. Its heat shines brightly in the endless shadows and silhouettes, and it blooms like a flower just as I extend an arm toward it.

Two bright hazel eyes flash on me as I sift aside the branches. They belong to a twiggy teenage girl with badly knotted hair and old, baggy clothes that have been haphazardly patched using stray bits of fabric. The hollow quality of her cheeks would suggest she hasn't eaten to her fill in weeks and the dirt beneath her nails is as thick as the silence standing between us.

"Sophia?" I say as our eyes meet.

Suspicion is etched into the lines parenthesizing her mouth. She lingers uneasily in the shade of a juvenile tree, where the light from a nearby lamppost casts playful shadow puppets on her porcelain complexion.

"How did you know?" Sophia asks.

I take another step toward her, prompting her to reestablish a comfortable distance between us.

"We used to work together at a place called The Establishment. Remember? I escorted you after you died."

Sophia wraps her arms tightly around herself.

"I don't remember The Establishment, but I remember you." She nods. "Sarah. Right?"

My heart is pounding. I wonder how many of us there are out here, caught in a crease between dimensions like loose change in a couch. If Sophia recognizes me, then maybe other people will, too.

"What happened?" I ask her.

"I don't know. I woke up under a bridge and now I'm here."

"How long ago was that?"

"I can't remember. Three or four days." Looking past me to the police station, Sophia adds, "I came here hoping to get help, but I don't think they can do anything for me."

"Well, that makes two of us." I look her over, noting the puffy tissue a few inches above her ear. I'm tempted to ask how she acquired the welt, but don't want her to feel like I'm prying. For all I know, her injury has nothing to do with the flash.

As if reading my mind, Sophia explains, "I don't know how it happened, but I woke up in a creek with a pounding headache and I've had this bump on my head ever since."

As if to emphasize her point, she gingerly prods the tender spot on her scalp. Her wound is in the exact same spot as mine— or at least where my swelling used to be, right before it inexplicably vanished.

"I take it you haven't seen a doctor," I deadpan.

210

"You think I'm going to show up at a hospital looking like *this*? They'll think I'm a homeless drug addict."

She has a point. It's tough to be discreet when she looks and smells like the wilderness from which she emerged.

"When did you last eat?" I ask, changing the topic.

Sophia shakes her head. Whether she's having difficulty remembering or is simply avoiding the question doesn't change the fact that she's trembling from malnutrition, something even the abundance of layers and the lack of light can't seem to hide. A stampede of unwelcome thoughts charges through my mind as I wonder how she managed to survive this long without the creature comforts of modern society. I need her to help me unlock the mystery of the missing Establishment, but first, I need to help her feel human again.

"My house isn't far from here," I say, which seems to pique her interest. "Come with me and I'll make you something to eat."

Just like that, I'm no longer alone.

○

It takes us nearly an hour to walk from the police station to my house. Despite having no attachment to the two-storey structure, I'm grateful for its beastly presence as it towers over the neighbourhood. This is not my neighbourhood, but it's as good a place as any to hunker down and figure out where to go from here.

Sophia shuffles along beside me with her head bowed and her oversized sweater hanging off her gaunt frame. She goes out of her way to avoid the puddles of light pooling beneath the street

211

lamps; I glance over at her just as she steps onto the grass and momentarily melts into the shadows. When she catches me watching her, she folds her arms and quickens her pace. She seems content to avoid eye contact, so I take the hint and direct my focus back to the asphalt.

"Were you alone?" I ask down to my shoes.

Confused, Sophia looks up from her determined trudging.

"When you woke up in the creek," I clarify, trying not to stare, "were you alone? Or was there anyone else?"

She leans into the incline as we begin to tackle the first big hill.

"It was just me," she says, her voice barely audible above the alternating rhythm of her footsteps. Sophia glimpses me sheepishly. "What about you?"

"I was with Gabe. We were in a car crash."

"Where is he now?"

"At the police station." When Sophia maintains her fixation on me, I explain, "Let's just say looks can be deceiving."

We crest the hill, where another circular patch of light awaits us. Sophia dodges it effortlessly, shimmying sideways along a well-pruned hedge before eventually rejoining me on the sidewalk.

"Does he remember what happened?" she asks.

"He does now." Sophia looks to me for clarification, so I sigh and say, "Ansel didn't have time to purge his vessel, so when he woke up in the hospital he thought his name was William and that I was his wife. Needless to say, it made things pretty difficult for us."

At the top of the next hill, I turn left and ascend the short flight of steps leading up to the house. Instead of keeping pace with me, Sophia remains rooted in the middle of the sidewalk, her jaw dangling with disbelief.

"You live here?" she asks.

"I didn't believe it either," I reply with a shrug. "But apparently..."

I turn back to the house. Even in the dark, it's magnificent, full of history and charm and untapped potential. I can picture it so clearly, somehow, and I find myself becoming entranced by these peculiar visions until Sophia slithers past me and puts an end to my gawking.

"You said you had food?" she says once we've reached the porch.

I channel my energy on my surroundings, filtering out the weathered wood and dusty windows in a blur of grey. I look around slowly, scouring every nook, cranny, and secret crevice, until my eyes distinguish the outline of a spare key sitting innocently on top of the doorframe.

I blink away my enhanced vision and reach for the key. When I make eye contact with Sophia again, I'm somewhat alarmed to find her staring at me.

"Whoa," she says.

"What?"

"Your eyes."

"What about them?"

"They went blue. Like, solid blue. Like someone switched on a supercomputer in your brain, blue."

I wriggle the key into the hole until it engages.

"You know, you might be onto something with the supercomputer reference." The lock snaps back and I twist the knob, shunting the door open with my shoulder.

"Did Ansel give you back your powers?"

"Yes, and a couple more, from the looks of things." I throw a glance over my shoulder at her. "Why? Do you have powers, too?"

"Sort of."

I usher her into the house. "Care to elaborate?"

Sophia lowers the hood of her sweater and turns her attention over to a lamp. Raising a hand, she aims it at the light and knots her brows in concentration. There's a low hum as the bulb begins to blush beneath the pale canvas lampshade. It snarls like an ornery dog, resisting Sophia's energy until her power becomes too much and the bulb shatters with a bang. Shards of glass sprinkle the antique wooden table, and then the foyer goes dark.

"Well," I say, shutting the door, "that clears a few things up."

"I wasn't sure if I should tell you. I didn't know how you would react."

Sophia kicks off her shoes and ventures into the house. I follow her into the kitchen just as she flips on a light and instantly goes rigid with shock.

"Whoa," she says again, her finger still hanging on the light switch. "Did someone die here or something?"

I come to a stop on Sophia's left, where I notice the now dried streaks of body fluid on the cabinets and the almost-black lake of blood spreading across the hardwood floor.

"Yeah," I sigh, "I did." I turn to her. "Tell you what. Why don't you get cleaned up and I'll fix us something to eat?"

She nods at the stain. "What about the Dead Sea over there?"

"I'll take care of it."

I lead Sophia up the extravagant staircase and into the bedroom where I'd spent my first three days. I provide her with a clean set of towels, a bar of soap, and a change of clothes, and once she's settled in, retreat back to the kitchen to mop up the crime scene.

I scour the kitchen for something to soak up the blood and discover an old cloth languishing in the sink. I work quickly, pausing intermittently to rinse the rag. Down on the floor on my hands and knees, there's no escaping the pungent aroma of death. I notice my reflection in the middle of the pool and spend several seconds staring at the halo of flyaway hair encircling my head.

That's when I see it: a second face—older, wiser, and decidedly masculine—beaming back at me from the macabre ruby mirror.

25

I whip around. I'm still crouched on the floor with the bloody towel balled in my fist when Ansel steps forward and offers a lukewarm smile.

"I see you found Gabe," he says.

"And Sophia."

He nods and gazes phlegmatically around the kitchen, appraising the tall, white cabinets and stainless-steel appliances.

"I figured you could use an ally," Ansel says simply.

Blood drips from the cloth, landing with a soft splat as I rise to my feet.

"What happened to Sophia?" I demand.

"She hasn't told you?"

"She doesn't remember."

Ansel begins patrolling the room, pausing to ogle an intricate porcelain figurine perched on the windowsill.

"Same thing that happened to the others," he says cryptically, cradling the sleeping fawn in his hand, "insubordination."

"And you thought dropping them off in the middle of nowhere was sufficient punishment?"

"Well, I can't say as I had any other options." He sets the figurine back on the sill. "With the malevolents running roughshod all over the facilities, I was forced to take drastic measures."

Ansel looks at me sideways. The conviction in his gaze causes me to tighten my grip on the rag, inspiring a fresh trickle of blood to gush through my fingers.

"Drastic measures," I repeat, eyeing him. "In what sense?"

"For one thing, I was forced to destroy the catalogue. If the malevolents had infiltrated the master files, who knows what might've happened?" Ansel continues, "After that, I suspended remote support so that the in-field malevolents couldn't contact Headquarters. Unfortunately, that also meant none of the staff could either."

"A lot of Catchers succumbed at that hospital," I say, digging my nails into the soggy fabric. "Was that part of your plan?"

"Collateral damage is never part of the plan, Miss Galloway."

"Those Catchers were good people," I persist, kneading the cloth in frustration, "they would've helped you, if you'd let them."

"I wouldn't doubt it."

"So why didn't you?"

Ansel is thoughtful. In the corner of my eye, I can see the pool of blood spreading slowly across the floor, filling the space I've already cleaned.

"I didn't want them to help me," he says softly. "It wasn't part of the plan."

"And what was the plan, exactly?"

"To stay in business, of course."

"But why destroy everything? If it was your intention to catalyze a mass die-off, why not just increase everyone's quotas?"

"Efficiency, my dear girl. Why squeeze every drop of energy out of my staff when the malevolents could accomplish the same task in half the time?" He sighs, casting me a look of pity. "From exceptional suffering comes extraordinary growth. Sometimes we need to lose everything to appreciate our own strength."

I look down at the blood. My reflection gazes disappointedly up at me, as if it understands the magnitude of my failures. I should have known better than to nurture my ignorance, and I should have never let my faith in Ansel's good intentions lull me into complacency. Gabe saw the situation for what it truly was, and I accused him of being disloyal. I was a fool—a well-meaning fool, but a fool nonetheless.

"So what happens now?" I ask him.

"Now, we rebuild."

"Rebuild."

Ansel chuckles.

"Dear girl," he says, looking me over, "what am I if not an architect? I've done my part; the malevolents are loose and free to do as they please. Now it's up to you to contain them."

He continues, "The souls will be the basis for your army. For every spirit you catch, I'll ensure there's a place for them in the hereafter. But be warned: your power is limited. If you fail to quarantine the malevolents before it expires, you and your recruits will be doomed to an eternity in the in-between. I don't think I need to explain the ramifications of this."

I shake my head. "When do I start?"

Ansel smiles as footsteps overwhelm the silence. I glance toward the stairs as Sophia appears wearing an old tracksuit I uncovered in the armoire.

"You already have," he tells me, and by the time Sophia reaches the bottom step, Ansel is already gone.

She falters. "Who were you talking to?" she asks me.

I glance at the empty space where Ansel had stood a heartbeat ago.

"No one," I mutter. I examine the rag as Sophia seals the distance between us.

She gestures to the spill.

"So are we going to talk about that?" she wonders.

Dropping to my knees, I resume my systematic cleaning from earlier. When the cloth becomes limp with blood, I run it under the tap while Sophia looks on in disgust.

"I needed to talk to Ansel," I tell her, "and the only way for me to do that was to cross the lifeline. The plan was to simply bleed out, but Gabe interfered." When comprehension fails to register on her slender face, I say, in the most apathetic tone, "He stabbed me."

"Did it hurt?"

"Not as much as I thought it would." I drain the cloth again and watch the blood spiral down the drain.

"Is that why Gabe's at the police station?"

"Yup."

"Are you going to save him?"

"Probably. It's what I do, after all." Sophia gives an inquisitive quirk of her brow, but doesn't press for an explanation.

She wanders over to the fridge. "So, food," she says, hopping onto the next train of thought. "What do you have?"

"My guess is as good as yours." I wring another wave of blood into the sink. "Besides muesli and almond milk, I don't honestly know."

Sophia ferrets around in the refrigerator. In her nutritionally deprived state, I'm surprised she doesn't grab the first thing she sees. She loads her arms with ingredients and then dumps what appears to be half of the refrigerator's contents onto the counter.

She frowns down at the food. Until now, I hadn't even realized my own hunger. Sharp, shooting pains alert me to my empty stomach as I stoop next to what remains of the blood, desperate to put the task behind me and move on to my more basal needs.

"You have a lot of food," Sophia says, halfheartedly attempting to organize the ingredients. "Have you eaten?"

"Not since I regenerated." Another trickle of bloody water splatters the stainless steel sink while my stomach growls in protest.

She turns to one of the cupboards, where she produces a pair of plates from a shelf and places them on the counter next to the food.

By the time I've conquered the mess, rinsed the rag, and scrubbed the lingering filth from my skin, Sophia has nearly devoured her entire sandwich and is well on her way to seconds. Various sauces and seasonings have blended together to form a sludgy film that is quickly obscuring the lower half of her face. Sophia consumes the sandwich with unbridled zest, with barely a breath between bites, until at last our eyes meet and she sheepishly wipes a streak of mayonnaise from the corner of her mouth.

"Sorry," she says, swallowing audibly.

"Don't be. It's good to have an appetite."

She returns to her unrestrained gobbling. I survey the plethora of offerings spread across the counter, including the loaf of organic rye bread, the jar of pickles swimming in their briny bath, the packages of pre-sliced deli meats, and a container of fat-free mayonnaise with a knife partially submerged in its quicksand-like consistency, before finally relenting and reaching for the other plate.

Half an hour later, Sophia and I have eaten to our fill and are now camped out in the living room with the curtains drawn and the lights off. A fire roars in the monstrous hearth as Sophia explores her surroundings, pausing occasionally to devote extra interest to random knickknacks and souvenirs. When she reaches the liquor cabinet, she uncaps a decanter of scotch and sniffs it cautiously.

"People drink this stuff?" she says reproachfully, setting the bottle back where she found it.

"Hard to believe, isn't it?" I slide back the metal screen and use the fire poker to reposition a smaller log that is on the brink of collapse.

Sophia directs her focus over to an oil painting on the wall. "Why here?" she asks, still studying the multitude of carefully applied brushstrokes.

"What do you mean?"

"Well, there had to be a reason Ansel decided to send us here, right? If he was going to send us anywhere, why not send us back the way we came?"

"You mean back to our old lives."

She nods.

"Well." I shut the screen and lean the implement against the bookshelf. "Maybe he thought that would be too jarring."

Sophia arches a brow. "More jarring than waking up in a place we don't know?"

She joins me on the sofa. Firelight warms the edges of her face and fills the gullies in the oversized sweater. She looks exactly the way I remember her, only with more hair and less resignation, and for the first time since discovering her huddled in the bush, I begin to see her for what she truly is: a soldier with a fighting spirit, rather than simply a victim of unfortunate circumstances.

"What else can you do?" I ask her.

Sophia glances at me and then raises a hand to the TV. It clicks on instantly, and she changes the channel with an imperceptible flick of her hand.

She looks at the bookcase. There's a small snow globe parked between a picture of Will and Tiffany on a yacht, and a collection of books arranged in descending order according to size. A slight twist of her wrist causes artificial snow to spiral around the miniature town, and then she shifts her energy over to the photograph and deftly tips it onto its face.

"When did you figure out you could do all this?" I ask her.

"Some time after I woke up in the creek. I noticed my fingers were tingling. You know how it feels when your arm falls asleep? That's what my arm felt like, except the feeling didn't go away. Some time later I found what I thought would be a good walking stick, but when I tried to pick it up, it moved on its own." Sophia shakes her head, adding, "Now you see why I was scared to get help? In addition to looking like a bum, I apparently had magical powers, too."

"It's a good thing you do. We'll need all the help we can get."

I explain Ansel's plan to rebuild The Establishment. Sophia is curious but standoffish, and when I finally arrive at the part about needing to consolidate the malevolents before my powers run out, she shakes her head.

"If your powers run out, you die," she informs me.

"Well, yes, but technically we all will. It's a classic case of the needs of many outweighing the needs of few."

"What makes you think Ansel will follow through? What if he lures us into defeating the malevolents and we still get stuck in the in-between?"

"Then we'd be of no use to him. It pays to keep his promise."

"I'm not doing it."

"Sophia—"

"No, listen. Ansel was the one who released the malevolents in the first place. Who's to say he's not just using us to make his own life easier?"

"That's the point of having staff, though, so the boss isn't stuck doing all the work."

"Maybe, but you have to admit: something isn't adding up. If he wants to reclaim The Establishment so badly, maybe he shouldn't have wrecked it in the first place." She spears me with a look of pure obstinacy. "I'm not doing it, and neither should you. Look, I know it's not ideal, but we could totally start over in this life. You, me, Gabe—"

"I didn't come all this way just to be stuck with Gabe."

"My point is, we're finally free. No more quotas, no more Ansel. We made it, Sarah. We made it to the next life. In a few days our powers will expire and we can just pretend none of this ever happened. It'll be like having amnesia."

I stare down at my hands. I don't want to have amnesia. Just because something fits doesn't make it mine. I don't want to live in this stuffy, suburban castle with a man who delights in antagonizing me. This is not my happy ending. And Sophia—

what's she going to do when she finally remembers who she is, and where she came from?

"So is that what you want?" I ask her. "To be forced to put on an act for the rest of your life?"

"There's no act, Sarah. All we have to do is adapt to our new lives."

"You were passed out in that creek because whoever owned your body died there. Do you really think you can handle cleaning up someone else's mess?"

Sophia becomes defensive. "What mess? I don't remember anything."

"Maybe not right now, but you will soon enough. Then what? You're just going to walk into someone else's life and make it all better? Don't be so naïve. This is a temporary arrangement for both of us."

"Well, maybe I like this life," Sophia snarls, glaring at me. "Sure I'm homeless, but at least I don't have cancer."

I can't argue with this, so instead, I sink into the couch and watch the firelight pulse on the contoured edges of the empty bottles littering the coffee table. At the far end of the sofa, Sophia pulls her knees to her chest and examines her stubby fingernails while I reflect on my ill-considered remarks.

Finally, I say, "I'm sorry. I hadn't thought of that." I look at her. "So you remember being Sophia?"

She nods and picks at a hangnail. "Most of it."

"But not the other girl."

"I'm not sure I want to. Nothing good ever ends with being unconscious under a bridge."

I nod. Even if she does manage to recover the owner's memories, something tells me she won't be returning to her life anytime soon. As far as allies go, I really couldn't ask for anyone better.

Rising from the couch, Sophia steers around the coffee table and heads for the stairs. "I'm tired. After three days of sleeping on the ground, I'm looking forward to a real bed."

I watch her until she's swallowed up by the shadows. I don't imagine sleep will come easily this morning either, so instead, I reach for the first photo album I see. Then I take a seat cross-legged on the floor and begin the tedious process of committing my own life to memory.

26

I awaken on the cold wooden floor with the photo album still open beside me. The fire burned itself out hours ago, leaving me with a stiff neck and a dry, scratchy throat that aches whenever I swallow.

I climb to my feet and try to get my bearings. It's too dark to read the wall clock, so I wander over to the window and peer through a crack in the curtains at the sleepy neighbourhood outside. A thick, white fog has settled over the tree-lined street and there's a line of dew dabbed along the base of the window. I observe the sidewalk for signs of life, but the only movement I see comes in the form of a small flock of birds that have converged on the lawn, beckoned by the promise of insects and whatever else the earth has to offer.

I let the curtain fall shut and make my way into the kitchen. I'm nearly halfway there when a draft flirts up my arm and I turn my head to find the front door standing wide open.

I step out onto the porch, where the wood is damp and the air is sweet with impending rain. A chill washes over me and I race back inside to check on Sophia.

"Sophia," I call upon reaching the top of the stairs. I locate the door to the guest bedroom and push it open, but all I find is a king-sized bed with its covers turned down on one side and the old tracksuit I lent her puddled on the bathroom floor. Her own clothes, which I'd washed shortly after she retired to her room, are nowhere to be seen.

I hurry back down the stairs and out the front door, stopping only once to pull on a pair of shoes. I have to find Sophia before anyone else does. Between her threadbare ensemble and her superhuman abilities, there's no telling what someone might do to her out here.

I trot down the steps and pause for a breath in the driveway. Even with her powers, she couldn't have gone very far without wheels—and neither will I.

I swivel around. Tucked out of sight beneath an overgrown tree sits a small drive shed. If memory serves, Will and Tiffany had two vehicles: the SUV they'd been driving the day of the accident, and the Camaro I'd seen in one of their many photographs. It's a long shot, but it's a chance I'm willing to take.

I reach for the handle and haul open the massive white door. Pale grey light falls over the Camaro's sleek black bumper and my heart summersaults into my throat. I can't remember the last time I drove a car, but it's the only hope I have of saving Sophia.

I slide into the driver's seat and lift the key off the rear view mirror. I jab it into the ignition and give it a fierce crank, my ecstasy turning to dismay, then panic, when the engine sputters and swiftly stalls.

I turn the key again. When the engine doesn't turn over, I clobber the steering wheel and try to ignore the pinpricks of hot, angry tears gathering behind my eyes. If I can't start the Camaro, what chance do I have of defeating Ansel's army of malevolents?

"Come on," I mutter, turning the key again, to which the engine's only response is a noisy putter of protest. Enraged by the car's lack of cooperation, I release the key and slam my hand on the dashboard.

The Camaro roars to life. I put it in gear and shoot backwards out of the driveway, just missing a minivan parked against the curb across the road.

I jerk the wheel to the left and shift again; the Camaro lurches forward. I've forgotten what it feels like to have this much power—not the kind of power that comes with catching spirits, but the power that only a muscle car and an open road can give you: the power and freedom of unlimited mobility.

I burn through the streets with both front windows down. I don't see Sophia anywhere, and now the first intrepid rays of sun are beginning to pierce the layer of fog.

I cruise down a street populated by several large houses and more vehicles than room to park them. I scan the sidewalk, but I don't see anyone I know. At the end of that street, I turn left and take my foot off the gas. A few other cars drift past me in the opposite direction, but I'm still searching for Sophia.

I've made it halfway to town when I spot a hooded figure shuffling along the sidewalk. The wobble in her walk is eerily familiar.

I pull up alongside her and lean across the seat. "Sophia," I call out the passenger window.

Sophia doesn't acknowledge me. Instead, she hunches her shoulders and soldiers on, her pale pink lips chapped from the chill and her sunken cheeks stained with tears.

"Sophia," I say again, in case she didn't hear me.

"I remember," she replies without looking at me.

"What do you remember?"

She glimpses me from under the hood, her hazel eyes ablaze with fury and fear in equal measure.

"Everything," she tells me. "I remember my parents, how I ended up on the streets... I remember it, Sarah. I remember everything." Sophia shakes her head. "I thought I was starting over, you know? But instead, I'm waking up in the middle of a nightmare."

"Sophia, get in the car."

She stops walking and reaches for the door before ducking into the passenger seat beside me.

"How long have you been out here?" I ask as I pull back into traffic.

Sophia's lips tremble with the effort of controlling her emotions. She places her fingers against the air vents, so I hinge forward and turn the heater to its highest setting.

"Not long." She rubs her hands together and gives me a pleading look. "What's happening to me?"

"I don't know."

Sophia draws her knees to her chest. I consider scolding her, and maybe insisting she wear a seatbelt, but given our present state of affairs, I let the impulse pass unheeded.

"Do you want to know what I remember?" Sophia asks.

"Sure."

"My parents were drug addicts. When they couldn't get their fix, they'd take it out on me. So I left."

"And you've been wandering the streets ever since?"

"I guess. Funny thing is I can't remember what happened in the twenty-four hours leading up to the creek. It's just a big, gaping hole in my memory." She changes the subject. "Can we get something to eat?"

"I don't have any money."

"But you have a big house."

"Lots of broke people live in big houses." I stop for a red light. "I'll make you some breakfast when we get back to the house. After that, we'll sit down and hammer out a plan."

"A plan for what?"

"To take care of the malevolents." I glimpse her face. "You do remember what we talked about last night, right?"

Sophia nods. "I still think it's a trap."

"It's not a trap. It's what we have to do to save The Establishment—and ourselves. Isn't that what you want?"

The light turns green and I speed through the intersection, with Sophia ruminating on my proposition in the passenger seat.

"If I help you do this," she begins, "does that mean I get to start over, for real?"

"I suppose it does." We pull into the driveway and up to the shed. I turn off the Camaro and then turn to Sophia. "One thing at a time, okay?"

She nods, and together we commence the trek back up to the house.

By the time we finally make it inside, there's a message on the answering machine.

27

The message is from the police station, saying they'd like to keep Gabe for further questioning. I'm assuming his powers haven't regenerated, or he'd have broken himself out of there a long time ago.

I look at Sophia, who's too busy raiding my refrigerator to devote much interest to this troubling new development.

"Who was that?" she asks as she reaches for the loaf of bread.

"The police. Looks like Gabe's in more trouble than we thought." I watch her spread mayonnaise on a slice of bread before smothering it with several layers of meat and cheese. "You still have your powers?"

Licking her fingers, Sophia extends a hand toward a jar of olives. The glass container glides across the granite before eventually coming to rest in the hook of her thumb.

"What's the plan? Are we doing a jailbreak?" she asks, unscrewing the lid.

"He's not in jail, just in police custody. The point is to keep him out of jail altogether."

Sophia picks up the sloppy sandwich and crams it into her mouth. For someone so petite, she has a gargantuan appetite.

"So go tell them he's innocent," she says, wiping sauce from her chin before diving in for another bite.

"I can't do that, Sophia. Not without evidence, anyway." I shake my head. "Look, they know what they saw, so at this point it would just be my word against theirs. We need a better strategy."

The meat in her sandwich is beginning to ooze out the other end, so she turns it around and resumes eating.

"You healed, right? So just show them that you're okay, and they'll let him go."

"Sure, but how's that going to look? I was stabbed. I crossed over, which means I was legally dead. If I march in there and show them I've healed completely in less than twenty-four hours, it'll create more problems than it'll solve."

She forces herself to swallow her most recent mouthful and throws me an exasperated eye roll. "You're not seeing the bigger picture here."

I recoil at her lukewarm accusation. "The bigger picture?"

Sophia doesn't respond immediately. Instead, she devours what remains of her breakfast, brushes the crumbs from her fingers, and then turns back to the refrigerator to hunt for something to drink.

"You have superpowers. If you want to save Gabe so badly, why not just use them?"

Too impatient to search for a glass, she unscrews the cap on the pitcher of almond milk and takes a long, satisfying drink. Then she drags a hand across her mouth, banishing the moustache dotting her upper lip, and waits for me to counter.

"Only if you help me," I say, to which she guzzles another mouthful. "You have powers, too, plus..."

Sophia squints. "Is there more to that thought?"

I smirk, looking her over. "You'd make an excellent decoy."

"Decoy? Like, a hunting decoy?"

"You said your parents are drug addicts, right? And that they kicked you out?"

"They didn't kick me out. I left. Big difference." She bristles. "Don't bring my parents into this. This is about you and Gabe."

"You're not hearing me, Sophia. If you walk into the station and tell them you're a homeless minor, it'll give them something to focus on while I free Gabe."

"So, you want me to distract them."

"Exactly." I add, "I know it's a long shot, but we can't afford for Gabe to go to jail. You said you wanted to start over, right? Well, this is your chance. Do me this favour and I'll do my best to convince Ansel to give you a better life."

She considers this quietly. Then, she nods.

I sigh in relief. "Thank you."

Sophia is silent a little longer, her eyes dancing over the assortment of ingredients that surround her.

"Do you think he'd consider it?" she asks me.

"Who?"

"Ansel. Do you think he'd really give me a better life?"

I don't want to inspire any false hope, but Sophia deserves a proper life. The least Ansel could do is consider it.

"Tell you what," I say slowly. "If you find yourself wandering the streets, come and find me. This house has plenty of room for one more."

Sophia's face lights up. "You mean that?"

"Of course I do."

"And Gabe would be okay with it?"

I flash back to my first conversation with Gabe after leaving the hospital. I'd asked him about our financial situation, and he'd said something so outrageous I'd dismissed it without a second thought. What was it?

Infertility.

"Yeah," I say at length, finally appreciating the gravity of his answer, "he'd be fine with it."

Sophia hurries to return all of the food to the fridge.

○

I steer the Camaro into the police station parking lot and drive slowly up to the front doors. It's been a long time since I've had a heartbeat, but something tells me it's not supposed to be this fast.

I turn to Sophia, who's sitting calmly in the passenger seat.

"Okay," I say, putting the car in park. "You know what to do?"

She nods.

"Are you sure? Because we only get one chance to do this."

"I know. Stop worrying."

I recline in the driver's seat and casually pan over our surroundings. I keep telling myself a half-baked plan is better than no plan at all, but it's hardly helping.

Sophia pops open the door and steps out.

"Where are you going?" I call through the open window.

She turns back to me with her hands in her pockets and her thin blonde hair flapping like a flag against her shoulders.

"Inside?" she calls back.

"You're sure you can do this?"

Sophia rolls her eyes and resumes walking.

I debate leaving the key in the ignition, but ultimately think better of it. With wheels like these, I'm asking to be carjacked. So instead, I pocket the keys, take one last breath, and then step out of the vehicle.

I walk through the doors to find Sophia sitting in one of the chairs. Several police officers are crowded around her, asking questions and taking notes as she sobs and spins a big pile of yarns about her broken household. It's a performance deserving of an Oscar, and by the time she's finished giving it, I've already made it around the corner and down a hallway.

My first obstacle comes in the form of a burly security guard, who's patrolling the halls in long, lumbering strides. I turn my Keepsake upside down and scan the area for a distraction. An abandoned mug of coffee sits on a table in a nearby break room, so I channel my energy and sweep it onto the floor.

The mug lands with a sharp clatter, sending leftover coffee and fragments of ceramic scattering in every direction. Alarmed by the commotion, the guard waddles off to investigate, giving me time to sneak past him and down another hallway.

Halfway to the holding cells, I remove my Keepsake and switch it to my right ring finger. The stone instantly turns silver, and before I know it I've reached the room where Gabe is being held.

"Freeze!"

I whip around. Another, more agile guard is rushing toward me, one hand already reaching for the Taser on his hip. I can't run, and hiding is officially out of the question.

That leaves me with only one option.

I turn around so that my back is facing him. I really don't want to do this, but it's the only hope I have of saving Gabe.

He liberates his Taser. "Hands where I can see them," he says, closing the distance between us.

I do as he says and raise my hands. I keep my back to him, even as inky black tears begin to well in my eyes.

"Where do you think you're going?" he asks as he comes up behind me. His footfalls are short and urgent as he holsters his weapon to reach for his handcuffs.

I turn around, stopping him dead in his tracks.

The young officer fumbles for his gun. The weapon trembles in his grip as he aims it at my head.

"Stay there," he warns, steadying his weapon, "or I will shoot."

I begin walking toward him. As expected, he backs away.

"You don't want to do that," I say as darkness encroaches on my vision.

He cocks the gun. Even if he shoots, the damage won't last. I'm positively unkillable.

"Ma'am," he says, his voice as shaky as his hands, "I don't want to shoot you, but I will."

I stop walking. My skin is cold as ice, but inside, I'm hotter than a furnace. Even with a gun, the young officer is completely powerless. After all, he may have a weapon, but I have the boundless potential of the blackness at my disposal.

I seize him by the shirt collar and lift him off the floor, causing him to drop the gun. He wraps both hands around my wrist, beads of sweat shimmering on his forehead as he thrashes helplessly in my grip.

"Where's William Foster?" I ask as he claws at the hand knotted in his shirt.

"I don't know who you're talking about."

I lift him a little higher. His heels scrape against the wall as he tries in vain to regain his footing.

"Yes you do," I say as his cheeks flush. "Where is he?"

"He's in a holding cell by himself," the officer croaks. "Word is he killed his wife—stabbed her to death with a kitchen knife over a disagreement about money."

I bore into him with my incinerating gaze. "I am his wife."

The officer's eyes go wide with terror. I tighten my grip on his collar, causing the veins in his temples to pop. I hold him until he succumbs to a lack of oxygen, and then watch as he sinks to the floor with his eyes bulging out of his skull.

I locate the holding cells, where I find Gabe sitting on his bed behind a reinforced steel door. I knock on the window and he leaps up to greet me.

"Ansel said you'd come," Gabe says, his voice garbled.

"When did you speak to Ansel?"

"Last night."

I give him a perplexed look. "Did you get your powers back?"

"Some of them."

"So why are you still here?"

"I can't unlock the door. Not from the inside, anyway."

I shift my attention over to the lock, where I examine the mechanism while Gabe looks on in silence.

I invert my Keepsake again, exposing the lock's internal components. I work quickly, manipulating the pins until they align and the lock disengages without much fanfare.

The cell door clangs open just as a flurry of voices fills the halls. Something in Gabe's posture catches my eye. I glance at his leg, which is straight, sturdy, and eerily devoid of a cast.

"Your leg healed," I say.

"So did your stomach," he replies, looking me over.

Gabe peers through the window at the hallway beyond. Then he turns back to me.

"I couldn't hold them off indefinitely," I say halfheartedly.

"It's okay. We can take them." In the midst of the tumult, he cracks the sincerest smile I've ever seen and says, "We're a team, right?"

For reasons I won't understand for another lifetime or so, I nod and smile back.

With that, he throws open the door and barrels down the hall, with me keeping pace less than ten feet behind him.

We race toward the front doors with a horde of armed officers hot on our heels. Where possible, I use our surroundings to our advantage, tossing various items into their path until we finally emerge in the lobby.

When Sophia sees us running toward her, she leaps up and charges toward the door. The three of us sprint toward the Camaro. I toss the keys to Gabe, who climbs into the driver's seat and starts the ignition in one fluid movement.

Sophia dives into the backseat; I hop in front. By the time the first gun goes off, we've made it across the parking lot and are flying at top speed toward the highway, with half a dozen cruisers in close pursuit.

I glance at the black and white vehicles zipping in and out of traffic behind us. "We need to lose them."

Gabe's eyes are glued to the road. "We will."

I twist in my seat to look at Sophia, who's sitting on the floor with her arms wrapped around her legs. When our eyes meet, I notice that she's crying. I don't try and comfort her—mainly because I don't know how.

I glimpse the speedometer. We're pushing 100 miles per hour and there's an exit fast approaching on the right. My eyes flicker toward Gabe, but he's too transfixed by our speed to acknowledge my pleading expression.

"Hold on," he says in a firm voice, and a second later we leave the highway behind.

28

I open my eyes to find Sophia asleep in the backseat and Gabe squinting into the sun beside me. We're driving through a forest, where the road is rough and the only proof of civilization is a series of well-positioned signs alerting us to sharp turns. The clock on the dash reads 4:02, meaning we've been driving for just over six hours.

I gaze up at the trees. Patches of pale pink sky poke through the gaps in the leaves and there's just enough light to illuminate the steel cables on the guardrails flanking the road.

"Where are we?" I ask, looking over at Gabe.

"A long way from home," he replies, steering into another turn.

I turn and look at Sophia, who's lying lengthwise across the seat with her hood pulled over her head and her hands tucked into her sleeves. Given the way things have been going lately, I wouldn't be surprised if she slept clear through to tomorrow.

"We need to find some place to make camp," I say, facing forward once again. "All this driving is making me car sick."

"Are you sure it's not your powers?"

"That, too." I look down at my lap. "Should we talk about what happened?"

"There's nothing to talk about. You died, I got arrested, and now we're on the run."

"There's a third level, Gabe—a third dimension. Ansel calls it the in-between."

We maneuver a bend overlooking a steep ravine. I shield my eyes from the sunlight slanting through the trees lining the ridge.

"I asked him about The Establishment," I continue. "He said it was still there, but not like I remember it."

"What did you see, exactly?"

"Nothing. The in-between is just a vacuum."

Gabe saws his jaw. I picture the void as we venture deeper into the wilderness, beckoned by the promise of solitude and a little time to sleep. I wonder if the in-between has always existed—not so much as its own reality, but as the foundation on which all the others are based. After all, just because you can't see something, doesn't mean it isn't there.

Where the road runs out of gravel, Gabe steers into the underbrush and drives until he reaches a clearing. There's a small lake on the far side of the meadow. Beyond that, a row of coniferous trees stands watch over the land. The sky is wide and pitted with stars; a few wisps of grey streak the otherwise endless sweep of blue and violet. I'm finally at peace, or maybe just too tired to care anymore.

Gabe puts the Camaro in park and turns off the engine.

"So are you going to do it?" he asks as Sophia begins to stir.

"Do what?"

"Ansel told me about the malevolents. He said you agreed to help him get them under control."

244

I stare at the slivers of moonlight carving the surface of the water. "I guess I did."

I brace myself for a lecture. Instead, Gabe stretches, yawns, and opens the door, inviting a blast of cool air into the cabin.

"We should make camp," he says as I emerge from the vehicle. "You and Sophia can go in search of wood and I'll work on building a fire pit."

"You're not worried someone will see us?" I ask.

"Out here? Hardly." Gabe leans on the roof of the Camaro. "If you're really worried, we can keep the fire low. And we'll rotate. That way, we all get a chance to recharge."

I scoff.

Gabe cocks a brow. "What?"

"Recharge. We're not Catchers anymore, Gabe."

He holds my gaze. I'm not sure if what I said is true, but one thing is for certain: nothing we do from this moment on will be anywhere near normal.

"I guess I should get started on that fire pit," he says, breaking the silence. I watch him set off across the meadow in search of a suitable campsite, and then shift my focus over to Sophia.

The woods cushioning the meadow are filled with vegetation of varying shapes and sizes. I task Sophia with gathering branches and dry leaves before slipping away to look for food.

Ten minutes later, Gabe, Sophia, and I have built a respectable fire with which to cook and keep warm. Gabe has parked the Camaro down by the water for safekeeping, as well as to give us somewhere to sleep. We manage to find a few fruit trees and line our pockets with bruised but still-edible apples. Until now, I hadn't realized how much I appreciate hot meals, hot showers, and warm beds. The view makes up for it, but just barely.

After Sophia falls asleep, Gabe and I pass the time making conversation. Despite my best efforts, Will's memories remain, so I allow Gabe to regale me with tales from the lives we've been forced to take. I have to say: looking at him now, stretched out in the grass with the smoke billowing around his face, it's not hard to see why Tiffany felt the way she did.

"How did you propose?" I ask as he tosses the apple core into the flames.

"I didn't. You did."

I lean back on my arms and study him through the swirling embers. "Go on."

Gabe smirks. "Let's just say you were in a rush."

"Was I?"

"You wanted kids. We both did. It took five years and all of our money before we realized it wasn't in the cards for us."

His gaze slips away from me. He wipes a smudge off the apple in his hand as I throw a glance in Sophia's direction and debate briefing him on our conversation from earlier.

Switching gears, Gabe says, "I meant what I said earlier, about us making a good team. It hasn't always been easy, but we've always managed to stick together."

I nod. I'm not sure who's speaking in this moment, but either way, he has a point.

"It's a shame we didn't start out that way," I say, clasping my arms around my knees.

Gabe reaches for a branch and uses the charred end to poke life back into the fire.

"It's not where you start that matters, Sarah—it's where you end up." A log crumbles to a pile of ashes, which are scooped up and scattered by a passing wind. Gabe finishes fussing over the fire, removes the smoking branch, and places it on the grass beside him.

Unsure of how to respond, I stand up and brush the debris from my clothes.

"Where are you going?" Gabe asks.

"For a walk. I need to think."

I trace the lake's perimeter. Overlooking the smooth obsidian mirror is a gentle knoll that descends into a sandy shelf. Time and time again, I find reasons to think about my brother. He was drawn to the ocean for the same reason I'm drawn to this lake: because the moments in which we feel most alive are usually the ones with the power to kill us.

I take off my shoes. The ground is cold beneath my bare feet as I undo the blouse, letting it slip from my shoulders to the sand below. It feels good to be numb again. As I unzip the pants, the wind reminds me that I may not be alone after all. I scan the tree line, but the rustling leaves reveal no danger.

After I finish undressing, I admire my reflection at the edge of the water. Long, healthy strands of hair whirl around my face. My skin is pale like the moon; thankfully, my eyes make up for the lack of colour. I give my two-dimensional twin a subtle nod of understanding and take my first step into the lake.

I gasp when the water meets my skin. The chill migrates up my legs, and by the time I'm waist-deep I can't feel a thing. I walk until the shelf disappears, then turn onto my back to gaze at the stars.

A flicker of movement steals my attention. I sit up and scan the woods, but can't see more than a few feet in every direction. I squint at the bushes fringing the lake, hoping with every fibre of my being that the wind is conspiring with my imagination. My heart begins to race as the rustling intensifies. I calculate my distance from the shore, shocked at how far I've managed to swim.

Gabe appears carrying an armload of sticks. When he sees me bobbing in the middle of the lake, he places the firewood on the ground and ambles down the grassy slope toward the water.

Neither of us speaks. Gabe pockets his hands and glimpses the heap of clothes deserted on the ground. Then he looks at me and heaves a sigh so deep I actually see his shoulders sink.

He bends down and tugs the knots out of his laces. His shoes removed, he sticks a hand under his shirt and lifts it over his head. His pants come off last, collapsing in a puddle at his feet.

Gabe wades in. He's so tense I can see the definition in his neck and arms, which hover indecisively at his sides. After a few cautious steps, he finally works up the nerve to submerge his hands, which he uses to propel himself toward me. Despite his initial reluctance, his strokes are long and self-assured and they part the water with confidence until at last we're face to face with each other.

"Hi," he says.

"Hi."

Gabe looks around, the water lapping at his chin as he turns his head.

"Nice night for a swim," he remarks through chattering teeth. He runs a hand through his hair, prompting a few enthusiastic locks to stand on end.

"It is," I agree. I tip my head back to look at the stars, but the clouds are blocking the view.

"Sophia's still sleeping," he informs me. "Where did you find her, anyway?"

"Outside the police station. She said she woke up under a bridge with no memory of how she got there."

"Was she hurt?"

"Not too badly. A few cuts and bruises."

Gabe nods as he continues treading water. Moonlight grabs the moisture dotting his skin, highlighting the angle of his jaw right before he turns to me and becomes just another shade in the monochrome of shadows.

"So are you going to do it?" he asks. "Carry out the orders, I mean."

"I don't really see any way around it."

"What will happen if you don't follow through?"

"Insubordination, I would assume."

A look of sadness comes over Gabe's face as he wraps his arms around my body. The warmth of his skin is a welcome surprise. I try to center my field, but all it does is pull me deeper into his presence like a pin to a magnet.

"I'm sorry I lied to you," Gabe says, even though it's Will who's actually speaking.

"It's okay," I say, still safe in his embrace. "You don't have to apologize for something I don't remember."

Gabe pulls back slightly. In his eyes, I see exactly what he does: the face of a woman who doesn't remember how it feels to be looked at like this.

My lips part, drawing him in. Our mouths meet with hungering insistence, and my energy plummets to the lower half of my body before I can stop it.

And then something pulls me under.

29

I open my eyes. Tentacles of filth spiral around my face as I try to right myself. I spot the hazy glow of the moon about ten feet above me and begin to swim toward it, only to be yanked back into the frigid depths of this watery grave less than a second later.

Through the rotating confusion of debris comes the serpentine outline of a mature malevolent. It wraps me in a column of bubbles, but not before I convert each and every one of them into micro orbs.

One by one, the bubbles pop. A miniature shockwave follows each eruption until the malevolent dives to the bottom of the lake, giving me just enough time to make my escape.

I break the surface and instinctively gasp for air. I look around for Gabe, but all I see is the reflection of the moon and the distant plume of smoke from our campfire.

From somewhere behind me comes the crash of flailing arms, followed by a brisk intake of air. Gabe explodes from the middle of the lake, looks around in fright, and then swims toward me as quickly as his frozen limbs will allow.

"Are you okay?" he asks, still fighting for a breath.

"I'm fine." I look around again. I don't see the malevolent anywhere.

That's when we hear the scream. It reverberates off the various trees and embankments, daring the wind to match its penetrating intensity. Gabe and I exchange looks, and then swim as fast as possible back to the shore.

My feet find traction on the wet sand as I gallop out of the lake with Gabe following closely behind. We wrestle our clothes back onto our bodies and then sprint blindly through the darkness toward the source of the sound.

Another scream carries on the wind. Its urgency intensifies as we race back to the campsite, where the fire is roaring and there's an enormous, hunchbacked figure clawing at the doors of the Camaro. Sophia is trapped in the backseat with her hood raised and her knees drawn to her chest, trying to form the smallest ball she can manage.

I form an orb and launch it at the malevolent. The beast emits an ear-splitting shriek as it rears backwards, abandoning the Camaro long enough for Sophia to escape. The creature claws at its own flesh, exposing a grotesque, red essence padded by sickly black organs.

The malevolent sets its sights on me and charges.

Gabe seizes a stick from the fire's infernal core. Flames shudder on the end of his crooked weapon, illuminating the unforgiving frown drawn across his face. He hollers as he waves the stick, trying to catch the malevolent's attention, but it continues advancing toward me instead.

I stand my ground as the malevolent rears back on its hind legs. It winds up its arm, preparing to strike. I do the same, calling a new batch of memories to the fore as my hand pulses with bright blue energy. Just as I'm about to diffuse the orb, the malevolent delivers a crushing blow. Its claws fit perfectly between my ribs, tearing the flesh from my bones as I'm viciously thrown to the ground.

The malevolent cries out as Gabe impales it with the branch. It swings its arms in an unrestrained fashion, failing in its attempts to free itself. Having immobilized the beast, Gabe then steers the malevolent toward the lake, where he drives it into the water and pins it facedown in the shallows until it drowns.

Gabe rushes over to me. I can't breathe. I'm not in much pain, but the blood pouring out of my body would fill a bathtub. I look around for Sophia and find her hurrying toward me as well, her champagne hair flapping against her shoulders with every step.

Gabe removes my hands to assess my wound. I peer unseeingly up at the stars until his eyes snap back to my face and he gives me a look of complete disbelief.

"What?" I ask.

Gabe and Sophia trade looks and say nothing. I peer down at my wound—except the wound is gone, along with all the blood. I check my shirt for damage, but the only evidence of an attack is a tear in the fabric that can easily be fixed using a careful hand and a stitch of thread.

Gabe helps me to my feet. The three of us approach the lake, where the malevolent lies in a heap at the edge of the water. Silence falls over the meadow, and in the sudden cessation of sound I become painfully aware of Sophia's tearful whimpers and my own heart hammering away in my chest.

Gabe reels me into a hug. He motions for Sophia to join us, and before I know it, he has one arm around her and the other around me. I never thought I'd welcome his affection, but that was before I used the memory of our kiss to grow my orb.

"Are you okay?" he asks me.

I look up at him and nod. My heart stumbles through the last of its surprise as I look over at the Camaro and then back at Sophia as she stares down at the malevolent. When a reflex causes the creature to twitch, she skitters backward and lands in the sand a short distance from the fire.

I begin to walk away, but not before Gabe grabs my arm and turns me toward him.

"Hey." Our eyes meet. "Where are you going?"

I survey the damage again then say, "To look for more firewood."

"I'll come with you."

"I'd rather go alone."

Gabe loosens his fingers. Sophia spins around and then leaps to her feet just as I wade into the overgrown grass separating the field from the surrounding forest.

I turn to look at her. "Where do you think you're going?" I ask as she comes up behind me.

A pained expression falls over Sophia's face. "With you."

"You should stay with Gabe. After all, he's the one who killed the malevolent."

"I'd rather go with you, though."

Too spent to debate where she'd be safest, I angle back to the forest and wait for her to catch up. We don't speak as we traverse the woods, but I don't mind; I could use a little peace and quiet, anyway.

Some time later, the three of us relocate to another spot along the lake. Gabe beds us down on pine bows and old blankets he keeps in the trunk while Sophia arranges our firewood in a neat little pile in the sand. As for me, I retreat to the privacy of the Camaro, where I fall asleep in the front seat after a long and ultimately fruitless quarrel with my inner demons.

When I'm inexplicably roused from slumber in the dead of the night, I gaze around and find Gabe and Sophia both sound asleep. I don't see the malevolent carcass anywhere.

30

Wake up, Sarah.

I'm jolted awake by a voice I don't recognize. It's morning and I'm alone in the car. I pan over the backseat, where the blankets have been pushed off to one side and Sophia's sweater is in a ball on the floor. There's a crick in my neck and my head is pounding from what I imagine is a combination of dehydration and not enough calories. I shake off the last of the sleep hangover, and then let myself out of the car.

I find Gabe and Sophia on the far side of the lake, which is the richest shade of turquoise I've ever seen. They've removed their shoes, rolled up their pant legs, and are standing knee-deep in the glittering green water, pointing to something in the distance. Despite the early hour, the sun is high and unobstructed. It's a spectacular autumn morning, with not a single cloud to speak of, and I catch myself smiling at Gabe and Sophia's shenanigans as I make my way toward them.

"Look who decided to wake up," Gabe teases, grinning at me over Sophia's head. She acknowledges me with a quick wave before turning back to the lake and skipping a rock across its dazzling face.

"You two look like you're having fun," I observe, taking a seat on a rock that's been warming in the sun. I slip off my shoes and set them on the rock beside me.

"Gabe's showing me how to skip rocks," Sophia says, turning to look at me. "Then we're going to try and catch some fish."

"We'll probably have to fish in another part of the lake. The rocks will have scared them all away by now." Gabe produces another smooth rock from his pocket and hands it to Sophia. "Okay, so this time, try and keep your hand flat. Remember, you're just flicking your wrist, not your whole arm."

Sophia plots the rock's trajectory and pulls back her arm, casting the stone across the water with ease. The rock bounces about five times before finally losing momentum and dipping beneath the surface to disappear forever.

"You got it now," Gabe says with a grin. He reaches into his pocket and hands her another rock, and when she's sufficiently occupied, turns and wades over to me.

"I thought you didn't like kids," I say as he emerges from the lake and takes a seat on the rock beside me.

"I wouldn't exactly call Sophia a kid," he counters, getting comfortable. "She's seen too much."

"All the same, I didn't peg you as the fatherly type."

He gives me a crooked smirk and shakes his head. "I'm just patching the holes in her childhood." His eyes crinkle mischievously as they slide over my face. "And you? She seems to follow you around like a puppy."

"That's usually what puppies do after you feed them."

Gabe chuckles and rolls his pants a little further up his legs.

"She's a good kid," he says.

"She is."

"Should we talk about last night?"

"Do we need to? You killed the malevolent."

Gabe lowers his voice and glimpses Sophia to ensure she's not listening. "I meant what happened at the lake."

I feign ignorance. "Well, malevolents are drawn to water and it was dark enough for them to sneak up on us. There. Mystery solved."

He smirks. "You're really trying to avoid this conversation, aren't you?"

"It was just a kiss, Gabe. Don't make it into something more."

I look at him. His skin is stubbled with midweek growth and his hair is dull from the sun, but he appears strong, healthy, and deliciously buff.

When did these words creep into my vocabulary?

Gabe rises from the rock and ambles down to the water to check on Sophia.

"If you say so," he says, grinning the whole time.

When they eventually tire of tossing rocks, Gabe and Sophia lead the way to an undisturbed part of the lake, where the water is calm and fish are snapping at the insects buzzing above the surface.

Gabe and Sophia fashion a spear out of a long, twisted branch they break off a nearby tree. I perch at the water's edge with my feet in the sand as Gabe uses a small pocketknife to sharpen the stick and sheer off any remaining twigs. They stand quietly in the shallows, their eyes trained on their target. When they finally isolate their victim, Sophia is giddy with impatience. She raises the spear, impaling her catch on the sharp end of the weaponized branch.

She squeals with delight as Gabe frees their kill. A radiant grin divides his face as he turns to me and holds up the fish, and I clap politely in a show of support for their surprisingly successful endeavor.

"Should we catch another one?" Sophia asks excitedly.

"Take it easy," Gabe says, exiting the water, "no sense killing more than we can consume."

She follows him out of the water. Gabe instructs her to go in search of firewood and she sets off toward the trees without another look back.

Gabe lays the fish on a rock. I watch it gasp for air until its gills go still and it surrenders the fight for survival.

Laying the spear in the grass, Gabe brushes his hands together and frowns down at the dead trout.

"I shouldn't feel guilty," he says softly. "I mean, it's just a fish, right? And we need to eat."

I nod. When we escorted souls to The Establishment, there was never any emotion involved—strictly business. So why am I suddenly squeamish at the sight of a dead fish?

Gabe picks up the fish. "You ever scaled one of these before?"

"No. Have you?"

"'Course. I did Scouts." He frowns apologetically. "But I guess you wouldn't remember any of that."

I get to my feet and brush the creases out of my pants. "I should check on Sophia."

"Sarah?"

I turn back to him. Gabe appears hesitant, but speaks all the same.

"Did you..." He pauses to chew the inside of his cheek. "Did you hear anything, when you woke up?"

"What do you mean?"

"I mean... did you hear any voices?"

I recall the disembodied voice rousing me from slumber. It didn't sound like Ansel at all, but for some reason, I don't mention this.

"No. I didn't." I squint at him. "Did you?"

Gabe shrugs and gives me his most disingenuous smile yet.

"Nope. Not a thing." Slipping back into his shoes, he ascends the hill with the fish in one hand and the spear in the other. "By the way, how do you like your fish?"

"Cooked."

"Well, that makes two of us, then." Amusement dimples his cheeks and he continues on his way, fading into the forest as he progresses toward our campsite.

○

Gabe insists on spending another night in the clearing. He says we'll be safe here, and it's the first time since outrunning the police that I've truly doubted him. Nevertheless, I help him build another fire and keep our wood supply well stocked. He and Sophia manage to catch another fish and the three of us enjoy a meal of smoked trout and apples while bantering about everything under the proverbial sun.

When Sophia finally turns in for the night, Gabe and I discuss Ansel's plan to rebuild The Establishment. Gabe is still trying to persuade me to defy the orders, but he knows as well as I do that neither of us belongs here. I tell him my word is my bond, and it puts a quick end to our halfhearted debate.

"Do you want to take a walk?" he asks after a couple of minutes pass in silence.

"Where?"

"Nowhere in particular," he replies with a shrug. Glancing at the Camaro, he adds, "I just don't want to wake Sophia."

"Do you really think we should leave her alone after what happened?"

"She'll be okay. I gave her my knife." He pulls himself into an upright position and offers his hand, which I accept.

Our stroll takes us around the top of the lake and into a meadow filled with rocks and wildflowers. The moon is full again tonight, and beautifully clear, thanks to the absence of clouds. Silver light drips like dew from every blade of grass, giving the entire field a quaint, milky glow.

We find a patch of dirt about fifty feet from the water's edge and sit down beside each other. Maybe Gabe is right: maybe we don't need Ansel, but the others do. Without The Establishment, the malevolents will destroy civilization and the victims of their ongoing havoc will be doomed to either haunt the earth or spend an eternity in an existential vacuum, with no purpose, no identity, and no hope for regeneration. It's a saddening prospect, and the only reason I'm still determined to see Ansel's orders to completion.

"It's not your fault," he assures me, leaning back on his elbows. "This was Ansel's doing—all of it."

"I should've stayed out of the basement. I'm afraid I've made the situation worse."

"You haven't. Those malevolents were bound to escape eventually." He sneaks a glance in my direction. "If there's anyone who should be sorry, it's me. I'm disgusted with myself for how poorly I treated you." Gabe looks me in the eyes. "I'm sorry, Sarah."

"I forgive you. You're not the self-serving asshole I thought you were."

"I was once, in a previous life. But I don't know that guy anymore." He sits up and nods at the lake. "Beautiful, isn't it?"

"It is."

"Reminds me of you, actually."

Warmth creeps into my face. I'm thankful for the darkness to disguise my reaction.

"I've never been compared to a lake," I say, hoping to divert the conversation from Gabe's unexpected compliment. "Or any body of water, for that matter."

He chuckles. "That could go either way."

Since we're alone and I'm curious, I decide to probe him for more of Will's memories. I've been thinking about Tiffany all day, wondering what she would think of all of this if she were in this body instead of me.

"Tell me about our wedding night," I prompt.

"We had a seaside ceremony. You wore flowers in your hair and no shoes. You were gorgeous—the stuff of dreams, really."

"I imagine heels and sand don't mix," I say.

He smiles. "That's exactly what you said," he whispers. "Two hundred dollars down the drain and you left the shoes in the hotel room, danced barefoot all night."

"What happened after that?"

"After that..." he smirks, "after we'd wined and dined and caroused to our hearts' content, you and I ran back to the hotel room and had our own private after party." There's a suggestive twinkle in his eyes and it sends tingles all the way down to my toes.

I lie on my back and stare up at the stars pulsing in the midnight sky. Gabe's face swoops into my field of view and he smiles when my gaze gravitates toward him.

"What?" I ask.

Gabe lowers his mouth to mine, grabbing my lips in a deep kiss. I place my hand on the back of his head, where his hair is thick and matted with knots, and wait for the rest of his body to settle over me like a blanket.

I shouldn't want this, but I do. When Gabe or Will or whoever he is begins to undo my blouse, I don't try to stop him.

"Are you sure you don't remember me?" he asks.

"I'm sure." I glance down at my stomach. Still no scar, but at least my amnesia is permanent.

Gabe's lips cup my mouth. He steals the air from my lungs, deflating my inhibitions as his manhood peaks against my warmth.

With a gentle twist of his thumb, the button on my jeans pops free. With every inch of skin that he exposes, the wind feels just a little cooler, the ground just a little harder, and my animosity just a little lighter. I may not remember him, but he remembers me perfectly.

"If Sophia asks," Gabe says, his lips skimming my neck, "this never happened."

When we return to our campsite some time later, all that remains of the fire is a pile of black wood dusted with fine, white ash. Sophia is still asleep in the back of the Camaro, and once we're closer, I notice a second figure standing next to the fire.

Ansel turns to address us.

"Nice evening for a constitutional," he remarks. He shifts his gaze to me. "I hope I'm not interrupting anything."

I shake my head and absently adjust the front of my blouse.

Ansel smiles at Gabe. "How's the leg?"

"Good as new."

"I hope you didn't forget about our little agreement."

I try to catch Gabe's eyes. "What's he talking about?"

"Nothing."

"Oh, it's far from nothing," Ansel says, striding toward us. "Mr. Conway and I had a long chat about personal accountability. Turns out, your companion owes me a debt of gratitude for saving his soul."

"Saving his soul?" I say incredulously. "Don't you mean protecting your assets?"

"That, too." He sighs and concentrates on Gabe. "And that's why I'm giving you another chance to make things right. Help Sarah contain the malevolents and I'll release you indefinitely from any future obligations."

"And if I don't?" Gabe retorts, eyeing Ansel uncertainly.

Ansel smiles dryly. "Then I have a special place in mind for you, and it's not the in-between." He nods and raises a hand, bracing his thumb against his middle finger. "Don't make me regret this," he says, and vanishes in a snap.

31

"Did you make some sort of deal with Ansel?" I ask, turning to Gabe.

"Maybe."

"This is a yes or no kind of question. Did you make a deal with Ansel?"

He hunches his shoulders.

"I wanted to protect you," he admits, "and the only way to do that was to sacrifice myself."

"But Ansel said—"

"I know what he said, but it's not the whole story. So long as Ansel is in power I'll never truly be free. Even if I regenerate, if Ansel needs me, I'm contractually obligated to report for duty. Those were the conditions I agreed to when I sold my soul."

"Why would you do that?"

"Why wouldn't I? My freedom is a small price to pay for eternal protection. As long as I don't go rogue, I never have to worry about ending up in the wrong place."

I crouch next to the fire and prod it with a stick until the dormant embers ignite. Flames lick along the steepled logs, throwing smoke ten feet into the air as Gabe squats in the dirt beside me.

"Ansel and I have a complicated relationship, but you're the one he chose to save humanity." Gabe plucks a twig off the ground and twirls it between his fingers while he thinks. "I got myself into this mess by making promises I couldn't keep. Now Ansel is giving me a chance to redeem myself. If you ask me, he's being very generous."

I can't look at him. "Where will you end up if you fail?"

Gabe sighs and tosses the sprig into the fire. "Where all defiant beings go—the blackness."

I don't speak. The only reason I haven't gone back on my word is because I actually believed that in helping Ansel I'd somehow be helping myself. I'd expected this life to be my reward for a job well done, but instead it feels more like punishment, especially if there's a possibility that Gabe and Sophia won't be present to celebrate our triumph over evil.

Gabe continues, "If we succeed in restoring order, then Ansel will grant me a reprieve. If we fail, then you, Sophia, and everyone who is yet to come will end up in the in-between and I'll go straight to the abyss."

"What about the contract?"

"It becomes null and void. If I can't live up to the stipulations, there's not much point in keeping me around."

"Can't he just rehabilitate you? Why go so far as to condemn you to an eternity of torture?"

"I know too much. Ansel was grooming me to be an advisor of sorts, and if he were to reintroduce me into the general spirit population there's a reasonable chance I could turn his troops against him." Gabe shrugs. "Like I said, you have more important things to worry about, like making sure the malevolents don't turn this planet into an existential wasteland."

"Maybe I should talk to him."

"I'd prefer if you didn't. Sometimes disaster is disguised as a good deed."

"But Gabe—"

"It's okay, Sarah. I'm not afraid."

Gabe rises to his feet and offers his hand, but I don't take it.

"What did you mean by protecting me?" I ask, looking past his hand to his face.

He heaves another sigh and stuffs his hand in his pocket.

"I negotiated with him, convinced him to give you a lighter sentence in the event that you should fail."

"I don't follow."

"Originally, Ansel was planning to condemn both of us to a lifetime of solitary confinement. I didn't think this was fair, given that you'd been unquestioningly loyal to him. After some cajoling on my part, I managed to work out a deal: if you failed, you would end up in the in-between with everyone else, and I'd end up being Hate bait until the end of time. It's far from ideal, but at least we'd both have some company."

He begins to turn away just as I push myself into an upright position. "Gabe?"

He faces me, his crestfallen expression vaguely illuminated by the fire's unreliable glow.

I swallow. "Thank you."

Gabe smiles and continues on his way, leaving me to tend to the fire with Ansel's words looping endlessly through my mind.

○

The next morning, I awaken on the cold, hard ground. My head is heavy and my stomach is sore. I feel nauseous. The clouds are black and bloated with rain and I can just make out the dull rumble of thunder on the horizon. I don't see Gabe or Sophia anywhere.

I stand up and brush the dirt from my clothes. Thinking they may have gone fishing, I scan the shore for their faces but only manage a fleeting glimpse before stumbling into the nearest bush to be sick.

By the time Gabe and Sophia return with their latest catch, I'm propped up against the side of the Camaro with my hands in my lap. I'm too weak to move, or even hold my head up. I notice Gabe and Sophia rushing toward me, but their voices are faint and garbled in the fishbowl of my foggy mind. My skin is scorching hot, and yet somehow cold and clammy. Everything around me has a distinct golden glow, and it's the last thing I see before I go unconscious.

○

I've lost track of time. Sleep comes to me in waves: short sessions of light, agitated slumber bookended by episodes of violent vomiting, and long, involuntary stretches of oblivion peppered with visions of shadowy figures with red eyes and pointy teeth. I lie beneath several layers of blankets in the backseat of the car, where an entire day seems to pass in minutes. Gabe has been standing vigil for hours, stroking my hair and encouraging me to sip water, but my body rejects his offerings, including the tiny morsels of fish and sliced fruit he keeps touching to my lips in an effort to persuade me to eat.

By the time the sun graces the horizon again, the only thing I manage to expel from my body is blood. Its bitter aftertaste plunges me into an endless cycle of coughing and dry heaving.

Sophia stands over Gabe, who's sitting in the front seat with his head in his hands. Both of their faces are blurry. Despite their muffled voices, I can still follow the thread of their conversation.

"What do we do?" Sophia asks in a thin, breakable voice.

"I don't know."

"Maybe we should go to the hospital."

"Sophia, please, just let me think."

"She's going to die."

"Sophia!" Gabe's head snaps up. He bores into her until she looks away. "Please. Just stop."

Tears grate on her mousy voice. "She needs help. Real help from a real doctor."

Gabe hangs his head and weeps.

○

By the third day, Gabe relents and drives us to the nearest town.

The Camaro hums with nervous energy. My survival demands an enormous risk: if anyone recognizes our faces, or even just our vehicle, it could jeopardize our whole operation. Ansel is counting on us to succeed, and that simply won't be possible if we're all incarcerated.

Still, I need help, and soon.

I sift aside the blankets and gaze at the power lines streaking past the window. We've reentered civilization and it's making me sick with fear. If I had anything left in me, I'm nearly certain I'd throw up.

"What if someone recognizes us?" Sophia, in the front seat, asks.

Gabe maintains his white-knuckle grip on the wheel. I watch him, waiting for his response between alternating pangs of nausea and fatigue.

Then he says, "No one will recognize us. We've traveled too far."

"TV travels faster."

Gabe roughs up his hair with his left hand.

"No one will recognize us," he says again, more softly this time, "I'll make sure of that."

Some time later, we arrive outside an austere building with pale yellow bricks and a pair of burning bushes on both sides of its covered entrance. Gabe locates a parking space a short distance from the doors, and then steals one more trepidatious breath before turning to me and offering a smile.

Though I'm weak from dehydration, I still insist on walking into the clinic. The doors slide open to admit us as we make our way across the floor and over to the registration counter, where a pudgy woman with crow's feet gives us a disparaging look.

Gabe speaks for me. "My wife needs help," he says, as if it isn't obvious. "We think she might've picked up a parasite of some sort."

The lady behind the desk nods curtly. "I'm going to need to see her health card."

Not one to miss a beat, Gabe pats his pockets for effect before turning back to her with a pleading look in his eyes.

"I must've left it at home," he says, "we were in a hurry."

She eyes me warily. "No doubt." Shaking her head, she reaches for a clipboard and hands it to Gabe. "Have a seat and fill this out."

He thanks her and guides me over to one of the chairs, with Sophia trailing us awkwardly.

I take a seat and tilt my head against the wall. Coming here has made me painfully aware of how much I've missed the creature comforts of modern society, such as indoor plumbing, reading material, and a roof to keep the elements off my head. I'm suddenly ravenous and my thirst is impossible to ignore. On my right, Gabe fills out the forms with the kind of confidence I'd expect from someone who's known me for years. Sophia is sitting on my left, gnawing at a hangnail and taking cursory interest in the TV in the corner of the ceiling.

I rest my head on Gabe's shoulder and close my eyes.

"Don't get too comfortable," he whispers, "we're just passing through."

"I know."

"Can we get something to eat after?" Sophia asks, leaning around me to address Gabe.

"I don't have any money."

She sighs and settles back into her seat. When she loses interest in the news segment, she helps herself to a parenting magazine and fans through the pages with a despondent gleam in her eyes. After everything we've been through, I'd love nothing more than to take her home and feed her everything in sight. I picture the sandwich she'd made shortly before we freed Gabe and have to cover my mouth to prevent myself from vomiting into his lap.

Some time later, we're led to a small examination room with a bed on one half and a chair on the other. The room has curtains instead of walls as well as a light box for viewing x-rays. As far as medical facilities go it's pretty rudimentary, but nothing worth complaining about.

The nurse hands me a gown. When she's out of sight and earshot, Gabe turns to me and shakes his head.

"In and out," he reminds me, and then takes the gown from my hands.

I lie down on the bed and stare up at the lights. I'm tired down to my bones, but I won't allow myself to be overpowered by sleep in a place where no one can be trusted.

Sophia folds herself into the chair and angles toward another TV while Gabe takes a seat at the foot of the bed.

"Shouldn't be too much longer," he says to no one in particular.

I massage my stomach with both hands. Sleep tugs at my eyes, so I make sure to keep them wide open.

"Thank you for bringing me here," I tell him. "I know you weren't exactly happy to do it."

Gabe's eyes dart around suspiciously before returning to my face.

"We need to be vigilant. You never know who's watching."

I tip my head back and try to relax. One crisis at a time: that's how we're going to get through this.

Sophia's voice reaches me. "Guys?"

We both look at her. She points to the TV, which is airing the same channel as the one in the waiting room. I squint at the images, shuddering as our faces flash across the screen.

Gabe wheels around to face me. "Get up," he hisses.

He pulls his keys from his pocket and hands them to Sophia. Unfortunately, we're not the only ones who've been watching the news. The whispering around us intensifies. One person even mentions the police.

I begin to slide off the bed, but Gabe stops me.

"I'm carrying you," he says. To Sophia, he says, "And you're leading the way. Whatever you do, do not make eye contact with anyone. Understood?"

She gives a frantic nod and tightens her grip on the keys.

Gabe hoists me into his arms. He pokes his head out of the room and glances furtively in both directions before motioning for Sophia to lead.

We make our way back toward the front doors. I can feel Gabe's heart hammering away in his chest as he adjusts his grip and quickens his pace in order to keep up with Sophia. His palms are slick with sweat and the feeling of his breath on my face is enough to trigger my nausea all over again. I keep my head down to avoid drawing attention to myself, but still manage to lock eyes with a stranger in the waiting room. She consults the TV again and immediately turns to the man seated beside her.

"Don't look at her," Gabe grits. We've nearly reached the door and I'm dizzy with relief and dehydration.

We run the last short distance over to the Camaro, where Gabe places me gingerly in the backseat and slams the door in my face.

I twist to look out the rear window, where the woman and her companion have just emerged from the building with cell phones against their ears.

"Keys," Gabe says as he and Sophia duck into the front. He tears them out of her hand, starts the car, and speeds off without even fastening his seatbelt.

32

The Camaro runs out of gas about three miles outside of town, where it sputters to a long, slow stop on the side of the road between a boarded up diner and a derelict gas station. Night is falling and we've had nothing to eat or drink since abandoning the campsite early this morning.

Gabe gets out of the car and instructs us to lay low while he investigates the gas station up ahead. It's a cool evening and the violet sky is laced with ruby and indigo clouds that look sweet enough to eat, but I'm too ill to devote much attention to my hunger.

As soon as the door closes, Sophia turns to me and frowns.

"I thought he had no money," she says, her eyes black with worry and juvenile innocence. "How can he get gas without money?"

Turning onto my back, I sigh and say, "Just let Gabe handle it. I'm sure he has a plan."

I prop myself onto my elbows and peer through the window at the craggy terrain that surrounds us. The horizon is an endless, tattered line of mountains with snowy peaks painted gold by the setting sun, and it makes me wonder how far we've traveled.

I lie back down just as Gabe appears at Sophia's window and signals for her to roll it down. They confer quietly about the unattended gas station before Gabe pops open my door and stoops to my level.

"How are you feeling?" he asks me.

I shrug. Everything on my body is aching, but I do my best to conceal my pain.

"Do you think you can walk?" Gabe continues, sounding apologetic.

The thought of hoofing it in my condition is ludicrous, but as long as we remain mobile, we stand a fair chance of outrunning the authorities. I just don't know how far we'll make it before my body decides to quit.

We consolidate the contents of the glovebox, including a pack of strike-anywhere matches, a pocketknife, a flashlight, a pack of gum, a few cheap napkins with a burger chain logo printed on the front, and a few rusty coins that add up to $4.27. Sophia is ecstatic and begs Gabe to put the money toward food, but he pockets the change and advises her to be patient.

Once we've finished pillaging the vehicle, Gabe tells Sophia to hop in the driver's seat and put the car in neutral, and together they push the car into the bushes.

"We should try and avoid roads," Gabe says as he and Sophia make their way back over to me. "And if we come across any towns, we'll go around them, not through." He holds my gaze. "You sure you're up for this?"

I nod.

He directs his words at Sophia. "You can be our canary," he tells her with a wry smirk.

She gives him a baleful look. "Your what?"

"The canary in the coal mine," I manage to say, even though I don't have the energy to speak right now. "It means you alert us to danger—hopefully without dropping dead."

Sophia's eyes go wide with fear.

To put her mind at ease, I say, "We need you to be our eyes and ears. If you notice anything suspicious, speak up." I wrap my arms a little more tightly around myself. "We should go. The desert gets pretty cold at night and we still need to make a fire."

United in our nostalgia, we throw one last glance at the Camaro and then set out on the next leg of our journey.

○

We walk as far as we can in the dark, using Gabe's flashlight to light the path. Shivers wrack my body as the chill settles into my bones. The fever has boiled off the last of my dignity, and when I eventually stray from the path to relieve myself behind a bush, I discover the same burn in an unmentionable place.

I'm losing my power. Sophia keeps turning back to check on me, and with every mile we cover I add another ten feet to the distance that separates us.

The three of us stop to make camp in the side of a hill. The hill—if you can call it that—is a stony outcropping peppered with tufts of sparse, hardy grass. The hill is merely a precursor to the mountains beyond: a smaller, more manageable ascent that promises fairer weather and fewer hazards.

Gabe locates a relatively flat area on an otherwise continuous slope and tasks Sophia with gathering rocks and anything that will burn. Though noticeably lethargic, she soldiers dutifully into the night, armed with the compact knife and a steely determination to carry as much fuel as possible in one trip.

Gabe unhooks the bungee cord and unfurls the makeshift bedroll. When he sees me sitting cross-legged on the ground a few feet away, he picks up one of the blankets and drapes it over my shoulders.

"You'll feel better once we get a fire going," he says. I nod, but I'm unconvinced. The pain is back, but it's not the dull, lazy ache I've grown accustomed to. Instead, it's a sharp, passionate throb: first in my head, then in my stomach, back, and joints. By the time Sophia emerges from the bush carrying enough stones to sink a small boat, even my eyelids are sore.

Gabe and Sophia work quickly, beginning with the ring of rocks and then adding sticks and dried vegetation. She's becoming quite the survivalist, and as soon as the fire is self-sufficient, she retreats into the shadows to hunt for hares and other rodents. I make it to the edge of the clearing just in time to spew vomit all over a thorny grey plant. A moment later, I feel the weight of my hair come off my neck.

Gabe frowns as I look at him over my shoulder.

"I made a vow," he says softly, "in sickness and in health."

After leading me back to the campsite, he spreads one blanket on the ground next to the fire and covers me with another. Despite the fever, I burrow deeper into the bed and fixate on the fire's nervous jig.

I don't eat any of the hare that Sophia hauls back to our camp. Gabe collects water in a bowl he fashioned out of tree bark, but

I can't drink. He becomes firm in his efforts to sustain me, saying I won't make it through the night if I don't cooperate, and I force myself to sip the water until it's gone.

Gabe stays up with me all night. Sophia grabs snatches of sleep here and there, but spends most of the darkest hours with us. The firelight makes her look older, somehow—or maybe it's just our treacherous circumstances chiseling away at her youth like whatever natural phenomenon was responsible for shaping the rocks towering over us.

Dawn makes its inevitable return, but my outlook is far from sunny. I pull the blanket up to my ears, but it doesn't put a dent in my discomfort. Gabe pulls me into his embrace. In doing so, he reveals his body to be less robust than I remember it. The blunt points of his hips become daggers against my back. Whatever's happening to us, it has nothing to do with the earth or her perennial perils.

Gabe lifts my hand to his face and squints at my ring. Then he sits up and studies it a little more closely.

I open my eyes as best I can, but everything within a twenty-foot radius is enveloped in a pale white aura.

"What?" I croak.

Gabe glances at me and folds my fingers protectively in his.

"There's something wrong with your ring," he says in a husky voice.

I blink furiously, trying to clear my vision. Sure enough, by the time my eyes adjust, I'm shocked to discover that my finger is black. I try to remove the ring, but it lodges itself more deeply into my skin, practically sinking into the bone below.

"Take it off, and she dies."

Gabe jerks his head sideways. Beside me, Sophia is petrified with fear. I imagine this was how the hare looked last night, right before she drove a rock through its skull and put an end to its misery.

Ansel looms over us, causing Gabe to stiffen. He lays a hand on my hip, but I'm afraid his gentle reassurance won't be enough to deter a being that materialized out of thin air.

"Were my instructions not clear?" Ansel asks after a second of tense silence.

I try to sit up, but Gabe applies the faintest pressure to my shoulder, coaxing me back to the ground.

Ansel cocks his head at me.

"You seem unwell," he observes, shifting his focus to Gabe. A look of disapproval clouds Ansel's gaze. "Surely it couldn't have anything to do with your companion's desire to prolong your little wilderness escapade."

Gabe leaps to his feet.

"You did this," he snaps, stepping over me in order to confront Ansel. "You sent that malevolent to kill Sophia, and you made Sarah sick. You can punish me all you want, but keep them out of it."

"Interesting." Ansel nods. "A hasty conclusion, I must say, but not an altogether unreasonable one."

"What good does any of this do you?" Gabe motions to Sophia and I. "There has to be a better way to make a point."

Ansel chuckles and walks over to the fire pit.

He collects a handful of fine, white ash and offers the remains of last night's fire to the passing wind. As the dust particles are lifted from his palm, a large, transparent orb appears. Sophia stands up and cautiously approaches the spherical illusion. The orb is filled with images—train wrecks, plane crashes, collapsed buildings. What I initially presumed to be the wind is actually the sound of people dying.

"What the hell was all of that?" Gabe asks.

"That," Ansel says, brushing his hands together, "was a preview of things to come—murder, mayhem, madness. And all because the malevolents have been allowed to multiply."

"If you're so powerful," Gabe spits, "why don't you stop them?"

"Why should I? They're doing a remarkable job." To me, he sighs and says, "But of course, you really can have too much of a good thing. I had assumed my orders would be carried out in a prompt and efficient manner, but clearly there's been a misunderstanding."

Gabe explains, "We've been on the run for days. Now's not exactly a great time to rally the troops."

"Oh, to the contrary, Mr. Conway—it's a wonderful time. Who do you suppose is influencing the media?"

"The justice system, of course."

"And who controls them?"

Gabe is silent, digesting Ansel's implications. Finally, he says, "This has nothing to do with the malevolents."

"Of course it does. I've given them unlimited range. They can assume any form they wish. Do you honestly believe you could cook up this much trouble on your own?" Ansel levels his gaze at Gabe. "Stop running, and they'll stop chasing you."

"You know it doesn't work that way. The malevolents won't stop until they get what they want."

"Then I suppose you have no choice. An organized resistance is imperative."

"And you're going to continue hounding us until it happens?"

"I wouldn't describe it as hounding. All I'm doing is following up."

"Sarah is sick," Gabe says, his anger building, "how do you expect her to act on your orders when she can't even feed herself?"

"Have you considered asking for help?"

"We're wanted criminals. If the wrong person sees us, jail will be the only outcome."

"You're thinking too linearly about this. I've endowed each of you with powers that transcend earthliness and mortality. You can call on anyone you want."

"And how do we know it won't cost us a place in the hereafter?"

Ansel smirks. "Where do you think the help is coming from?"

"I don't believe it," Gabe says, turning back to me. "We're going to get you help, but it won't be from him, or anyone he knows."

"You're working on borrowed time, Mr. Conway," Ansel reminds him. "Compliance or insubordination—those are your options. I suggest you choose wisely."

By the time the sun peeks over the horizon, Ansel is long gone.

I stare down at my fingers. The necrosis that was once spreading through my hand has receded, leaving my skin sleek and unmarred. Time is slipping away from me, not just in the metaphorical sense, but in the physical sense, too, like water pulling back from the shore at low tide, dragging sand and free floating debris behind it.

Gabe helps me to my feet and holds me until my legs regain their strength. Then we gather our belongings and continue walking toward the mountains.

33

On our third day in the desert, I've nearly succumbed to my mysterious illness. I lie in my makeshift bed with Gabe's limbs twisted around my body and his face buried in my hair, which muffles his sporadic sobs. He holds me tightly as I slip away from him, breath by cloudy breath, and all I can think about as the walls close in around me is how miserably I have failed.

○

"Wake up, Sarah."

I awaken on a stretcher, swaddled in several layers of blankets. I glance out the window just as the rugged, untamed wilderness gives way to long, curling ribbons of asphalt and skyscrapers that glisten in the sun as we pass.

I search for Gabe and Sophia and find them sitting on the opposite side of the helicopter looking dirty and spent. Relief slithers through me, followed quickly by a crushing wave of panic.

I try to sit up, but the straps are too tight. I begin to thrash, desperate to free myself in spite of any injuries, when the paramedic who originally woke me lays a hand on my shoulder and gently coaxes me back into a horizontal position.

"Take it easy," he says in a mellifluous voice, holding me down until I surrender. "You're okay. You're safe now—and just in time, too."

"Where are we?" I look at Gabe. "How did they find us?"

The paramedic explains, "Your friend here flagged us down. You appeared to be in distress, so we agreed to transport you back to the city. We'll be landing soon."

Gabe hovers over the stretcher with a serene expression on his face. His eyes are lucid and glassy with emotion as he feels for my hand under the blankets, causing my stomach to stir with a flurry of competing emotions.

"Do you trust me?" he asks in a whisper.

I nod. I don't have a choice, and even if I did, I'm not in any condition to pursue it. Gabe, Sophia, and I are in this together, bound by our superhuman abilities and the knowledge that Ansel is counting on us to restore order in the known universe.

Held down and helpless to defend myself, the dread hits me like a humid summer day. I strain against the imposition of the nylon belts, but they hold fast. If I breathe any harder, I'll surely hyperventilate.

Gabe cups my face in his hands in an effort to soothe me, but all it doesn't help. I jerk my head sideways, liberating myself from his calloused caress, only to have the paramedic tighten the straps until my limbs tingle.

Gabe turns my head toward him and brings his mouth to my ear. "Just trust me, Sarah," he whispers.

He returns to his seat. Beside him, Sophia shifts her hair out of her eyes and goes back to admiring the view. When my gaze catches hers, she gives me a subtle nod, making me wonder if she and Gabe have a plan that I don't know about.

When we touch down on the helipad a few minutes later, I've managed to get a handle on my runaway emotions. Although I'm still quaking in my blanket cocoon, I'm able to take several deep breaths. As I'm lowered to the rooftop and escorted to the elevator by a blizzard of white coats, the fear I've fought so hard to suppress gurgles up again. Gabe and Sophia follow me in, and as the door slides shut, I feel his hand wriggle beneath the covers to find mine.

I'm wheeled into a room and fussed over by a slew of doctors and nurses, who banter about their weekend plans in between evaluating my symptoms. I'm swept away in a landslide of technicalities, and after some time, given a robust cocktail of medications to combat what has evolved into a serious—and potentially fatal—infection.

And then they put me in a room of my own and leave me there.

I sit up and appraise my antiseptic prison. The IV line embedded in my hand has been affixed with clear, itchy, unbreathable tape, and it pinches my skin every time I move. I follow the line over the bedrail and up the metal pole to a bag dripping with a transparent solution. Another, slightly smaller bag is suspended behind it, and it's filled with a toxic-looking yellow elixir that goes only by AR40.

I flip the sheets off my body. Lowering the bedrail, I swing my legs over the edge and stare at my bare feet through the stars sprinkling my vision. I look around for my clothes, but the only thing in this room that belongs to me is the cold, unyielding realization that I'm being treated for something far more sinister than a run-of-the-mill parasitic infection.

In a panic, I check my left hand—the one tethered to the IV stand—and find my Keepsake missing.

A man in a flowing white coat appears in the doorway; he's wielding a clipboard and chewing absently on the earpiece of his glasses. When our eyes connect, he gives me a trite smile and tucks the paperwork under his arm.

"What did you do to me?" I ask as he slips his glasses back onto his face. "And where are all my things?"

"Your things?" he says, consulting the clipboard.

"My personal effects—my clothes, my ring, all of that."

"Not to worry. You won't be needing any of that here." He gives me a long, calculating look.

I set my jaw. "The ring was a gift from my husband," I fib, "and I'd like it back, please."

"Interesting," the doctor says, lifting the stethoscope from around his neck, "it's not the first of its kind I've seen today." He holds up the instrument. "May I?"

I look him over, from his crop of thin, peppery hair to the meticulously creased khakis he wears under his doctor's coat, and give a tiny nod of consent.

The aging practitioner applies the stethoscope to my chest and tells me to breathe deeply. I do as he says, but I'm wary, especially when my mind circles back to my ring. It's not the kind of jewelry you can buy on planet earth; the stone isn't even made from organic material, and the band is engraved with a pattern as unique as a human fingerprint—my fingerprint, that is.

Now I understand why I've been robbed.

He moves the stethoscope around my chest, repeating his simple instructions with each new position. When his attention momentarily drifts elsewhere, I continue my assessment of his outfit. To my horror, I discover a large syringe filled with a pale blue liquid lying at the bottom of his coat pocket.

"Nervous?" he asks.

"What makes you say that?"

The doctor removes the scope and drapes it over his shoulders again.

"Your heart took a bit of stumble there for a second. I thought perhaps you might have been… concerned about something."

I hold his gaze. "No, doctor. Not a thing." My thumbnail catches the corner of the tape and I carefully begin to peel it back, all the while keeping my eyes trained on his.

The doctor's hand moves to his pocket. "In that case—"

I tear the tape off my hand and yank the needle out of my skin. The doctor topples like toy blocks as I shove him out of the way and run as fast as my legs will carry me out the door.

I find Gabe in a room down the hall. He's alert but surprisingly mellow, perched on the side of his bed with a pair of tubes burrowing into his hand. He looks up as soon as I appear in the doorway, but his excitement is rapidly extinguished by the abrasive quality of my voice.

"Sarah—"

"No time for talking. Just trust me." Without warning, I seize his hand and rip off the tape, inspiring a yowl of pain from my hopelessly flustered companion. A perfectly round glob of blood forms on his skin as I remove the needle amidst the ruckus of frantic doctors scrambling to locate me.

"What are you doing?" Gabe asks.

My eyes flicker over his ashen expression.

"Getting you out of here. These people aren't on our side." I point to the bag of AR40. "They know the truth. They know we're not like them."

With Gabe liberated, I inch toward the door, pausing to check in both directions before taking his hand and leading him down the hall.

Sophia has been given a room of her own too, but someone has turned off the lights and shut the door—for what reason, I couldn't tell you, although I suspect the AR40 has something to do with it.

She doesn't stir as we enter the room. A vivid purple contusion is blooming on her neck and her face is slick with sweat. I try desperately to wake her, but she lapses into incoherent mumbling and goes unconscious seconds later.

"They've already given her the injection," I say as Gabe attempts to shake Sophia from her medicated slumber. Outside, the voices are growing louder.

Gabe hoists Sophia into his arms. Her bare legs are mottled with bruises and the skin on her arms is laced with scratches.

Until now, I hadn't realized the extent of the damage done to her lithe little body.

I usher Gabe through the door. He pauses to adjust his grip on Sophia and then assumes a rigorous pace as we search for an exit, or at the very least a place to hide. Despite being unencumbered, I'm struggling to keep up with him.

Gabe turns to me. "I hope you have a plan."

"I wish."

"What's this about an injection, anyway? I didn't get an injection."

"But you would've. Don't you see what's happening here? They're exterminating us, Gabe. They know we're... different."

"Who's exterminating us?"

I reply without thinking. "The malevolents." I catch Gabe's perturbed expression. "Ansel said the malevolents can assume any form, right? So who's to say they aren't masquerading as doctors?"

"That's absurd. The doctors are just doctors and they're all following protocol."

"By pumping us full of chemicals?"

"If that's what it takes, sure."

I grab his elbow and pull him to a stop.

"How could you?" I say, gesturing to Sophia. "Gabe, look at her. Look at us. This isn't normal." I hold up my left hand. "They took my ring. Apparently I'm not the only one with a Keepsake around here."

This seems to pique Gabe's curiosity. He adjusts his grip on Sophia as we resume walking.

"Did you ask for it back?" he wonders.

"Of course I did. But the doctor told me I wouldn't need it. Do you know what that means, Gabe? It means he knows the truth. A Catcher without a Keepsake is practically blind."

A steep crescendo of voices cuts our conversation short. Gabe and I duck down an empty hallway and shoulder through a set of doors leading to a large room that looks like it was abandoned mid-renovation. Plastic curtains partition the stuffy space, which is dark and littered with scraps of demolished drywall. We pick our way across the floor, watching for stray nails and fragments of glass, until we discover a table carpeted with construction plans in the corner.

I sweep the papers onto the floor and motion for Gabe to lay Sophia on the table, which he does with noticeable care. Then he steps aside so I can check her over.

"Sophia?" I say quietly, wiping a stream of saliva from her lips. I massage her cheeks until the circular motion of my thumbs drives away the last of her drowsiness.

Her hazel eyes flutter open. She squints at me, and then Gabe, before attempting to sit up.

"Careful." I gently coerce her back down. "How do you feel?"

Sophia rubs her head in the same spot where her welt had bloomed on her first night in the creek.

"Does your head hurt?" I ask her.

Sophia nods. "I don't understand. I thought I'd healed."

I turn to Gabe. "How's your leg?"

"Fine."

Sophia tries to sit up again, but is quickly thwarted by a wave of pain. I pry back her fingers, subsequently uncovering a glistening red gash slashed across her scalp.

"What happened after they took you to your room?" I ask.

Sophia shields the injury while Gabe roots around for something to staunch the bleeding.

"I don't know. I don't remember." She licks her lips and blinks back tears.

"Did a doctor come in and talk to you?" I persist as Gabe nudges my arm. I accept a dirty rag from his outstretched hand. It's not ideal, but it'll have to do.

I give the rag to Sophia, who winces when the fabric meets her skin.

"I don't... I mean, I don't think—" Her eyes widen and fly over to me. "He hit me."

"Who hit you?"

"The doctor."

"What did he look like?" I cover her hand with mine and apply the faintest bit of pressure to her scalp, which causes Sophia to squirm.

She combs her memories as Gabe crosses his arms and patrols the deserted floor.

"Doctorly," Sophia says, trying to pull away from the pressure on her head, "tall, kind of old, white coat."

"Beige pants?"

"I think so."

"And his hair—was it a silver colour?"

She nods. "Did he come see you, too?"

"Briefly. He didn't stay long… or rather, I didn't stay long." She gives me a skeptical look, to which I reply, "He was going to give me an injection of some sort, and so, I ran."

"Injection." Sophia appears to reflect on this a moment longer. Her eyes grab mine. "Was it a weird blue substance?"

My stomach is doing more flips than a circus performer. "Yes, exactly. And the AR40 was yellow."

"He tried to inject me too, right before—" Sophia breaks off and touches a finger to her scalp once again. "He must've hit me. I don't remember it exactly, but…" She shakes her head. "When I saw the needle, I panicked. I hate needles. Do you think he did something?"

"You mean like bash your head in so you couldn't fight back? Yes. Yes, I do."

I remove the rag, turn it inside out, and reapply it to Sophia's wound. I'm queasy with rage and fear, and now I can't shake the image of an unscrupulous practitioner flooding Sophia's system with unidentified toxins.

I look away until the thought clears. On the table, Sophia gives me a look of concern.

"What was in the needle, Sarah?"

I sigh. "I don't know."

Sophia's eyes wander to something in the background. Gabe has finished his assessment of the site and is now making his way back over to us with his arms still linked together against his chest.

"I don't understand," he says, "where is everyone?"

"Maybe the project got cancelled," I reply.

"No, I mean, where are the other Catchers? You said there were others, right?"

"There are others?" Sophia says in a voice that is equal parts appalled and hopeful.

"I don't know for sure," I say, turning my attention back over to Sophia's cut, which is sticky with clotting blood, "but the doctor—or whatever he was—said he'd seen other rings that looked just like mine. That can't be a coincidence, right? I mean, Keepsakes are so—"

"Rare?" Gabe proffers. "Otherworldly?"

"Exactly."

Sophia dodges my hand and props herself up on her elbows. "So, wait. If there are others, then that means—"

"We're not alone, which means we have allies. And if we have allies, then that means—"

"We can build an army." Gabe nods slowly at me. "Looks like you might be able to pull this off after all."

"How? I don't have a Keepsake."

"You don't need one. Just look for the people who've been injected." He points to the flower of veins on Sophia's neck, which she automatically covers with her hand.

"And if they're all unconscious?" I say.

"The only reason Sophia was unconscious was because of blunt force trauma. We don't know what the injection does, although I'm sure we will soon enough." To her, he says, "I just hope it isn't something catastrophic."

A look of terror comes over her slender face. I place my hand on her knee in a gesture of consolation.

"Okay," I say to no one in particular, "so where do we start? If we go back out there, it might be the last thing we do."

"We don't even have proper clothes," Sophia protests. "Shouldn't we try and find something to wear first?"

"She's right," Gabe agrees. "These gowns will make us easy targets. If we're going to blend in, we need to look the part."

"What are you suggesting?"

A sober look comes over Gabe's face. "Something tells me you're not going to like it."

"I don't think we have much choice at this point."

His gaze waffles between us. Then he sighs and says, "We steal them… from the doctors."

"Oh, no. Gabe—"

"Look, you just said we're out of options. I know it's not a perfect plan, but time's not on our side right now. Either we rob the doctors or we stick out like sore thumbs."

I relent and angle back to Sophia.

"It's not the worst thing we've done," Gabe adds with a sly smile.

I mirror his congenial gesture, and then nod.

"Maybe you should go first," I suggest. "That way, you can show us how it's done."

"It would be my pleasure." Gabe gives an exaggerated bow, making Sophia giggle. We watch his ghostly figure navigate the plastic curtains, and soon he's out of sight.

34

Gabe fastens the last button on the crisp white shirt and turns his attention over to the cufflinks. Ten minutes ago, I watched him drag an unconscious doctor into our dusty hideout and strip him down to his underwear. He then snapped the dust out of the shirt and pants before wrestling both pieces of clothing onto his body, surprising me with both his efficiency and stone-cold indifference. Soon, Sophia and I will need to hunt down our own changes of clothes, but for now, I'm too busy wondering what to do with the body.

"Will you be okay out there?" Gabe asks as he stuffs the shirttails into the waist of his pants.

I nod. "It's Sophia I'm worried about."

He pulls on the socks and shoes and draws the laces tight.

"She'll be okay," he assures me as he brushes the dust from his knees. "If she can survive several days in the bush, then she can steal clothes from a stranger."

Gabe gestures to the doctor, wearing nothing but a pair of briefs. Chalky white dust has settled into his eyebrows and the hair on his head is tousled and dull with age. I keep expecting him to jolt up, but he's as still as a board and doesn't seem likely to move anytime soon.

"When you attack, attack from behind. If you land a blow in the right spot, you should be able to knock them out cold the first time. And if that doesn't work..." Gabe's eyes sweep over my face. "Well, you can figure it out. Aim for the back of the head and you shouldn't have any trouble."

I lean around one of the curtains to check on Sophia, who's sitting on the table with her legs crossed at the ankles. Her slender fingers are restless and dotted with blood as she fiddles with the edge of her hospital gown. Without knowing the reason for the injection, it's hard to anticipate how she'll react to it. For all I know, she already has.

Gabe reaches down and takes the doctor by the ankles. He then hauls him behind a pile of scrap drywall, carving a wide trail through the powdery residue coating the floor.

"That should do it. Sweet dreams, comrade." Gabe brushes his hands together and turns back to me. "Ready?"

"Not at all."

"You'll be fine. And don't worry about Sophia. I'll keep an eye on her."

Outside the wing, the halls are hauntingly quiet. Safety hazards aside, I'm grateful for my bare feet, which mute my harried footfalls. I take short, cautious strides, pausing often to evaluate my surroundings. The distant trill of a telephone spurs me on.

Just as I'm about to turn down another hallway, a soft, rhythmic squeak grabs my attention. I hold my breath, straining to pinpoint the source of the sound. I need to find a place to hide, and fast.

I look around quickly and spot a vending machine in a waiting room on my left. As the footsteps become louder, I duck behind the refrigerator in time to avoid being seen by a young nurse in sky-blue scrubs.

I peek around the corner at her shrinking figure. Then I shadow her closely, matching her curt, determined strides as she steers left and heads toward the abandoned wing.

My takedown is swift and savage. Clamping my left hand over her mouth, I use my right arm to lock her in a chokehold until she loses consciousness. I look around again before laying her gently on the floor.

Something in her misshapen form stirs my suspicion. When I flatten two fingers against her neck, I find an unsettling stillness where the flutter of a pulse should be instead.

Bile rises in my throat as I stare down at her lifeless body. Memories drip from her fingers in big, shiny, ink-like drops. The story of her life is being unwritten before my very eyes, plucked word for word from the invisible pages of her existence. It takes everything I have not to scream.

"There you are," Gabe says when I appear a few minutes later. He's sitting on the table with Sophia, whose eyes are drooping with exhaustion.

I lay the body of the young nurse outside the curtained room and turn to them in horror.

"She's dead," I croak.

Gabe stares at me, wide-eyed and speechless.

He leaps off the table. Behind him, Sophia blinks rapidly as she tries to process what she's seeing.

Gabe crouches and checks for a pulse. When his search turns up empty, he flashes on me with an incinerating look.

"Sarah—"

"It was an accident. Gabe, I swear, I was just trying to knock her out."

"Oh, you knocked her out, all right." He pushes himself to his feet and rubs the back of his neck. "Okay. Let's not panic just yet. Maybe we can still revive her."

"How?"

"I don't know. I'm just trying to diffuse the situation." Gabe's whole body shrugs. "We don't have much time. You get dressed and I'll hide the body."

He helps me to remove her clothes and I slip behind a curtain to change. Not wanting another mishap, Gabe then vanishes to hunt down our third victim. The girl he brings back draped over his shoulder is only a few years older than Sophia and drooling from the impact he's delivered to her skull. He drops her like a sack of grain and waits for Sophia to do the honours.

Gabe approaches me as I stand over the deceased nurse, feeling dirty and sinful in her still-warm clothes.

Sensing my unease, Gabe rests his hands in his pockets and takes a deep breath to alleviate some of the tension in the air.

"Ansel will understand," he says to the corpse, "he'll know it had to be done. Besides, what's a war without casualties?"

"Impossible." I unlink my arms and turn to him. "I can't do this, Gabe. I'm not cut out to lead an army."

"Yes, you are. You wouldn't have made it this far if you weren't."

"But what do I have to show for it? You'd think by now we'd have made some actual progress."

"Who says we haven't? You survived not one, not two, but *three* near-death experiences. You saved me from going to jail, and you gave Sophia a chance to escape her broken home. I think it's safe to say the victories outnumber the failures here."

Gabe places a hand on my shoulder. "This wasn't your fault," he says. "For all you know, it was Ansel's will. Maybe he's just doing this to test you."

I shrug, trying to loosen Gabe's grip. His warmth seeps through the shirt and into my skin, reminding me of my own mortality as I search for somewhere to plant my gaze. I refuse to cry at all, but especially in front of him.

Sophia saunters over to examine my victim. She's thin but healthy, with smooth, sandy skin and long legs fortified by endless trips around the hospital. She has a pale copper beauty mark about two inches above her right hip and a necklace shaped like a child's doodle languishing between her breasts. Her beauty is raw and simple, interrupted only by the pinkish tinge to her neck where my elbow had tightened on her trachea. I can't look at her anymore, so I reach for the discarded gown and spread it over her body.

"What now?" Sophia asks.

"Now," I say with a sigh, "we find the others."

Her gaze slides down to the floor. "What do we do about her?"

On my left, Gabe bends to reach for her ankles.

"Try not to worry too much. Like I said, Ansel is full of mystery and murderous tendencies."

"But he didn't kill her, Gabe. I did."

"Ansel kills everyone. It's his job."

He proceeds to drag her away. The gown snags on a corner and I wait until Gabe has laid her next to the doctor before covering her again.

I study the outline of the nurse's nose through the white fabric veiling her face. As the dust settles, so does the realization that I've grossly overestimated my own abilities. I'm too flawed to be a Catcher, and too empty to be human. So what does that make me?

"I'm sorry," I say.

"Are you?"

A figure manifests in my peripheral vision. Sunlight streams through the gaps in her hair, giving her a fractured, angelic glow. But it doesn't stop at her edges—it flows through her like water, lending a strange opacity to an otherwise solid form. The source of the voice steps forward, deserting her spotlight as she drifts toward me.

"I am," I say as the young nurse stands next to her body. "I swear I didn't mean for this to happen."

"Any way you can put me back?"

"No."

"Why not?"

"Because I'm not authorized to do so. And even if I were…"

The nurse looks past my shoulder. When Gabe sees her standing next to her vessel, he shakes off his surprise and turns to me for an explanation.

"So what's next?" she says as Gabe and I trade looks. "Should I go toward the light or…?"

"There is no light. In fact, there's nothing at the moment—just a big hollow void called the in-between. Let's just say the afterlife is under construction."

The nurse surveys the dilapidated room with palpable apathy. There are strict rules surrounding the care and transport of a human soul, without which we would undoubtedly descend into anarchy, but to my knowledge, there's no protocol for escorting an improperly claimed spirit. After all, Catchers aren't responsible for initiating the separation process. I would ask for clarification, but without my Keepsake my connection to The Establishment—or whatever's left of it—is spotty at best, and nonexistent at worst.

"The in-between, eh?" she finally says, studying her semi-transparent skin. "You'd think they'd have thought up a better name for it by now."

"It used to be called The Establishment, before the malevolents destroyed it. Ansel's working on salvaging what he can, but there are no guarantees." I force a smile for courtesy's sake. "What's your name?"

"Rebecca Harding. Yours?"

I make a mental note of her name and then say, "I'm Sarah. This is my partner Gabe, and the girl in the corner is Sophia."

"Are you ghosts, too?"

"Not exactly. Ansel has a pretty strict policy against hauntings."

"Is Ansel a friend of yours?"

"Not anymore," Gabe chimes in, his lips twisting into a grimace. "Hell if he ever was."

"He's our boss," I explain. "We used to work for him at The Establishment, but when that fell apart, we ended up here. We're still not entirely sure how it happened, but we're almost certain the malevolents are to blame."

"You're saying a lot of things I don't understand," Rebecca says. "If you're not ghosts, then what are you, exactly?"

Gabe answers for me. "Technically, we're Spirit Catchers—"

"That means nothing to her, Gabe," I remind him. "We might as well keep it simple and call ourselves the undead."

"But we're not dead. We have heartbeats."

His voice rings with despair and sadness. I've made love to this man and tasted life on his lips. We're as alive as we're ever going to be, but only because there's no alternative.

I approach one of the windows and rest my forehead against the glass. I'm too close to see anything beyond my own reflection, and now there's a hazy circle of condensation blocking whatever remains of my view.

Gabe stands beside me as Rebecca continues to explore her environment.

"What are you thinking?" he asks.

I let out a long breath and watch it spread across the transparent barrier.

"That I'm too close to the problem to see a solution," I reply, minding my limited visibility. To test my theory, I take a couple of steps back from the window and watch the landscape come into focus, first in bold colour, and then in fine detail. I wonder if this approach would work on my current predicament.

I turn back to Rebecca, who's exercising her newfound permeability on a table saw in the corner. Ironically, the absence of danger has only made her more cautious. I watch her negotiate the next hazard with visible apprehension before directing my words back at Gabe.

"What if Ansel's not expecting an army of Catchers? What if he's expecting something else? Something... simpler."

Gabe crosses his arms. "What did you have in mind?"

"Even if we do manage to locate the other Catchers, there's no guarantee they'll cooperate after what Ansel did to them. But spirits don't have a choice—they can't stay here, and they don't know what comes next. All they can do is what we tell them."

"And what are we going to tell them?"

"That a supreme being with questionable but altruistic motives is building an empire that defies the laws of nature, and that he needs our help to rid the world of evil."

"And if they ask what's in it for them?"

"I'll tell them exactly what Ansel told me: anyone who helps fight the good fight will be given a chance to regenerate."

"That assumes this isn't a trap. Even we don't know that for sure." He shakes his head and separates his arms. "Why bring Ansel into this at all? Why not just convince them to follow you?"

"Why would anyone follow me? I'm just a pawn."

"So are they. Ansel's not human. He's never been human, and he never will be human. Who do you honestly think they're going to trust: a godly divinity with no real connection to earth, or someone who looks, sounds, and acts exactly like them?" Gabe nods, keeping his gaze steady on me. "We're Spirit Catchers. This is what we do. If there was ever a time we needed the spirits, this is it."

I nod slowly, digesting everything he's thrown at me. As Catchers we may have more power, but our energy is inorganic. Human spirits are the purest and most powerful force in the universe. All they need is someone to organize them.

"If Ansel didn't want you to lead, he wouldn't have given you a human form," Gabe continues. "Familiarity is an advantage. Why waste it?"

"Not that I should have to remind you, but my human form has given me no shortage of trouble."

"And every time it does, you find a way to heal yourself. But Ansel didn't choose the human form for its infallibility. He chose it because that's the one the spirits will recognize."

"In that case..." I turn back to the room, where Rebecca is flickering in and out of view. I scan the space again, and turn back to Gabe a second later.

"Where's Sophia?" I ask him.

He straightens and looks around, but there's nothing to see except for a single, lonely spirit who's poring over a rusty nail with exaggerated interest.

"Sophia?" Gabe calls, right before I shush him. "Where is she?"

"Hey, Rebecca?" She looks up. "Did you see which way Sophia went?"

Confusion crinkles her brow. "Who?"

"The girl who was with us," I clarify.

Rebecca's expression is eerily blank.

"I didn't see a girl," she replies, "just you two."

I spin back to Gabe, but he's already striding toward the door, churning my dread along with the dust.

"She couldn't have gone far," he says as I hurry to keep up. "If we're lucky, she's just stepped out for some air and isn't wandering around in a drugged-up stupor." To Rebecca, he says, "You're coming with us. I'll be damned if I lose two people in the same breath."

"She can't come with us, Gabe. What if someone sees her?"

"Who's going to see her? She's a spirit, for Christ's sake. No one can see her but us."

"You don't know that. All it takes is one medium to blow our cover. Do you really want to take that risk right now?"

"Would you prefer she stay here and haunt the place?"

I turn to Rebecca and explain, "No one can see you. I mean *no one*. Keep your distance from us and try not to walk through anything."

"What's a medium?" she asks.

"Someone who can see spirits as clearly as they can see living, breathing people."

Gabe adds, "They're a blight on the trade and a pain in our collective ass. But that doesn't matter. What matters now is finding Sophia before someone else does."

I nod. Even in nursing garb, the needle bruise will be a dead giveaway. I can only imagine what will happen if someone encounters her roaming the halls, and it's not a pretty picture at all.

Gabe is the first one to exit the wing, followed by Rebecca. I steal a breath and a moment to center myself, and then abandon the safe haven without another look back.

35

Gabe insists on splitting up, even at the risk of losing one another. After a few parting words, he veers down a narrow hallway and disappears around the corner, leaving Rebecca and I to scour the east end of the hospital alone. I'm worried about Gabe, but I'm more worried about Sophia, especially since she knows better than to wander off without telling us where she's going. I keep envisioning the needle mark on her neck and wonder if her recent scuffle with the doctor had anything to do with her sudden disappearance.

"So this girl," Rebecca says, falling into step beside me, "who is she, exactly? And what's going to happen if we don't find her?"

"We used to work together. I found her outside the police station a few days after The Establishment collapsed and she's been tagging along ever since."

"The police station, huh?" A look of mockery comes over her face. "Seems like you're no stranger to the law, although I'm sure it'll come in handy when you're on trial for murder."

"First of all, it was an accident. And even if it weren't, who's going to press charges? You?"

"Why not? I can see the headline now: Vengeful Ghost Gets Justice." Rebecca slants me with a smug grin. Even if she is just trying to lighten the mood, I'm too busy fretting over Sophia's safety to flatter the joke with a reaction.

"You won't press charges," I say, growing tired of her presence. "Maybe your family will, but you'll be long gone by the time they ever see the inside of a courtroom."

Rebecca tears her eyes from my face. I follow her gaze as it settles on a solid grey door about six feet to her right. "Should we check the bathrooms?" she asks.

"Yes."

She starts walking. Before she can get too far, though, I reach for her arm and reel her back in.

"Rule number one," I say as she rips free, "never transcend a barrier unless you can see what's on the other side. You never know who might be watching."

"You mean like a medium?"

"Exactly. They're not as bad as malevolents, but you should still avoid them. Point is, always be aware of your surroundings. Just because the Living can't see you doesn't mean you're invisible."

After glancing in both directions, I lay my hand against the door. A large circle forms around my fingers, revealing the room on the other side. Rebecca's eyes widen accordingly.

"Magic?" she asks.

"Space compression. You'll learn all about this during orientation." I remove my hand and the temporary window fades from sight. "You're clear. Make it quick."

With a perfunctory nod, Rebecca steps over the threshold. I don't even hear her feet hit the floor.

A moment later, she reappears looking confused and dismayed.

"She's not in there," she announces.

I turn away and continue walking, forcing Rebecca to catch up.

A cacophony of voices greets us at the next turn, so I shove Rebecca into a supply closet and urge her to remain quiet. She may be a ghost, but they have a reputation for being noisy—or at least, this one does.

Hunkered down in the dark, we watch a pair of shadows creep across the patch of light on the floor. The voices evolve from a distant murmur to a loud, raucous banter as the doctors pass, oblivious to our presence. When I'm certain they have no intention of returning, I pull myself up and banish the dust from the back of my pants. Or Rebecca's pants, I suppose.

"So this is your grand plan?" Rebecca taunts. "Hide in a supply closet and hope for the best?"

I shrug. "It beats the alternative."

"Being dead?"

"Being turned into a lab rat. The doctors have been handing out injections like candy. The problem is we don't know what the injections do. All we know is they're being given in combination with a mysterious substance called AR40."

"You mean Alien Repellent?"

My eyes snap toward her face. I wonder why she didn't say something sooner.

"You know about this?" I ask, no doubt looking every bit as surprised as I feel.

Rebecca lifts a shoulder. "Not really. It's a fairly new cure."

"Cure for what, exactly?"

"For foreign sicknesses. And by foreign I mean not of this world."

She gazes down at her lap and continues.

"A few weeks ago, we noticed a large influx of patients with self-inflicted injuries. This set off some alarm bells and prompted a hospital-wide quarantine to identify and isolate the cause of the outbreak.

"The first batch of patients was subjected to a battery of tests. Some time later we started to notice that these people could heal themselves instantaneously. This sparked a wave of panic and several doctors began toying with the idea of introducing the AR40. It's not a cheap solution, but it's ninety-nine percent effective, especially when combined with CX10."

"CX10?"

"Compound X. Recent blood tests revealed an unidentified compound that supposedly allows the alien subjects to manipulate time and space. The CX10 keeps the patient calm so that the AR40 can be safely administered."

"So it's a sedative?"

"Partly. We use it to manage pain. The drowsiness is just a side effect."

My head is whirling. On the other side of the closet, Rebecca gazes idly around at our cramped quarters. She's staggeringly indifferent to my mounting anxiety, and it dulls my guilt about killing her.

"What does the AR40 do?" I ask her.

"It purifies the body," she explains, "everything from bones to soft tissue. Of course, I wasn't part of the team that developed it, but from what I understand the solution basically replaces all of the cells in an affected body with new cells—right after it destroys the old ones. The process can take up to forty days, hence AR40."

"And the CX10?"

"Ten doses spread over forty days, or one every four days. By the end of the third day, most people are pleading for mercy." Rebecca heaves a deep but inauthentic sigh, presumably for dramatic effect.

My knees go weak as I sink to the floor. Sophia could be anywhere by now, and who knows what condition she's in? For that matter, where the hell is Gabe?

Rebecca checks her surroundings before stepping into the hall. After I've pulled myself together, I open the door and slip outside, where Rebecca is standing in front of a bulletin board poring over a bunch of pamphlets.

"We need to find Gabe and Sophia," I tell her.

"What about the rest of your people?"

"Do you know where they are?"

She skates a finger down the edge of a brochure while I wait for her to speak.

"Most of them don't make it to the fortieth day," she says in a deadpan voice. "The human body isn't exactly designed to be recoded on a cellular level."

"So you're saying—"

"It's not a cure, okay? It's genocide." She composes herself. "The doctors know it's not a cure. Hell, even the patients know it's not a cure. If you make it to forty days—and so far no one has—all that awaits you is a long, slow, agonizing death. It's far from ethical, but at least it keeps the masses calm."

"Has there been a lot of civil unrest?"

"What do you think? Our world's been flooded with people who can heal themselves and move objects with their minds. If that's not a pandemic, then I don't know what is." When I fail to reply, Rebecca adds, "It's been all over the news."

"Well, we've been avoiding TV like the plague, for obvious reasons."

She cocks her head, recognition wrinkling her brow.

"That's where I know you from," she says. "You're wanted for murder."

"I don't know about me, but Gabe certainly is. I should also add that it was an accident."

"What is with you two accidentally killing people?"

I shrug; I have to find Gabe and Sophia. The remaining Catchers I'll worry about later, once we've had a chance to wrap

315

our heads around everything. I wish I had my Keepsake to help me navigate, but for today, my instinct will have to do.

As the activity around us builds, I begin to feel uneasy. Crowds tend to possess a certain nervous energy as it is, but you don't usually see this much commotion in a hospital. Everyone is looking for us. It's only a matter of time before we're found.

Rebecca keeps her distance from me, but I can still feel her cool, clammy presence like a draft on the back of my neck. I know she's scared, but I'm in no position to comfort her right now.

As we pass a nurse's station, she stops to stare at her former coworkers. She raises a hand in greeting, but no one waves back. The reality of her circumstances sinks in as her arm falls straight at her side. Rebecca turns to me, but all I can do is watch.

"Can they see me?" she asks.

I glance at the women behind the desk to ensure they aren't looking before I shake my head.

A swarm of voices surges through the main entrance. I inch toward the wall and lean around the corner just as a horde of police officers comes barreling into the waiting room.

That's when I spot Gabe hurtling toward us, a pair of security guards hot on his heels. I motion for Rebecca to flee as Gabe shoots past, hooking me into a heart-pounding sprint that transforms our surroundings into a blur of colour.

We race across the hospital. Before long, Gabe drags me through a door and up an endless flight of stairs until we emerge on the roof. We've gained a slight lead on our pursuers, but it's not enough for me to catch my breath or process the magnitude of Gabe's error. We're trapped, and the voices in the stairwell are getting louder by the second.

"Where's Sophia?" I manage to choke out.

"I don't know." Gabe approaches the edge of the roof, causing my heart to flutter violently in protest.

He rushes back over to me. When our eyes meet, I see everything we've been fighting for going up in flames.

"We have to go back for Sophia," I say in a last-ditch effort to delay the inevitable.

Gabe seizes my shoulders. I can't believe it's come down to this. Until now, I didn't think we had anything left to give. I was wrong.

"If she found us once, she'll find us again," he assures me, his voice softening. "But right now, I need you to trust me."

The door bursts open. Gabe grabs my hand and tugs me toward our doom. I match him stride for stride, watching the skyline come into focus against the hazy arc of blue. I see the trees in a thousand shades of bronze and copper, and beneath that, a glinting sea of cars flowing like blood through the arteries of the city. The people are the last things I notice, and a second later we fling ourselves over the edge.

36

Wake up, Sarah.

Everything opens at once—my eyes, my airways, my mind. I'm lying on my back on an old concrete floor. On my right is a row of windows that goes on forever. On my left, there's nothing to see except for more concrete: concrete pillars, concrete walls, and a lattice of beams draped in cobwebs. I try to establish my location, but I'm too afraid to move.

The fall comes back in fragments: first the assault of the stairs on my knees, then the burn of the wind on my face as we tumbled through gravity's merciless clutches. By the time I'd concluded my descent, the tender embrace of oblivion had already swallowed me whole.

I sit up slowly and turn toward one of the windows. It's impossible to see anything through the dirty yellow glass, but a little bit of sunlight still manages to sneak through. I search for my shadow in the rectangular spotlight, but the only things standing between the window and the floor are a few particles of dust riding the shifting currents of air.

I look around for Gabe, but he's nowhere to be seen.

"Hello?" I call. My own voice answers back.

As the echo fades, a giggle takes its place. I turn toward the sound and find a young child with fiery red hair peering out at me from behind a column. Tiny white polka dots splatter her navy blue dress. I recognize the mismatched socks. It's the girl from the train, but what's she doing in a place like this?

I hold out my hand to her, but before I can get too close, she pushes away from the pillar and speeds off like a rabbit.

She leads me deep into the labyrinth. I push myself to catch up, but she's too quick to be caught. Before long, we desert the well-lit warehouse for a dark tunnel that reeks of sewage. The walls are covered in a slimy green residue and the air is so cold, it hurts just to breathe.

The tunnel eventually opens into a dank, windowless room bursting with activity. The little girl blends into the sea of bodies and is soon reunited with a young couple in the front row.

I gaze around incredulously. At the front of the room, a large man beats his hand against a stone podium as he speaks. Hundreds of people stand before him, nodding and cheering and waving their fists. I'm still trying to count the attendees when a comforting voice penetrates the man's tireless monologue.

"Sarah!"

Gabe fights his way through the crowd, ignoring the disapproving glares that come his way. As he emerges from the melee, I reach forward and wrap my arms around his shoulders. I'm so overcome with relief that it takes me a moment to realize that the man with the megaphone voice has suddenly stopped talking.

He clears his throat. Gabe and I direct our attention toward the front of the room, but I can tell from the edge to Gabe's energy that he isn't tolerating the interruption.

"Do you mind?" the man says in a tone that suggests he minds very much.

Gabe scowls. "No, but you certainly do."

The man furrows his brows. Gabe folds his arms, looking both bored and impatient as he waits for the speaker to continue.

"Rule number one of fighting the malevolents," the unidentified man says, piquing my interest, "nothing is more important than fighting the malevolents. If you don't understand this, then you're under no obligation to stay."

"With respect, comrade," Gabe says, smirking, "there are plenty of things more important than fighting the malevolents. If you don't understand this, then perhaps you should reconsider your role in this war."

"My role is not up for negotiation, and as far as I'm concerned, neither is yours."

"Gabe and I have been fighting this war far longer than you have," I chime in, "so I suggest you show some respect."

"And I suggest you stand down before you are forcibly removed from the premises."

Two beefy men converge on us. Before they can get too close, Gabe takes my hand and leads me into the crowd.

No one turns to look at us. They're all focused on their leader, whose gaze lingers on my face as I shift closer to Gabe.

"Where's Sophia?" I ask as the man soldiers on.

Gabe pretends not to hear me, even though we're standing close enough to touch.

"Is she okay?" I persist as he saws his gaze back and forth over the room. "Is she here?"

"I didn't see her," he whispers. "I looked everywhere, but I don't think she's here."

"Where is here?"

"No one knows," he replies, "but it's not the in-between."

I look around again. The man with a bloated sense of self-worth smolders with passion. His cheeks burn with rage. Despite his obvious fatigue, he continues fueling the frenzy with increasingly ambitious promises. His followers applaud wildly.

"Who is he?" I ask Gabe, hoping he can still hear me.

"I don't know," he calls back. "He never said what his name was."

Gabe continues, "After we jumped I woke up in an empty room. I didn't see you anywhere. I thought maybe you'd survived, somehow. Some time later, I saw this little girl. She told me to follow her, so I did. And that's how I ended up here."

"Did she have red hair?"

"Yes. Red hair, blue dress."

"They must be using her as bait."

Just when I think the crowd can't get any louder, it does. There's an intense pounding in my head and the lack of personal space is making my field hum with interference. I scan for an exit, but the only way out is the way we came in.

I begin to pull Gabe toward the tunnel. I wonder if he can feel it too—the tension in the air, and the lack of camaraderie that

Catchers usually exhibit when brought together for a common cause.

We elbow our way through the riotous group. We've nearly freed ourselves from the commotion when one of the guards intercepts us and abruptly shoves me back.

"No one leaves," he booms. I try to swat his hand away, but the guard grabs my arm instead, nearly wrenching it out of its socket.

Gabe tries to liberate me, but is swiftly apprehended by the second guard, who twists his arms behind his back and immobilizes him in an instant.

The clamor dies down. One by one, the heads swivel toward us, their faces painted red with exertion and thinly veiled condemnation.

The man huffs as he descends his podium. A gap forms in the crowd as he makes his way toward us. Gabe lunges forward again, only to be jerked back by a curt tug of the bigger guard's hands.

The man gives me an apologetic smile, which I don't reciprocate.

"Still working for the man, are we?" he says in a voice laced with pity. "You do know the malevolents were his idea, don't you?"

"Ansel did what he had to do," I say, quelling the desire to spit in his face, "and so will I—with or without your input."

He chuckles and turns back to the room, but the other spirits are as emotionless as gargoyles. In my periphery, the second guard seizes a handful of Gabe's hair and snaps back his head, eliciting a fierce growl of pain.

"It's a shame, really," the man is saying now, "something tells me you would've made a fine soldier."

"I already am."

"To what end? Has Ansel not exploited you at every turn?"

"You call it exploitation. I call it leveraging one's strength."

"Yes, he did say you have plenty of those." He clasps his hands behind his back and studies the floor. When our eyes meet again, his are blacker than a starless sky. "Perhaps you'd like to demonstrate?"

I look around the room. All the eyes staring back at me are pitch-black, except for Gabe's, which are wide with terror.

This isn't a spirit convention. It's a malevolent lair.

Gabe and I exchange looks. I don't know how many powers we have left, or if they will even work, but I'd rather go down fighting than give myself over to a room full of evil spirits masquerading as human beings.

The malevolents advance forward, eyeing us hungrily. Gabe's head is bent so far back I can clearly see the protrusion of his larynx in his throat. On my other side, the little girl with garish red hair is smiling, her innocent expression offset by her penetrating, ebony gaze. She raises a hand to wave at me. I nod once to acknowledge the gesture, then I direct my focus back to the man with the improperly fitted shirt, and grin.

"It would be my pleasure," I say, my hand forming a fist behind my back. From there, the orb begins. Gabe eyes me nervously, but I keep my gaze firmly planted on the man's face.

"You do realize you're outnumbered," he says mockingly. "If I were you, I'd admit defeat."

"Never. The world needs The Establishment."

"What the world needs is a little housekeeping," the man replies, pointed teeth bared in a devilish grin. "Wouldn't you rather be on the side that wins?"

"You'll never win. Even if you do manage to overpower Ansel, it won't be long before you engineer your own demise."

"Impossible. The more of us there are, the stronger we become."

"Desperation will eventually force you to turn on each other. When resources become scarce, you'll resort to cannibalism. Your numbers will dwindle and ours will rebound. It's the law of nature."

"Laws were made to be broken."

"And so were you."

I open my hand. The guard restraining me rears back as thousands of bright, blue bees descend on him. The second guard releases Gabe to swat at the insects buzzing around his head. It's no use: the bees sting him anyway, causing hundreds of blisters to form on his face and arms.

One by one, the blisters erupt. As the attack continues, the guard's human form falls away to reveal a hideous creature with charred skin and a skeletal physique. With one final, demonic cry, the malevolent is condemned to its vessel: the little girl with inhumanly red hair.

The remaining malevolents rise toward the ceiling like smoke. A long, black funnel siphons them into the little girl's mouth. She internalizes their wickedness before turning calmly to me. The room begins to implode around her, but she remains upright, smiling, and soaked in a river of black tears.

Her presence is like a magnet. It bends the beams in the walls, practically ripping the concrete from its steel skeleton. The ceiling buckles, groaning as the roof collapses on top of it.

I look down at the floor. A trickle of water slithers between my feet. I turn around. Sure enough, the water is coming from the tunnel—and it shows no signs of letting up.

I face the girl, who's smiling in the midst of the chaos.

"We have to let go now," I say as the water reaches my knees. Pale blue light shoots through the gaps between my fingers. Meanwhile, Gabe struggles to keep his balance. His face and hair are white from the dust raining down on him. As the water rises, he grabs one of the beams and holds on for dear life.

I open my hand, freeing the last of the bees. They shatter the girl like glass, scattering the shards in every direction.

As the water reaches my stomach, a vortex appears in the middle of the room, sweeping my legs out from under me. As I disappear beneath the surface, all I can see is darkness. Pieces of the vessel rake across my skin, cutting my arms as I'm sucked down into the depths of the drain.

I'm drowning.

As I lose consciousness, a face emerges from the shadows. My heart skips a beat, then another—not from suffocation, but from surprise.

Brody offers his hand, and I take it. We swim back toward the surface, where the water is warm enough to melt the ice crystals on my skin. Just when I think I'm going to succumb to a lack of oxygen, a hand grabs my arm and yanks me out of the water.

"I got you," Gabe says as I gasp for air. He wraps his arm around my body as the water begins to recede, taking Brody's memory with it.

The pressure finally eases long enough for us to regain our footing. Chunks of concrete splash into the water below, vanishing into a place where nothing can escape.

With nothing to support its weight, the ceiling decides to follow.

Gabe pushes me into the tunnel. With a final, mighty crack, the roof drops toward the floor, sealing the opening behind us.

37

The world outside the lair is bleak and desolate. We make our way down the road, passing parked cars and piles of garbage, but there isn't a single soul to speak of other than our own.

A storm is brewing. Lightning strobes against the sky, but it isn't thunder that follows the flash. Instead, each indistinct pulse releases a blood-curdling wail. Hundreds of faces are trapped behind what appears to be a giant sheet of glass, beyond which there is a dense layer of dust and debris. It looks like some kind of mega-orb, but instead of memories, it's filled with malevolents. Thousands of them.

"What is this place?" I ask.

Gabe climbs onto a nearby dumpster and gazes around. The wind whips my hair across my face just as he completes his surveillance and hops down off his perch.

"I don't know," he replies. Our eyes meet. "How are you holding up?"

"I've been worse."

"We need to find shelter." Gabe surveys our surroundings again and points to an abandoned shop wedged between two skyscrapers.

We cross the street and stride through the door. The old floor is littered with needles and there's so much dust that my throat burns with the effort of stifling a cough. I cover my nose with my shirt, but it does little to aid my breathing or block out the pungent odors.

Gabe flips the switch on the wall, to no avail. I'm still patrolling our hideout.

"Well, it's not a five-star resort, but at least it gets us out of the wind." He cups a hand over the lower half of his face and squints at the discarded syringes. "As long as we remain standing, we should be fine."

I take a seat on the counter. I've adjusted to the smell and the darkness, but not the feeling that the worst is yet to come.

Gabe sits down beside me. Aside from some rips in his shirt and a handful of nicks on his face, he's surprisingly unscathed for someone who just crawled out of a malevolent lair.

"So what do we do now?" I ask him.

"Look for the others?"

"There are no others."

"You don't know that. Maybe they're taking shelter, too."

I allow myself to entertain this possibility, but my hope is waning. A vicious wind rattles the door, but Gabe doesn't seem to notice.

"I should've known," he says down to his hands.

"About the lair?"

He nods. "Ansel chose you. That should've been all the proof I needed that I'd stumbled into a trap." He clears his throat and picks a point on the wall to rest his weary gaze. "Do you think Sophia's okay?"

My skin prickles with shame; this is the first time I've thought of her since we took our fatal plunge off the roof. Despite my fledgling optimism, I can't help but assume the worst: that Sophia was captured and destroyed along with all the others. I just can't believe Ansel would approve of such grisly treatment. We were his soldiers, his children. He wouldn't let the malevolents do this to us.

Would he?

Gabe embraces me. Whenever I remember Sophia, it will be in exaggerated eye rolls, obscene quantities of mayonnaise, fearless forays into the bush, and an insatiable appetite for adventure. I miss her quirky mannerisms. I miss the narrow, slightly upturned tip of her freckled nose peeking out from under her oversized hood. I miss the creak of her laugh and how she doted on Gabe like a daughter.

He holds me as I sob.

"Next life," he says into the side of my neck, "we'll find each other and be a family. I promise."

He lifts a lock of hair over my ear. I picture him standing at the edge of the lake with his pants rolled up to his knees and his pockets sagging with stones. He may have given Sophia a childhood, but she gave him the chance to be a father—something I alone could never have done.

Gabe kisses me. A single, salty tear scurries down my cheek as I lean into him, desperate to feel anything other than the sting of my own grief.

He pulls away. His eyes mirror my sorrow as I dry my face with my hand.

"What happened to us?" I ask him.

"Enlightenment," comes a voice from the darkest corners of the store.

Ansel appears, first as a silhouette, and then as a fully formed apparition.

He approaches the counter and looks at Gabe, who seems strangely unruffled by the older entity's arrival. After everything we've been through, I suppose you could say he's become accustomed to our boss dropping in on a whim.

Ansel directs his words back at me.

"Nice work, soldier. It appears you've put a monumental dent in the malevolent population."

"Where are we?" I ask him. "Because it's not the in-between, and it's not The Establishment. So, what is it?"

Ansel seems taken aback.

"This is The Establishment," he informs me, "or at least, the foundation of it."

"But where are the others? Shouldn't they be here, too?"

"Who says they aren't?"

"But the malevolents—"

"Are contained, thanks in large part to your quick wit and selfless heroism. The world owes you an enormous debt of gratitude for your sacrifice."

"Sacrifice." I look at Gabe. "What sacrifice?"

He turns to Ansel. "This isn't The Establishment. The Establishment would have structure and protocol. This is a lawless hellscape."

"Is it?"

"The eyes don't lie. Look at where we're standing. Is this really the foundation of the greatest empire in existence?"

This seems to please Ansel, whose mouth curls upwards slightly at the corners. He walks toward the door, keeping his back to us as he admires the destruction.

"They all start out this way," Ansel says as Gabe helps me down from the counter, "barren, infertile, a once prosperous land devastated by her inability to sustain life. If earth were a woman, would you overlook her worth on account of her deficiency?"

"Of course not, but you're comparing apples to oranges. The earth is not a womb demanding a tenant," Gabe argues.

"Oh, but she is, and what better way to flatter her potential than to employ her as the fulcrum on which the fate of humanity will forever pivot?"

Ansel returns to his assessment of the uninhabited city.

"Mother Earth needs her children, and I need their spirits. She provides me with the necessary space in which to operate and I, in turn, ensure a consistent turnover of human servants to cultivate her land and make the most of her abundant natural resources."

"When you say they all start out this way, are you suggesting there's more than one earth?" Gabe asks.

Ansel smirks. "What do you think?"

"How many?"

"Too many to enumerate. You may think this makes matters more confusing, but it's the only way to prevent déjà vu—that is, sending a spirit back to a life they've already lived.

"Ever since The Establishment was destroyed, it's made me reconsider my approach to managing spirits—good and bad. Now that the malevolents have been consolidated, I'm eager to proceed with the next stage of the process."

"Which is?"

"Rebirth. The next iteration of The Establishment will take into account the malevolents' unlimited and highly volatile power. Advanced security measures will be necessary to prevent history from repeating itself."

Gabe bristles. "Why do I get the feeling you're about to ask a colossal favour of us?"

"Because I am. Why else would I have gone out of my way to contact you directly?" Ansel continues, "The malevolents that you see out there account for nearly ninety percent of the evil in the universe. Your job is to quarantine the lot."

"Sounds like there's a caveat in there somewhere."

"There's always a caveat, Mr. Conway." Ansel's eyes slide back to me. "This final task will demand every skill in your repertoire. After all, it's not just the future of mankind that will be in jeopardy, but my existence as well."

Ansel folds his hands in front of his body. The look on his face is darker than the tenuous mass of monsters floating over this sordid planet. I can't imagine a universe—or multiple universes, for that matter—without Ansel.

"I have a proposition for you," Ansel says as he makes eye contact with Gabe. They exchange looks that transcend the usual nonverbal pleasantries and moments later Gabe indicates his interest with a singular tip of his chin.

"It concerns your contract," Ansel adds, glancing at me.

"She knows," Gabe says. "Given her role in this war, I wanted her to have all the facts."

"You signed a non-disclosure agreement."

"I'm aware of the conditions."

"And yet you chose to violate them."

"Sarah has been tasked with mobilizing an army of unprecedented proportions. As her second in command, I weighed the risks and concluded that her knowledge of any prior agreements between yourself and I was necessary to devise and execute a viable strategy."

Ansel nods slowly. Finally, he speaks.

"Your troops have been stationed at a base north of the city. Once you have assembled your army and briefed them on the mission, you will receive your final set of instructions. But beware: your powers will expire before the next lunar cycle.

Once that happens, my powers alone will be insufficient to contain the malevolents. Keep an eye on the horizon at all times. Once the sun disappears, so, too, will everything else."

Just like that, he's gone again.

Gabe wanders over to the door and presses his forehead against the glass in frustration.

"How much time do we have?" I ask.

He lifts his head.

"Hard to say. The malevolents are blotting out the sun." He lowers his arms and angles back to me. "If this doesn't work, I just want you to know that I will continue to fight alongside you. Victory is an ambitious goal, but one must be equally prepared to accept defeat, especially under these conditions."

"If failure were an option, we would have achieved it by now."

Gabe walks over to me and sets his hands on my shoulders. A smile hedges his lips, but his eyes tell an entirely different story.

"I'm doing this for Sophia," I tell him, sounding oddly confident despite the catch in my voice.

He sweeps his thumbs across my cheeks. Tears pummel my eyes and throat, but I don't have the strength to let them flow.

"I know," he replies. His hands return to his sides. "We should go. Perhaps the skies will be clearer closer to base."

Gabe leads the way outside, where the wind has evolved into a devastating gale and the rotating mass of malevolents is showing signs of instability. A few impetuous beings have managed to disentangle themselves from the group and are now orbiting the others in an erratic fashion.

"We don't have a car," I say. "There's no way we're going to make it to the base in time."

Gabe twists around and shields his eyes from the furious wind. A devious smile spreads across his face.

"Sarah," he roars, "come on. It's me, Gabe Conway."

"I know who you are."

"I used to be a mechanic. I can hot-wire anything."

"A mechanic? Don't you mean carjacker?"

"That too."

He turns his focus back to the street and raises a hand to point at an old, forgotten motorcycle stashed against the curb. Despite my apprehension, I nod and jog after him, my body fighting to remain upright in the fierce bellows of hot, dense air gusting across the street.

I hover over Gabe as he bypasses the ignition. Moments later, he picks up the helmet and turns to me.

"What about you?" I ask.

"The way I see it your brain is a lot more valuable than mine right now." He guides the helmet onto my head and fastens the strap under my chin. Then he peers at me through the face shield and flashes me a reassuring grin.

Gabe slings a leg over the seat and waits for me to clamber on behind him. I wrap my arms around his waist, and moments later we're mobile.

38

We wind our way out of the city with the help of several well-positioned skyscrapers, whose glass façades function like enormous mirrors. Despite their numbers, the malevolents show astoundingly little interest in us. Instead, they spiral through the sky in a throbbing, amorphous clump, sucking up garbage and other debris as they go.

Our journey leads us into the outlying counties, where we eventually spot a long, thin tendril of smoke. Contrary to Gabe's assumption, the sky out here is murky and ominous, but at least we have an unimpeded view of the horizon.

Gabe leans into a turn, which takes us along the edge of a field and over a succession of small hills. As a cluster of tents materializes from behind a line of trees, Gabe deviates from the road and surges through the mud toward the settlement.

We sputter to a stop behind one of the crudely erected structures. I dismount quickly and remove the helmet just as Gabe leans the bike on its kickstand and rakes his fingers through his violently tousled hair.

"Don't get your hopes up," he says as I pass him the helmet.

I falter. "What do you mean?"

Sympathy pushes to the surface of his weathered face.

"I saw you looking for her," he says softly. "I don't want you to be disappointed if she isn't here."

I feign disinterest and turn away. I'm prepared for disappointment, but won't reject hope if it decides to drop in unannounced.

"Sarah?"

I angle back to Gabe, who smirks as he ambles past me.

"Nice hair," he teases. I swat him on the arm, wiping the playful grin right off his face.

At least a hundred spirits are flowing in and around the tents. Half a dozen rusty barrels full of dried leaves and sticks smolder at the edges of a sandy clearing, where the squatters have constructed an elevated platform using wooden palettes and some cinderblocks. It appears as though they've lived here for weeks—no doubt waiting for Ansel to provide them with some much-needed guidance.

"So how many souls do you estimate?" Gabe asks as we maneuver the hub of activity.

"At least a hundred, maybe more."

"Will that be enough?"

"I hope so. If they're strong, their numbers won't matter. It's not the size of the army that wins the war."

"It's the quality of the leader, and you're as good as it gets."

"Flattery won't win a war either, Mr. Conway. But thank you."

A few spirits acknowledge our arrival, but show no interest in approaching us. I try to read their energy, but the bulk of them appear unconcerned by our presence or the increasingly powerful wind promising to reduce their precarious homes to piles of debris.

"Hey!" a voice bellows out of nowhere, and we turn in time to see a burly spirit charging toward us.

"Who's that?" I ask.

Gabe shrugs. "Self-appointed leader, I would assume. Don't worry—I'll take him down a notch."

The instigator concludes his jaunt across the clearing just as Gabe raises his hand.

"Take it easy, comrade. Ansel sent us."

"You talked to Ansel?"

I explain, "We just came from the city. The malevolents are gaining strength and Ansel has urged us to act—preferably before sundown."

"Sarah will head the resistance," Gabe adds. "She's been to the Ward and has extensive experience in mass quarantines."

The surly spirit scoffs. "Does she now?"

"She destroyed a lair less than two hours ago. Unassisted, I may add."

"Listen, pal. I don't know who you are or what gives you the right to rush in and save the day, but we've been getting on just fine without Ansel or his pet."

Gabe indicates the multitude of tents. "Seems like you've gotten pretty comfortable."

"This was a temporary arrangement. We needed a place to assemble and strategize our next move."

"Of course you did, comrade."

"As I said, the situation is under control. If you want to help, the wood pile needs restocking."

"Sarah will lead the charge," Gabe insists, "and seeing as Ansel's orders are absolute, I'd caution you against defying them."

"I refuse to take orders from anyone, including Ansel."

"Then there's no need to concern yourself with defeating the malevolents, since Ansel will undoubtedly make you their next meal."

The bigger spirit cocks a finger at me. "We already have a leader. No sense spoiling the broth."

Gabe once again comes to my defense.

"Don't worry, comrade. No proverbial broth will be spoiled so long as we observe Ansel's request to have Miss Galloway mobilize the troops. I suggest you see to it that she has everything she needs."

The rival spirit huffs and stalks off. Our would-be altercation has gone unnoticed by the others, but given the current climate, I can't say as I blame them for keeping their heads down.

"Thank you," I say.

"No need. After what happened in the lair, the least I can do is make sure no one stands in your way."

Satisfied with this response, I gaze at the surrounding bustle. A handful of spirits duck into a nearby tent; several more are wedging sticks into the barrels. No one appears to be actively working toward a plan to confront the malevolents, and it's making my head spin with worry.

That's when I hear my name—high, sharp, and brittle with relief.

Sophia throws her arms around my waist, wrapping me in a fierce but refreshing hug. I don't know how she made it out of that hospital, but it doesn't matter. All that matters is that she's here and we're together, quite possibly for the last time.

Sophia removes her head from my chest.

"I can't believe I found you guys," she exclaims. "When you said there were others, I thought maybe I could find them, but when I got back to the wing you guys were gone."

"We were out looking for you," I tell her, smoothing back her hair. "Why didn't you tell us where you were going?"

Sophia becomes sheepish. "I didn't want you to worry. And I wanted to help." She turns to Gabe. "You're not mad, are you?"

He sighs and pulls her into his embrace, ignoring the question completely.

"Are you Sarah?"

The three of us turn around. From the far side of the clearing comes a tall, modestly dressed woman; a small entourage flanks her on both sides. When our gazes connect, she smiles and offers her hand.

"I am," I say as our palms meet. "And who might you be?"

"Alexandra," she replies, smiling, "but Ansel calls me sister."

I stare at her, stunned. "You're Ansel's sister?"

"In a word, yes. My brother may be the creator of life and death, but he needed an earthlier embodiment to oversee the day-to-day operations."

"So you know about the malevolents then."

Alexandra nods. "Seems my brother has been overly generous about expanding their range as of late."

"And so he sent here you to regain control of the situation."

"He sent me to supervise. You're the one he's asked to bottle the genie."

I nod slowly. By now the other spirits have taken interest in our dialogue and are crowded around us looking equal parts baffled and amazed.

Alexandra turns to address them.

"Spirits," she begins. "You are being confronted by a monumental challenge—one that will demand every ounce of power, courage, and faith. Ansel has asked that I watch over you, but expects that you will honour and respect Sarah as your leader. Until such times as the malevolents have been safely contained, you will defer to her on any and all matters concerning the resistance. She is your last hope for salvation. I would ask that you treat her as such." Alexandra meets my eyes. "We should get started. There's much to discuss."

341

I shoot Gabe and Sophia one last look and then follow Alexandra into the nearest tent.

39

The tent where Alexandra and I convene features dark green walls and an overturned barrel serving as a table. Wind rustles the sheet of tarp pulled across the door and there's a pile of wood staying dry and burnable in the corner. The tent has enough room for ten spirits to stand comfortably, but Alexandra and I are the only ones here.

"Ansel tells me you have experience with malevolents," Alexandra says. "He also mentioned that you have certain abilities that preclude possession."

"Prior to The Establishment's destruction, I was escorted to the Ward and asked to quarantine a delinquent. Unbeknownst to me, I had resorted to an impure memory and was subsequently immunized against future infections."

Alexandra circles the makeshift table, her arms folded across her chest and her thoughtful expression trained on the ground.

"It's rare, but it happens. Have you experienced many side effects?"

"Only when I channel my immunity in self-defense."

"Inadvisable, and quite frankly reckless. My brother has strict rules against exposing the Living to evil."

She clasps her hands behind her back.

"That being said, exceptional circumstances demand exceptional measures. Assuming you acted in the interest of the larger whole, I don't imagine my brother would consider your behaviour grounds for insubordination."

I brace myself against an avalanche of guilt. "Perhaps not, but you should know that my actions resulted in two unauthorized claims: a male police officer whose name was never given, and a young nurse by the name of Rebecca Harding. I'm prepared to accept whatever punishment Ansel deems fit."

Alexandra holds my gaze. She appears neither upset about nor indifferent to this admission, and after a brief spell of silence she nods and resumes pacing.

"My brother is a reasonable entity. I'd be happy to lobby for a lighter penalty should he choose to pursue one."

I indicate my gratitude with a discreet tip of my chin. For now, at least, I'm too concerned about the impending Armageddon to devote much thought to Ansel's choice of disciplinary action.

Alexandra steers the conversation back on track.

"The malevolents are expected to disband prior to attacking. When that happens, it will become exceedingly difficult to contain them. Seeing as you possess the bulk of the experience in this situation, I would ask that you initiate the orb."

"Can I expect reinforcement?"

"Only if you're prepared to educate the rest of the spirits on orb formation. Given our limited resources, I would recommend you put your energy toward more promising endeavors."

"Understood." I guide the discussion elsewhere. "Ansel stated that anyone who contributes to the fight against the malevolents would be guaranteed a place in the hereafter. Does his word stand?"

"Absolutely."

"In that case, I'd like to make a request." I study her ageless complexion. "I would ask that Ansel grant Sophia Jacobson more favourable conditions in the next iteration of her life. Failing that, I would ask that he sees to it that she have access to our home, without interference from child protection services or law enforcement officials."

Alexandra considers my proposition in silence. "Granted."

Relief fills my chest as she reverts back to the issue at hand.

"Ansel has asked that I refrain from inundating you with too many details. My involvement in this matter will be minimal, as I simply do not possess the spiritual fortitude to assist you."

"I don't understand. I thought you and Ansel were related."

"My powers encompass the natural: everything that can be seen, touched, mined, and harvested falls within my domain. Ansel is the overseer of the supernatural. He is the creator of everything beyond sensory perception: life, death, presence, absence, energy, space, and spirit. So, while we're each responsible for vastly different functions, we are very much related, and very supportive of one another's work."

I smile as comprehension settles over me. "Mother Nature."

Alexandra seems pleased. "Rally your troops, Miss Galloway. You have a war to win."

The wind blows, tearing through the gaps in the tent wall, and a moment later Alexandra returns to the earth.

○

I part the tent flaps and slip outside. On the far side of the clearing, a group of spirits is bickering amongst themselves. One of the signal fires is dwindling from neglect, so I retreat back into the tent and emerge a minute later with an armload of sticks. I direct my focus back to the skirmish, but I'm too far away to catch the thread of their conversation.

Gabe comes up behind me.

"It's getting dark," he says.

I glance at him. "I know." Nodding at the group, I ask, "How long has this been going on for?"

"A couple of minutes. Apparently they want to split up."

"Split up?"

"A few spirits have been talking about abandoning the resistance. They say it's not worth the risk."

"Well, that's just perfect," I grumble.

"If it makes you feel any better, there really isn't anywhere for them to go. Even if they do leave, it won't take long for them to realize their mistake and come crawling back to you."

Gabe pockets his hands.

"I talked to Sophia," he says, "she feels terrible."

"She shouldn't."

"She thinks she caused this."

346

"She didn't. Where is she, anyway?"

"Recharging in one of the smaller tents."

I debate telling him about my request, but ultimately decide against it. It'll be my gift to him in the next life—if there is a next life.

"How was your meeting with Alexandra?" Gabe asks.

"Fruitful. But she won't be able to help us, at least not directly."

For some reason, Gabe doesn't even flinch.

"You won't need it. Ansel chose you for a reason."

I nod. I'm suddenly tired down to my bones and would love nothing more than to disappear someplace quiet and let the malevolents consume whatever's left of this sickly planet. But I made a promise to Ansel, and I will see it through even if it kills me.

A shadow bleeds across the meadow, putting a quick end to the ongoing chatter. Gabe and I, along with most of the other spirits, all turn our attention to the sky, where the mass of malevolents is rapidly encroaching on our safe haven. The wind transforms from a constant but tolerable breeze into a seething gale, snuffing the signal fires and sending a handful of spirits scrambling for cover.

I direct my words at Gabe.

"Go wake Sophia." He obliges with a half-nod and speeds toward one of the tents.

As for myself, I hurry in the opposite direction—across the clearing and straight onto the platform.

A female spirit turns to me and grimaces.

"Who are you?" she asks.

"I'm Sarah. Ansel sent me to organize the resistance."

"There is no resistance—only chaos. If Ansel truly valued us, he'd come and put an end to this maelstrom himself."

"Ansel needs us. He's not strong enough on his own." I recall our discussion in the Ward and the comment he'd made about a king's army being a reflection of his strength. At the time he'd been referring to Hate, but now I wonder if he was also referring to himself.

The female spirit dismisses me with a quick headshake. A few of her companions turn to leave, even as the settlement's other occupants begin to gather around my stage. I spot Gabe in the front row, along with Sophia, who is surprisingly alert despite being recently roused from slumber.

Panic grips me. "Where are you going?" I call after the spirit who challenged me.

She and her posse turn around. I can barely hear them over the wind.

"Does it matter? We'll all be history soon enough."

A tingle radiates down my arm, where thousands of tiny lightning bolts zigzag along my skin. The tingling sensation intensifies, and when the mega-orb develops its first crack, I feel the shockwave in the deepest, darkest reaches of my being.

I aim a finger at one of the tents. Like a bullet from a gun, a bolt of electricity shoots out, igniting the tarp instantly. Seconds later, a trickle of warmth runs down my throat.

I double over and cough, splattering the sand with blood. The frightened spirits take a collective step back, except for Gabe, who rushes forward to comfort me.

"What's happening?" he asks.

"Nothing I wasn't expecting," I murmur. I make eye contact with him. "I want you to stay with Sophia. Things are about to get a lot worse and I don't want her running off again."

Gabe holds my gaze a moment longer, and then vanishes into the gathering without another look back.

The crack on the orb begins to spread. From this enormous fissure streams a vicious, unrelenting wind a hundred times more devastating than the hurricane already raging around us. Too afraid to even contemplate fleeing, the spirits huddle together in the centre of the clearing. Nervous energy surrounds them like a fog, and I reach out to capture it.

The memories follow swiftly. They enter through the tips of my fingers before whizzing up my arm and into my essence. Another crack in the monstrous orb causes the ground to shake, and still the energy flow continues, filling me to capacity.

After I've harvested every last recollection, I motion for the group to step forward. When they are all safely contained within the consolidation zone, I prepare myself for the onslaught.

A few bold malevolents detach from the orb, but don't attack. Individually, they don't stand a chance—and neither do we. After all, war is, and has always been, a numbers game.

The crack widens, delivering another blow to the earth. Several tents collapse in response to the shifting soil and the last of the barrels are catapulted across the meadow, scattering their contents in every direction.

The spirits lower themselves to the ground. I raise my hand to summon the malevolents.

And then the orb shatters.

A staggering number of malevolents plummet toward the earth. I clutch the smaller orb in my left hand, hardly noticing when the heat of all those mixed up memories causes my skin to blister and peel away.

The malevolents circle us like sharks, herding the already dense group into an even more concentrated mass. The sky is black and starless and the wind hurtling across the meadow has rendered the settlement history. There's nothing left—no tents, no barrels, not even the motorcycle we arrived on. All that remains are the polar ends of the only life we've ever known: good and evil, presence and oblivion, Spirit Catchers and malevolents.

I close my eyes and diffuse the orb.

The shockwave flattens everything: trees, buildings, highway overpasses. A protective dome encases the clearing, preventing the more ambitious malevolents from preying on the spirits within. The larger ones fasten themselves to the transparent shield, desperately seeking an entry point. Their claws rake across the smooth shell; the trails they leave are temporary, and soon the monsters surrender with an apoplectic shriek.

Except for one that manages to penetrate. There's a weak spot in the orb, and it's directly above Sophia's head.

Gabe looks up, sees the hole in the barrier, and holds her a little more tightly.

"Hey!" At the sound of my voice, the malevolent whips around. Its growl is deep, blood-red eyes narrowed like knives. "Looking for me?"

As it lunges, I feed it the mental image of Tiffany on her wedding day. The creature explodes, scattering its remains in every direction.

One by one, the memories vanquish the malevolents, obliterating them on contact. Overhead, the sky is a terrific, shimmering band of colour—pastel blues, sensual violets, blushing fuchsias, and splendid golds, all blended together and ornamented with the last, sparkling traces of the once formidable malevolent orb.

Bit by bit, the wind dies down. It careens through the tall grass before finally fading into a delicate, defeated breath of air. The silence returns, but not before the last, fledgling malevolents, visibly outnumbered and too disoriented to retaliate, unleash a final, primitive wail and zip off into the void.

My essence fades out, and seconds later I fall to the ground.

40

The dreams I have during my stay at the infirmary are vivid and terrifying. I dream of being cast adrift in a smoky grey universe where there are no stars, no planets, and no galaxies. Malevolents roam freely throughout this existential vacuum, and the chill that surrounds me is deep and penetrating. Hate crops up on the fringes of my awareness, but before it can devour me, I'm yanked into a dense, suffocating darkness and made to linger there for an unspecified length of time.

Catchers come and go. Of all the entities that make time to visit, only two bring me any comfort: Gabe, whose voice is smooth and orotund, and Sophia, who answers in her usual, mousy lilt. Their words echo around me like a gentle, soothing wind, carrying me through the long stretches of loneliness.

The table on which my body lies is a thin, slightly curved sheet of metal that sits roughly four feet off the floor. A sleek, white machine with a holographic screen and a cluster of wires sprouting from a port on its side stands beside me.

There are four wires in total: one on my temple to record brainwaves, dreams, and memories; one on my chest to monitor my essence; one on my wrist to repair my lifeblood; and one on my ankle to ensure I don't wander away.

The healing process takes a week to complete. During that time, I only sense Ansel's presence once. After several moments of observing me in my infirm state, his energy disappears.

On the seventh day, a Healer is sent in to bring me out of my coma. Ansel accompanies him. The machine beeps as it delivers a mild electric shock, and a second later my eyes fly open.

Ansel smiles down at me. The Healer stands across from him, but is too preoccupied with the machine to devote much interest to me.

"Well done, soldier," Ansel says proudly. "The citizens of the world thank you, and so do I."

"System's stable, sir," the Healer says. "Shall I initiate the decontamination process?"

"Please." Ansel smirks at the skeptical crease rumpling my brow. "For the machine, not you. You've already been sufficiently decontaminated."

The Healer removes the probes. The screen goes red as the wires are sucked back into the machine. A warning appears, followed by a robotic voice announcing that the sterilization process is about to begin, and then the Healer leaves us alone to talk.

"How do you feel?" Ansel asks as I sit up.

I test my newly repaired joints, which are as smooth as oiled hinges. My skin is a uniform paleness and my hair is thick and shiny with health. Looking at myself now, it's almost as if I never left.

"Brand new. Thank you."

Ansel smiles and removes his hand from behind his back. I'm expecting to see a perfectly folded black uniform, but the ensemble he hands me isn't black, or even silver.

It's red.

"I don't usually do this," he says as the material changes hands, "but in light of recent events, I decided to make an exception."

I set the boots on the table beside me. The uniform is a one-piece outfit with a sturdy but flexible plastic exterior, black gloves, and a hood that zips into a transparent mask. In the midst of my stupefied ogling, I catch sight of a narrow strip of material on the breast pocket, along which my last name is printed.

I point to the label.

"Why does it have my name on it?"

Ansel explains, "The Hunters make up a small but elite group. In a department consisting of fewer than fifty employees, I can afford to customize." He backs away. "I'll give you a minute to dress. Then I'd like to show you around."

By the time I exit the infirmary, Ansel is leaning against a metal railing and conversing with Gabe, who is standing next to Sophia. When they spot me walking toward them, both of their faces light up in grins.

"Well, look at you," Gabe says, doing precisely that. "You're moving up in the world."

"Believe me, I'm as surprised as you are." I shift my focus to Ansel. "You wanted to show me something?"

He smirks and wags a finger, indicating for the three of us to follow.

"After The Establishment was destroyed, I endeavored to create a new home for the spirits, one that could withstand a tremendous amount of force in the event of a security breach or other mishap."

Ansel leads the way down a long, curving flight of stairs. In the centre of this grand entryway is an enormous, holographic globe that displays birth and death rates in real time, as well as the distribution of Catchers across the world. A ring of futuristic computers similar to the one that nursed me back to health encircles the hologram, with each screen responsible for tracking and displaying a specific set of demographic details.

Across the room, a line of Catchers waits to register their recruits. Some of them give me an appreciative nod. I smile politely back as Ansel steers toward a door and leads us into an elevator.

"Does the projection replace the catalogue?" I ask as the door closes and we lift off.

"It complements it. Originally, I designed the globe with the intention of isolating any remaining malevolents, but in the interest of convenience, I decided to expand the hologram's functions."

"Does it have a name?"

"I call it Eye on the World, or The Eye, for short."

"The Eye," I say, nodding. The elevator door opens. "I like that."

Our expedition takes us down a hallway, past a window, and up a flight of stairs that eventually ends in a series of metal doors.

Ansel approaches the third door on the right and it rolls open as if it has been expecting us.

"Is this your office?" I ask as Ansel gestures for us to enter.

"Actually, it's yours."

The three of us turn around. Astonishment takes shape on my face and I glance at Gabe and Sophia to see if either of them shares my disbelief.

Ansel waves a hand around the spacious room, with its ornate wooden desk, mind-boggling assortment of books, and carefully concealed closets. The window behind the desk overlooks a courtyard rife with flowering trees. A second later, the courtyard is replaced by a beach. I watch the waves tumble across the alabaster sand before being dragged back into the ocean, taking the secrets of the sea with them.

"It's a dynamic landscape," Ansel says as Gabe, Sophia, and I line up along the window. "The software is synced to your Keepsake, so if there's a place in your heart that you'd like to revisit, now, you can."

I lay my left hand against the window, channeling my fondest memories onto the living canvas. Grain by grain, the beach where Brody and I once frolicked materializes, and as it does, a tickle of emotion stirs in my throat.

I lower my hand and turn back to Ansel. He smiles.

"I know it's a lot to take in, especially given your recently acquired status." He nods at my uniform for emphasis. "But the truth is, I need someone to help run this place. Someone I can trust, and who's witnessed the result of poor planning firsthand. In short, I need an advisor."

"You want me to advise you?" I hope he doesn't confuse my surprise for self-doubt.

"The fact that you were able to seek out and subsequently destroy not just a malevolent lair, but the rest of the hive as well tells me that you're more than capable of assuming a tremendous amount of responsibility, and I would be delighted to work alongside you."

"You want to mentor me?" I'm so stunned I can barely think.

"It would be an honour and a privilege."

I look at Gabe, who smiles and says, "Take it. You've earned it."

I turn back to Ansel. On my other side, Sophia is beaming, looking as beautiful as ever with her oceanic eyes and waves of rippling, honey hair.

"When do I start?" I ask.

○

It's Gabe's last day at The Establishment. Ansel has already approved his regeneration, as well as assigned Sophia a new mentor. As for me, it's my first day of training with the Hunters, so I'm trying to focus on my shiny new position in order to dull the sting of a surprisingly difficult goodbye.

I walk Gabe to the regeneration chamber, which sits at the end of a long hallway filled with light and hope. Once there, he'll be sealed in a specialized pod that will simultaneously extract his energy and destroy his vessel. I myself will not see the inside of the regeneration chamber for another two or three generations, but at least Ansel has guaranteed that Gabe and Sophia will spawn into the same life.

Gabe stops and turns to me. The light from the hallway washes over his face as I search for somewhere else to rest my gaze.

He smiles. "I guess this is goodbye, then."

I smirk. "Don't sound too devastated, Mr. Conway."

Gabe chuckles and stuffs his hands in his pockets. I'm going to miss that laugh, and even that stupid tuft of hair that never behaves.

"Well, Miss Galloway. It's been a pleasure."

I nod and force a smile. My chest is tight and my vision is cloudy, but I don't want him to see me as a sloppy, blubbering mess.

I extend my hand, and Gabe takes it.

"Take care of Sophia," I tell him, "and yourself."

"Don't worry about us. We're not the ones running down malevolents."

I take my hand back. Being a Hunter is one of the most dangerous jobs at The Establishment, but I have faith in my team, and in myself. In four weeks, I will have completed my basic training, at which time I will join a crew of five on an expedition that is expected to last two years. I'm excited, but also, predictably, a little afraid.

Gabe nods at the hallway. "I should be going," he says. "Take care of yourself, Sarah."

Then he pulls me into a hug and holds me there for a very long time.

We let go. I bring my hands together in front of my body and then watch as Gabe steps over the threshold and into the light for the last time.

○

The Commander 4 is one of five spacecrafts in Ansel's fleet and boasts technology that the Living could only dream about. Though piloted by two, the cockpit has room for six, and since we're constantly rotating, everyone gets a turn in the driver's seat.

The Commander 4 has an average cruising speed of just over 760 miles per hour. Despite the speed, the environment inside the Commander 4 is as calm as a smooth sea, enabling us to move freely between rooms and the portable holding tank wherein we keep our malevolents.

We take turns guarding the tank. Ironically, it's the quietest place on the Commander 4, and I welcome the opportunity to temporarily abandon the jubilant banter of the cockpit for the peaceful solitude of the lower level.

Down in the tank, my thoughts have room to wander. I think about Gabe and Sophia often. Sophia is still working at The Establishment, and if my math is correct, then Gabe is just over a year old in earth time. It'll be another three decades before their paths cross. I know this because I saw the post-regeneration report in the master files, and because I know Ansel is a man of his word. I'm not worried. If there's one thing I can always count on, it's Ansel keeping his promise.

Having completed my rounds, I make my way back up to the main deck. Our two-year malevolent-trapping mission is coming to a close, and now that we've filled the tank to capacity, the only place to go is home.

"All okay below deck?" Damien Matheson, who is manning the controls, asks.

I take a seat on his right and secure the various restraints. Once we're on route to The Establishment we'll be blazing through space at the speed of sound, and though it won't cause us any physical harm, at least the restraints will minimize the destabilization sickness.

"All malevolents present and accounted for," I reply. "All fifty-five thousand of them."

"Nice work, Galloway."

"Thank you." I slip on the headset and join the conversation that is taking place between the Commander 4 and The Establishment.

"Headquarters is in sight," comes a voice from the cockpit's rear. "Shall I announce our approach?"

"Already covered," Damien says. He angles the microphone toward his mouth and presses a button to speak.

"Headquarters, this is Commander 4. We have you on radar and will be approaching shortly."

The headset crackles. "Approach acknowledged, Commander 4. Cargo status?"

I jump in. "Fifty-five thousand counted and contained. No incidents to report."

Damien pushes several buttons and turns a couple of dials. Then he reaches for a lever and fires us straight across the universe.

When The Establishment comes into focus some time later, my essence bubbles with a mixture of relief and sadness. It's been a long two years, with nearly half a million stops spread across hundreds of overlapping universes. I've seen every kind of planet there is: thriving green planets unburdened by human life; parched, ailing planets where the animals are disfigured and the vegetation is nonexistent; planets that defy logic and the laws of nature. Small planets. Big planets. But the one I miss most is the one where Gabe lives, and where Sophia will soon be joining him. It's the only one that ever felt like home.

Damien pushes the button on his headset again.

"Headquarters, this is Commander 4. Docking bay is in sight. Seeking permission to dock."

A moment later, Headquarters replies. "Permission to dock granted. Welcome home, Commander 4."

"Okay, Galloway," Damien says, "put her down nice and easy."

I consult the multitude of gages. When the Commander 4 is aligned with the docking bay, I reduce our speed and focus on keeping the spacecraft level. It clicks smoothly into position, with the cockpit on the top half of the bay and the tank directly beneath it, where the malevolents can be wheeled straight into the basement. Ansel raises a hand to wave as the Commander 4 is secured in place using cables, chains, and more than a few wires. A swarm of technicians converge on the spacecraft, and then the six of us disembark.

"Welcome back, soldiers," Ansel says, shaking each of our hands. "I trust you had a good trip?"

"Any trip that brings us back to The Establishment is a good one," Damien replies.

Ansel leads us toward a door.

"You're actually just in time. A new batch of recruits is about to commence the next stage of their training, and I'd like each of you to serve as mentors."

"How many students, sir?" one of the Hunters, Lisa, asks.

"Ten each. I'm sure you'll recognize the occasional face here and there." Smirking, Ansel cocks a brow at me. "I've allowed the recruits to choose their mentors. Can you guess who Miss Jacobson requested?"

Despite my diminished energy, I feel a spark of pride ignite in my chest. "I'd be honoured, although it's hard to believe she's already at level three."

"I recently boosted her quotas. She's proving herself to be an exceptional Catcher."

We stop outside a wide metal door. Unlike the old, change room-style barracks, the new barracks feature a decompression chamber and adjoining common room. The decompression chamber is for Hunters returning from missions or third-level Catchers undergoing training in the Ward. The common room satisfies a more basic need: the need for companionship and belonging.

Ansel takes me aside.

"I appreciate you staying on," he says when the others are out of earshot. "I know it ultimately delayed your regeneration, but you should know that your work here is not without my deepest gratitude."

"It's all right. As long as Sophia is taken care of, I'm happy."

"And Gabe," he adds with a capricious twinkle in his eye.

I fold my arms and smirk. "He was an excellent soldier, and an unrivalled ally. I trust he'll live up to whatever challenge you've designed for him."

"I'm sure of it." Waving a hand at the door, Ansel says, "I won't take any more of your time right now. Better rest up, Miss Galloway. You have a long six months of mentoring ahead of you."

I nod only once, and like waking from a dream, our conversation ends and Ansel disappears—there one minute, gone the next.

JESSICA INGOLD is the author of three books for young adult readers as well as countless blogs and newspaper articles. With over ten years of experience in writing and self-publishing, her goal is to craft stories that resonate with book enthusiasts of all ages.

Twitter.com/JessieIngold

Facebook.com/jessingoldbooks

Lulu.com/spotlight/jessicaingold